Shards of Anomie

Morgan Briese

ISBN-13: 978-0-9966350-0-4

MorganBrieseWrites.com

DEDICATION

To all those who said I couldn't, I did.

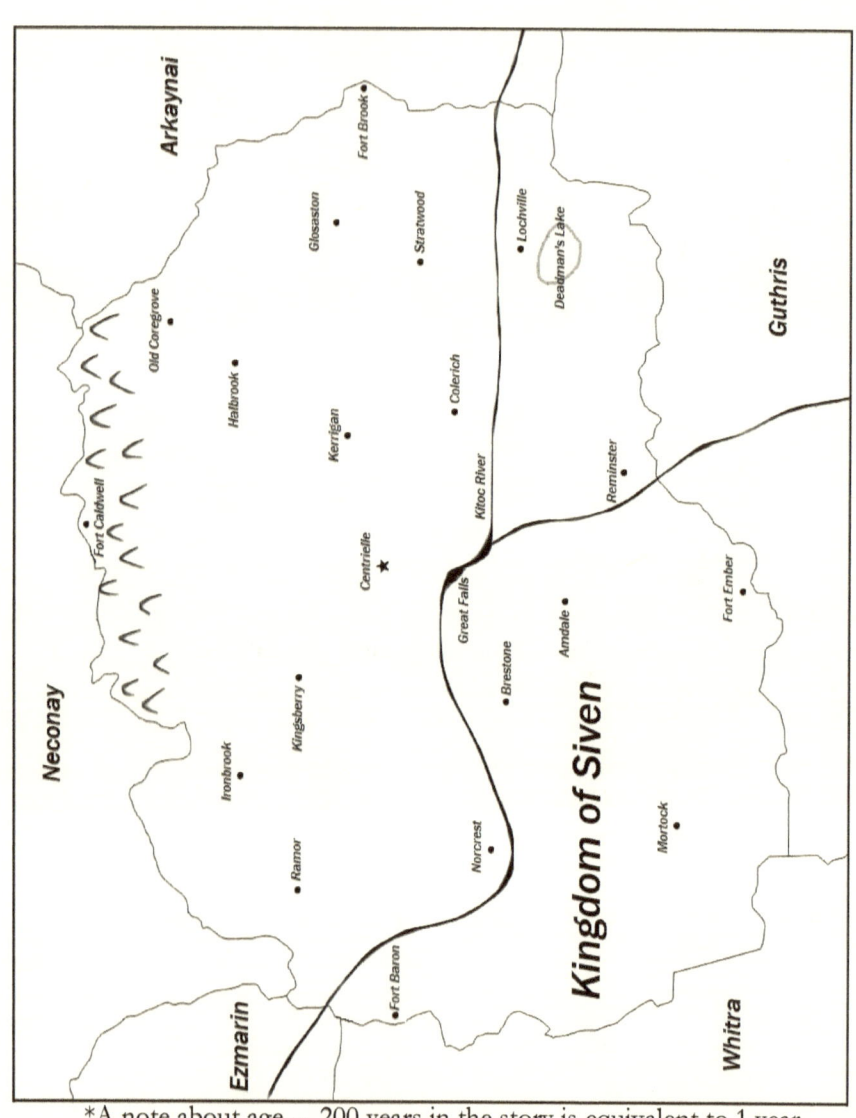

*A note about age… 200 years in the story is equivalent to 1 year

TABLE OF CONTENTS

1   The Fateful Day   7

2   Out of Uniform   13

3   The Real Traitor   18

4   Trust in the Enemy   27

5   A Second Chance   35

6   Memories to Believe In   41

7   Brothers   50

8   Voice of Reason   56

9   Had to Be Wrong   64

10   Paint an Umbrella   72

11   Lesson Learned   78

12   Close Your Eyes   86

13   Someone's Daughter   92

14   Checkmate   99

15   Filthy Mouth   106

16   Not Alone   114

17   Blind   122

18   Braided Together   129

19   Responsibility   135

20   Crisis of the Snake   145

21   Monster and Darkness   153

22   Swimming With Dolphins   162

THE FATEFUL DAY

The darkness consumed me, even when I swore to every divine being that I'd continue to seek the light. My wishful thinking wasn't enough to keep the hopelessness at bay. I naively overestimated my fragile resolve only to be left broken and scarred, no longer having the will to fight. Could anyone really blame me though? Seven centuries was a long time to be isolated to my own relentless thoughts.

My cries echoed through the darkness, bouncing off the colorless stone walls to encircle me. How long had I been shedding these stinging tears? How many more days would it take for the tears to completely dry? Would I ever escape from this cold, musky dungeon, or would my final days be lived in despair?

The desperate sobs were not meaningless though. They were not cried out of pity for my own life. If that had been the case, I would have gladly accepted my fate to rot away with the darkness; because I deserved this. A failure like me – someone who couldn't even protect that which matters most – deserved a fate of isolation, unfit for the title of human.

"William." His name slipped from my lips in remorseful whispers over and over again. I couldn't protect him from the spell, and I failed to break it. I came so close to freeing him only to end up here.

I didn't deserve to continue taking up air. This isolated dungeon was too luxurious for me. The cell was too spacious and the stone too soft. The few scraps of bread and murky water I ate were wasted on a being without the will to live.

Even so, the darkness tortured the last fragment of hope which refused to die. Loneliness in a pitch black world trampled upon it, and eerie silence ate at its corners to whittle it into shavings at my feet. Hope lay dormant in scraps of its former self – no longer enough to keep away the demons of my mind, and I couldn't fight against them alone. I was too tired, too exhausted, too broken. There was no point in struggling anymore.

I was powerless against the threads of fate. The fleeting moments – the actions which were out of my control – proved that all too well.

"If it comes down to a civil war, which side would you choose?"

William and I had had this discussion countless times in the past few decades. It wasn't an easy decision for the two of us to make. We were expected to lay down our lives for the king and queen; it was our duty as their royal guard captains. But as knights, we had a far greater duty to protect the civilians of Siven, especially if their royalty refused to.

Under the rule of King Caldwell and Queen Ember, Siven suffered greatly. It started as isolating Siven from the five surrounding countries' conflicts. To lessen the number of refugees seeking safety within Siven's borders, King Caldwell sanctioned discriminating laws against anyone who wasn't a citizen of Siven. Even if the refugee wanted to become a citizen to escape the discrimination, their citizenship would be denied. Most wouldn't dare to even apply, because with the denial came deportation and in some cases death.

Over the course of a few decades, it became evident that refugees weren't the only people being targeted. The discrimination moved up the ladder to anyone not of Siven blood – regardless of citizenship. Entire families seemingly disappeared without a trace, and neighbors turned a blind eye to it. But I can't bring myself to blame the neighbors for doing nothing; because with martial law newly instated, knights had the right to deal with delinquencies as they saw fit.

If you asked me, I'd say martial law resulted in even more intolerance. With power came great responsibility that many knights were too inexperienced to shoulder. The lack of proper training and regulations gave way to violence against those considered weak – those who were different, poor, or simply unable to meet society's expectations.

Those who called Siven home decided to take matters into their own hands. The rebellion started out strong as protests in the streets, but the spilling of their own blood forced the rebels to retreat with their tails between their legs. In the last few years, the unjust laws became more severe, and the rebellion's numbers started to grow again.

William and I were now caught in the middle. *"This is neither the appropriate time nor place to be discussing it,"* I scolded Will. *"The king and queen are only a few yards away."*

King Caldwell and Queen Ember sat on a beautifully carved oak bench in their private flower garden. Golden crowns accented with sparkling jewels perched atop graying hair, and the gold glinted with each slight turn of a head. Quiet murmurs of their conversation flew with the warm breeze to reach the grand fountain situated in the middle of the garden. The soft dribbling of water drowned out the king's and queen's exact words.

Sitting beside me on the edge of the fountain, William insisted, *"They can't hear us."* His hand rubbed the nape of his neck as deep walnut orbs lowered to stare at his boots. *"This is an important decision. It can mean life or death."*

As in William's life or death.

The Bates family did not originate from Siven. Will's parents fled the eastern country of Arkaynai during the bloody border war between Arkaynai and the southern country of Guthris. While his family had been granted citizenship under the former monarch's reign, not all refugees shared in that luck. Because of that, William had a personal tie in the current conflict boiling in Siven. Although he's a legal citizen, Will worried the only thing standing between him and imminent death was his rank as a knight. If he lost that rank – or if discrimination climbed further up the rungs of the ladder – where would that leave him?

"I've already told you. I will stand by your side no matter the choice you make," I told my partner, placing a comforting hand on his armor-clad thigh.

A weary sigh escaped his parted lips. "What if I wasn't here? What path would you take then?" William's head rose to turn anxious eyes at me.

"I can't say for sure. To be honest, I haven't made a decision, and I believe it's best to wait. We have more authority as captains than we do as deserted knights."

William placed his hand atop mine, squeezing gently. "But if you had to choose right here, right now; which side would it be – the crown or the people?"

I huffed out a breath of air and stared into his dark irises. When he phrased it in such a way, it was hard to choose anything other than the people of Siven. To follow the crown meant saving my own hide – putting my life above that of hundreds of thousands of others. But to follow the people of Siven, I'd risk not only my life but the lives of my family. Being asked to choose between the lives of a handful of those dearest to me and the lives of entire populations of people was unfair. I wanted to say my family, but I wasn't selfish enough to believe my family was the only one that mattered. Because in those entire populations of people were families exactly like mine with people who cared as deeply for one another.

"I'm sorry, but I honestly can't decide. Not right now at least. I guess I'll know when the time comes."

"But–"

The blaring echo of trumpets rang throughout the castle. The nearest sentry shouted, "Intruders! The rebel force has invaded!"

William's hand detached from mine as we jumped to our feet in unison. Darting across the span of grass and stone pathway, I heard the chaos of heavy footfalls, clashing swords, and vicious shouts from outside the garden's entrance. My right hand instinctively drew the blade at my hip as I reached the startled king and queen.

"Your Majesties," William calmly addressed them, "we must get you to the safety of the castle. Stay close and follow me." Will ushered the king and queen into motion, leading the way to the arched stone entry as I guarded their retreating backs.

"Well, well, what do we have here?" a sickeningly tranquil voice questioned from the entryway as two cloaked figures manifested from thin air. "Finding the almighty king and queen was much easier than even I could have imaged," the front man said, addressing nobody in particular.

He wore an onyx cape wrapped around him, hood down to reveal golden blond locks pulled back in a high ponytail. The strands of bright hair silhouetted fair beige skin only to contrast against the pitch black of the cloak where it rested on the man's shoulder. His icy blue eyes pierced through everything in his way until they landed on King

Caldwell. At the sight of the disheveled king, a sadistic leer overcame the man's original nonchalant expression.

The second man stood behind the blond, veiled completely from head to toe in a matching onyx cloak. Broad back to his comrade, he played lookout for his partner in crime.

"Stay where you are!" William shouted. In one swiftly fluid motion, William drew both of his swords from the sheaths secured to his lower back.

The blond took two slow, deliberate steps toward William. "You must be Sir William, the only knight in the kingdom who utilizes dual weapons successfully. I highly recommend you step aside. I mean, I'd hate to accidentally miss my real target and harm such a well-respected captain." The man's threatening words were accompanied with the slight tilt of his head and an intent stare.

"I'm afraid I can't do that," William said.

With a shrug of his shoulders, the intruder replied indifferently, "Suit yourself. You can't blame me if I miss." The man's hand darted out from under his cloak to sweep through the air in a wide arc before a long index finger zeroed in on the king.

A low sizzle broke the unnatural silence as summery green sparks lit up the pad of the blond's finger. Without a single word of incantation, miniscule sparks leapt from the fingertip to be camouflaged by the manicured grass before fizzling out completely. In the blink of an eye, the remaining sparks shot from the man's finger in a tightly wound ball aimed at King Caldwell.

William lunged forward to become a wall between the intruder and the king. The ball of magic connected with William's chest plate to splatter across the glinting steel before seeping through the metal. A single, shaky breath exhaled through his lips as his shining blades slipped through trembling fingers to clatter on the stepping stones. Lids closed over hazy brown eyes, and knees buckled, allowing gravity to pull William's body toward the ground.

"Will!"

The pounding of boots rushing toward the garden from the courtyard drowned out the cry of my partner's name. "Sir," the gruff voice of the second intruder drew the blond's attention to the hastily charging knights.

I dashed to the falling form of my partner, the clatter of my own sword in my wake. I reached for him — my hands ghosting over his forearms. My fingernail nicked the metal of his armor, but his weight never fell upon me.

The olive tone of his skin paled to a deathly white, and the tussled locks of chocolate hair lost its sheen and color. He faded, growing transparent until the roughness of the stone wall could be seen right through him. Merely an outline of a man, even that brief afterimage disintegrated.

The only proof he ever stood before me crashed into the stone pathway piece by piece, the armor still warm from his body heat. The last piece — his navy cloak — fluttered down like a fallen leaf to settle over the jumbled pile of metal. Shimmering dust lingered above the pile and slowly conformed to each other. As the dust gathered, it shaped and shifted until it took the form of a pristine longsword.

The weapon slowly descended from the sky. I reached out with open palms; but as I tried to grab it, it jerked back from my reach. I was left with no other option but to stare at it through blurred vision.

Shaped from a single piece of steel; the hilt, guard, and blade flowed smoothly together, not a single impurity fracturing the metal. Accents of gold ran down the blade, circling back countless times to create a mesmerizing maze. At the entrance of the maze sat a sapphire droplet. The droplet's bulb was encased in steel near the guard to securely hold the jewel in its rightful place. A new labyrinth of gold crisscrossed along the guard before dipping to the hilt and winding its way down in a woven pattern.

A single crack appeared in the middle of the golden maze of the blade. The crevice grew in all directions – inching its way up and down the blade, crossing over the guard, and streaking down the hilt like a strike of lightning. The sword shattered into countless pieces, and each tiny shard floated in midair for only a single beat of the heart. Like an exploding display of fireworks, they burst into the sky to soar above the clouds – disappearing altogether.

The intruder sighed. "Tsk. I guess that would be my cue to depart." He glanced sidelong in my direction. "I humbly apologize for my horrible aim. To show my sincerity, I will give you instructions to break the spell. Meet me at the Great Falls at sundown." He smirked, his lips quirking and his irises piercing. Both his body and the form of his companion grew translucent, fading to only a brief afterimage.

I couldn't think – couldn't process the flurry of stomping boots upon stone or the angry shouts of the king. Even the wind was silent in my ears. Unable to hear anything but the thumping of my own heart, I stared at what little remained of my partner.

It didn't matter what choice I made now. Whether to remain loyal to the crown or the people – none of it mattered. The worst case scenario – losing my loved ones – was already happening. Right before me, William disappeared – taken from me while I stood powerlessly by, unable to do a damn thing. There was no choosing; my choice was made for me.

I abandoned the jumbled armor and unmanned swords – retrieving only the navy cloak to tie it around my neck – turned on my heels, and marched past the perplexed knights to stand directly before the king and queen, their pale and wrinkled cheeks flushing with anger. Dropping to one knee with my head bowed, I placed the balled fist of my right hand directly over my heart. "Your Majesty, I wish to pursue the sorcerer and his companion. With your permission, I'd also like to meet him at the predetermined destination alone."

"I want their heads, but I'll send a whole squadron after them."

My head shot up to lock gazes with the king's infuriated coppery yellow orbs. "This is personal. I go alone, or I cut down every knight you send with me." I rose to my feet, towering a couple inches above the aging king. "I'm going alone."

King Caldwell scrutinized me from head to toe. He dared a glance at the subordinates pausing by the garden's entryway. After a few too many moments of contemplation, he barked out thunderously, "Fine! But so help me, if you don't return within twenty-four hours, it'll be your life on the line instead! Understood?"

As a final sayonara, I saluted King Caldwell one last time. "Understood, Sir." Dropping my arm to my side, I turned my back on the king and queen. I marched through the arched entry of the garden, catching the curious gaze of a fiery redhead. A single shake of my head had him nodding in understanding and stepping aside for me to pass.

After hurrying through the inner courtyard, I paused under the arch looking out upon the main yard. For a rebel invasion, the intruders were certainly generous in leaving most people and property intact. Aside from the occasional broken crate or hacked wagon wheel, the destruction was minimal. Not a single drop of blood stained the courtyard stone.

While assessing the minor damage, my eyes focused on a head of strawberry blonde hair. The small head turned, and ochre orbs brightened with a face splitting smile. "Dawn!" the high pitched voice squealed as the child dashed in my direction. Twin braids bounced against the girl's slender shoulders with each swift footfall.

Squatting down, I caught the petite body as the child jumped at me. My arms wrapped securely around the girl, and I quickly stood to my full height. Energized giggles escaped dusty pink lips when I spun in a few complete circles. Coming to a standstill, I leaned back to peer at the rosy face of the child. "Are you okay? You're not hurt, are you, Rose?"

She squirmed in my grasp, lightly swinging her legs to bump into the lower half of my chest plate. "I'm fine. See," Rose squeaked as she extended her palms to show me.

I huffed out a breath of relief. Other than a few stray strands of hair, all was in its rightful spot. My lips pressed to Rose's forehead, placing a kiss upon the rosy skin. "Thank heavens."

The relief that washed through me was so powerful it caused a slight shiver to run down my spine. Rose was my baby girl, not through biology but through mutual love. Four hundred years ago, during a border skirmish with the northern country of Neconay, Rose's parents were killed by Siven knights. While surveying the carnage, William and I happened upon her cowering form hiding in a closest of her family home — the bodies of her murdered parents right outside the door. Siven stole the only people Rose could count on to care for her, but William and I couldn't allow her to become a starving, unwanted orphan in the middle of a war zone. The two of us returned to Siven with Rose, adopting her as our own. Over a short period of time, Rose gradually came to trust William and me. That trust bloomed into an unwavering love as an indestructible bond formed between the three of us.

"Where's Will?" Rose asked, twisting in my grip to search for the man.

OUT OF UNIFORM

"Rose," I began, touching my hand to her cheek. Vivid orbs stared expectantly at me. "Will's gone, and he might be in danger."

Her vibrant face darkened to a mixture of grief and sorrow. Pooling in the corners of saddened eyes, tears threatened to overflow, but Rose blinked against them. "Where did he go?"

"I don't know, but I'm going to find out. And I need your help. Can you do me a favor?"

Wiping at her eyes, Rose nodded.

"I need you to stay with Grandma and Grandpa for a while." Rose threw her arms around my neck, nodding as she buried her face. At the sound of muffled sniffles, I cupped the back of her head to rub rhythmic circles with my thumb through the soft strands of hair.

Holding tight to Rose, I hastily crossed the yard to the outer stable. A row of identical white pegasi stood tied to multiple hitching posts. "Hang on tight," I instructed as I placed Rose atop the nearest mount. After unwrapping the reins from the post, I placed my left foot in the stirrup and swung up to sit behind Rose. I pulled her flush against my torso, keeping one arm securely around her small frame.

Urging the pegasus into motion, its snowy hooves clicked against the flagstone. We rode to the gatehouse and waited for the wrought iron gate to rise. Once it rose, I dug my heels into my mount's side. The equine took off at a speedy lope. Silvery wings unfolded and elongated as we crossed through the gatehouse. With a few quick flaps of its feathers, the pegasus lifted into the open sky.

We quickly abandoned the castle, leaving behind the open meadow in which it was nestled. The field of manicured lawn shifted to thick, dense forests for as far as the eye could see. We rode far above the lush treetops with a clear sky before us and swirling clouds above us.

A couple hours passed before the concentrated forest abruptly ended to surround a quaint family house and the farm's multiple outbuildings. My mount steadied itself in one spot and lowered in altitude until its hooves touched down upon the dusty earth of the barnyard. I swung from the saddle and took Rose in my arms. Placing the child on her own feet, I told her, "Go to the house and get Grandma."

Rose nodded before running across the yard to the two-story farmhouse. As she reached the door, I turned to lead the pegasus in the opposite direction, tying it to a *hitching post outside the first of three stables.*

"Dawn!"

I turned at the call of my name. Standing in the open doorway with Rose snuggled to her chest, stood Raven Lockwood – my mother. Her dark auburn hair was tied in a loose ponytail and draped over her right shoulder, messily hanging opposite of Rose. She was clothed in an off-white button up and muddied overalls. The sleeves of the cotton shirt were pushed up to her elbows, and sooty brown gloves shrouded each hand. Wrinkles creased her forehead as olive green orbs drew together to analyze my sudden appearance.

Leaving the ivory equine tied, I crossed the yard to meet my mother beneath the door's threshold. "As nice as it is to see you, I'm guessing this isn't a social visit."

Meeting her gaze, I nodded.

Olive eyes peered at the disheartened child held within her warm embrace. The inquiring orbs locked with mine. "What happened?"

"Will's in trouble. Could you please watch Rose for a while?"

The gloved hand resting upon Rose's back left the child to land gently on my shoulder guard. Reassurance emanated from the soft touch – strong enough to penetrate the metal. She tenderly prodded, "What happened?

I wanted nothing more than to melt under her gaze, throw my arms around her, and spill everything. But I couldn't. To do so would put my family in danger, and I wasn't selfish enough to risk their lives along with mine. The less they knew about my future actions, the safer they'd be. "Will has been sealed away, and I'm going after him. Please take care of Rose."

"Of course," my mother said as her hand retreated once again to Rose's slender back. "Take anything you need. We'll tack Cobalt for you." Raven stepped past me, brushing her hand against my upper arm. Placing Rose on her own feet, the two of them strolled to the middle stable while interlocking their fingers together. A lighthearted giggle broke through any remaining tension as the linked hands swung freely between the pair.

Tearing my eyes from the heartwarming duo, I entered my childhood home. Even after all these years, not a single thing had changed. The small, accommodating kitchen welcomed me back. Dusters hung on copper hooks, their coattails brushing against the tops of leather boots. The wood grained walls encircled a dark-stained oak table with four matching chairs surrounding it. Maroon drapes were tied back, allowing the sun's rays to illuminate the pine floors. Chestnut cabinets followed after the window on the far wall, to turn at the corner and end at the cast iron stove.

My boots clicked against the wood with each step I took to travel further into my old home. I passed by a separating wall to enter the family room. An old rocking chair and a soft armchair sat opposite each other near their respective windows. Situated between the two was a light sage settee with a coffee table standing before it. Pictures stood proudly on the mantle of the fireplace that was nestled in the corner. A corncob tobacco pipe lay dormant atop a small stack of wood beside the fireplace, only an arm's reach from the rocking chair.

I passed behind the settee and reached the staircase leading to the second floor. The boards groaned as my weight shifted from stair to stair. I stepped up on the first platform, rounded the corner, and climbed the last handful of creaky stairs. Before me were three doors to choose from – one on each side and another a few paces forward. My hand reached for the doorknob on the left; and slowly turning it, I pushed in the door.

The subtle rays of light spilling in from a single window irradiated pastel purple walls. Beneath the window was a twin-sized bed complete with violet bedding. A bookshelf displaying more knickknacks than books overlooked the foot of the bed on the opposite wall. Entering the room, an elongated oaken dresser was immediately on my left, and cozied in that same corner was an elaborate full-body mirror.

I crossed the room to stand at the edge of the bed I slept in every night for the first few millennia of my life. Untying the navy fabric from around my neck, I draped the garment across the violet blanket. I unknotted my own cape and let scarlet lay beside navy blue.

Turning my back to the garments, I took one step toward the dresser when my eyes zeroed in on my reflection in the mirror. I paused midstep, unsure of my own image. What did I stand for? Was the armor I wore a symbol of justice for all or justice for the small few deemed worthy by the king and queen? Did the golden star engraved on the armor above my heart show loyalty to the crown or to the country? Was I a dog to the royal family or a respected protector of the common people? Where did I truly stand in this boiling conflict that threatened to tear my country in two?

Staring at my armor clad form, I already knew my answer. Piece by scarred piece, I stripped myself of all connections to the crown until I was left staring at my pale skin barely kissed by the sun. The armor I so proudly wore to defend Siven crashed to the floorboards in a jumbled mess. I stepped over the meaningless hunks of metal and grabbed hold of brass knobs to pull the top dresser drawer open. I hastily changed into a fresh cotton long sleeve and a dark pair of denim jeans. After grabbing out a second set of clothes, I retrieved both capes from the bed and exited my room.

I ran down the achy stairs, taking them two at a time. Crossing through the family room to the kitchen, I headed straight for the closet situated beneath the stairwell. I pulled the door open and quickly lit the kerosene lamp mounted on the wall. As light flooded the dark space, I hastily collected the few supplies my journey would require. After shoving it all in a saddlebag, I gave the closet a final once over and extinguished the kerosene-fueled light. I grabbed a dark oil duster off the hook on the wall and slipped into it before stepping out of the farmhouse.

The ivory pegasus I rode in on was replaced with my personal mount. Innocently pure white ran from the stallion's large head, curved with his arched neck, and continued across the length of a muscular back to end at a rounded rump. All four of the steed's athletic legs were dipped jet black. Onyx ears pricked forward and protruded from a dark silky mane that matched his long tail. Folded at his sides, intricately woven feathers were as bold and dark as the night sky. He turned his crescent marked forehead and black speckled muzzle in my direction before a high pitched whinny erupted through dusty pink lips.

"Hey there, my boy," I answered his warm greeting as I stepped to stand before my steed. "How have you been?" My hand outstretched, gently petting the length of his face;

15

and in response, the equine pranced lightly in place.

A string of giddy giggles sounded from atop the pegasus' back where Rose grabbed hold of the saddle horn. Gliding one hand from Cobalt's face to the side of his neck, I side stepped to stand at his shoulder so I could drape the saddlebag behind the saddle. After gaining a free arm, I wrapped it around Rose's torso. The child beamed brightly at me, showing off her pearly whites. "He missed us!" she exclaimed with pride.

A few feet to my right, my mother added, "We all did."

I glanced at Raven. "I'm sorry."

"Don't apologize," she chided me. "Cam and I are proud of you. We understand you have a tight schedule."

"Where is Dad?"

My mother's expression visibly grew sullen. "He's renewing our contract in Centrielle." As quickly as her demeanor turned sour, Raven's eyes softened, and her lips upturned ever so slightly. "Don't fret over something as minute as that. Go rescue your knight."

"Yes, Ma'am," I said.

Turning to Rose, both my hands carefully grasped her small frame. I lifted her from the pegasus' back and embraced her tightly. Delicate arms clung around my neck, and strawberry blonde locks pressed against my shoulder. I pivoted on my left foot, placing myself between her and Cobalt. Squatting to the ground, the soles of Rose's shoes touched the dusty earth. Her grip on my neck gradually loosened as she lifted her head from my shoulder. "I love you now and forever more," I solemnly vowed, pressing my lips to her forehead.

Rubbing fervidly at her eyes, Rose forced a small smile to grace her trembling lips. "Come home soon, and don't forget to bring Will back. Okay?"

"I promise."

Rose stretched up on her tiptoes to place a swift peck on my cheek. "Bye-bye," she whispered before spinning on the balls of her feet to dash toward Raven. Being lifted from the ground once more, Rose buried her face in the crook of Raven's neck.

While comforting my little girl, Raven slowly nodded once — effectively prodding my departure. With a final wave goodbye, I mounted my pegasus. I grasped the reins in my right hand and directed Cobalt south. With subtle pressure on his ribs, the stallion took off at a lope. Onyx feathers unfolded after a few long strides and flapped to lift us off the ground.

With an uncontrollably racing heart, I steered Cobalt high in the evening sky and refused to sneak even a glance over my shoulder. No matter how far we flew, I longed to hightail it back to my daughter. My right hand twitched, aching to feel the warmth of Rose's fingers intertwined with mine. What I wouldn't have given to be relaxing in front of the fireplace with Rose cuddled in my lap and William's strong arm draped around the both of us.

But that wasn't what life had planned for me. A rebel sorcerer complicated my already chaotic duty as not only a mother and lover but as a knight entrusted to protect Siven. How was that young sorcerer skilled enough to sneak a small militia into the castle yard without the repercussions of detection? The task would have been nearly impossible for an aged, experienced sorcerer, but the blond couldn't have been more than 4,500 years old. Even if he had been training since birth, the power he possessed shouldn't have been at his disposal for another few millennia at its earliest.

The sun hung low on the horizon and dusted the sky a brilliant pink and vibrant orange by the time Cobalt's hooves touched down on lush grass. Mere moments after our landing, a single dark figure emerged from the shadows atop a pitch black unicorn and left a second figure masked in the darkness of the trees. An onyx hood was pushed back so the rays of the setting sun could shine upon golden locks. "You're out of uniform," the sorcerer observed, ever present smirk plastering his face.

While an irritated sigh blew past my lips, my fingers pinched the bridge of my nose. "Skip the small talk. How do I break the spell?"

"Nice to meet you too. My name's Kent. What's yours?" the sorcerer chatted, either oblivious to my radiating anger or purposefully stoking the fire of malice. Upon receiving a glare of daggers and a soft snarl, the sorcerer's smirk morphed into a hard somber line. "I apologize for missing my initial target. I had no intention of harming any of the royal guard members."

My tongue clicked at the man's arrogance. "An apology won't bring my partner back. Take responsibility, and tell me how to break the spell. Then we can go our separate ways."

Liquid blue orbs danced with genuine curiosity as Kent asked, "You're not going to slaughter me where I stand?"

"I'm not that stupid," I scoffed at him.

Every muscle veiled under the dark fabric visibly relaxed, and the sorcerer's childlike grin faintly softened his features. Hands rustled beneath the onyx cloak and released a cylindrical object from the confines of an inner pocket. "Catch," Kent said, effortlessly tossing the object at me.

Rough parchment met my palm as Kent began his explanation, "That scroll will lead you to exactly one thousand metal shards. Connect those pieces to form a longsword. Once the sword is completed, your partner will return."

"It's that simple?"

"Not quite. The time limit is one thousand years." The sorcerer let his new information sink in before asking, "Any other questions?"

"No."

"Then I'll be on my way," Kent stated before backtracking into the cover of the forest. "Don't die."

"Same to you. Hopefully the next time we meet will be on better terms," he called over his shoulder with a halfhearted wave.

Staring at the scroll within my grasp, I sincerely wished to never again see that sorcerer's face. I would gladly live my entire life without associating with that man even a single moment longer.

THE REAL TRAITOR

Enter the monsters' lair used once every seven hundred years to find the needle in the haystack.

The delicately stroked calligraphy rested upon the surface of the unrolled parchment within my grasp. Its ink seemed to perch atop the parchment as if refusing to dissipate into the layered fibers. If I ran my finger through the prideful words, would they smear into a muddied reminiscence of their former selves? Too terrified of losing the first clue to my reunion with William, I gingerly gripped the paper's edges.

Staring at the imperious directions, I analyzed the clue word by word. Monsters' lair *and* once every seven hundred years *were the keys.* Needle in the haystack *was the final swing to hit the nail on the head. Could the clue be any clearer?*

With a tender touch, I rerolled the parchment before storing it in my saddlebag. "Let's go," I said to my steed. Taking off, I steered Cobalt's flight directly over the Great Falls to dip down the path of free falling water. I soared mere feet above the billowing cloud of mist and followed the natural flow of the currents until the broad pool narrowed to a single strip of blue cutting through the forested terrain. As the shades of pink and orange in the sky were consumed by the utter darkness, the noise of rushing currents butting heads guided my journey east.

The lightless night prevailed over the typical starry sky, and the darkness had shivers running down my spine. My grip tightened on the reins as the hair on the back of my neck stood tall. A racing heart had blood scrambling through my veins and echoing in my ears to drown out the rushing water below.

The chill night air encircled me but didn't offer any warm comfort. It made me long for William's reassurance. A tranquil whisper or a soft caress would have easily stilled the trepidation of my limbs, but it was selfish on my part to assume I was the only one yearning for the other.

Where was William now? Had his mind and body been sealed away in some foreign world? Were his body and soul even connected, or had they been torn apart? Did consciousness evade him or was he fully aware of the circumstances at hand?

My basic understanding of sorcery wasn't enough to find the answers on my own. I knew sorcery revolved around the four elements of air, water, earth, and fire. It wasn't some almighty power that lacked limitations; it was an ability to manipulate the elements and their compounds as the user saw fit. But even knowing that didn't put my mind at ease. How did Kent manipulate the compounds of the human body to transform it into steel? Or was that even what he did? How many techniques went into creating that one spell to bind the body and soul of a man to a shattered sword? William's mind couldn't have been destroyed, so where was it now? Was it broken into a thousand pieces and infused into the shards? Or did it have nothing to do with the sword, and his mind was sealed away in a completely separate space?

Even with so many questions bouncing around in my head, I couldn't find a single answer. If I hadn't been in such haste to begin this search, would my mind had been clear enough to think of these questions earlier when confronting Kent? Whether that would've been the case or not, it was too late to let my mind contemplate the what-ifs. One thousand years was not a substantial amount of time, but I'd be damned to squander even a single millisecond. Even if I had to endure sleep deprivation and nutrient deficiency, I'd break this spell in less than a fifth of my allotted time.

When the sun finally peaked its head above the treetops, a vast clearing and peccable body of water slumbered to the south of my river route. Veering from the Kitoc River, Cobalt and I ventured into the treeless plain. The closer we flew, the more distinct the monsters' lair became.

Soaring well above the notorious water, I crossed the length of Deadman's Lake. Below me, dark figures loomed within the water's depths. The obscure blobs glided through the murky liquid, some so close to the surface that the scales of their backs shined in the sunlight. Nearer to the lake's sloping banks, the creatures were nowhere to be found – thankfully preferring the depths at the center of the lake.

Nestled at the water's edge with the plain on one side and the start of the dense forest on the other stood the mouth of an ominous stone cavern. Cobalt landed on the grassy clearing just beside the cave, staying a respectable distance from both the rock structure and the lake.

After loosely tying the reins around the saddle horn, I slid from my steed's back. I stripped myself of my clothes and shoes to pile them on the ground. Clad only in my undergarments, I padded to the lake's bank, digging my heels into the soil to slide down the slope and splash into the water.

Deadman's Lake easily welcomed my intrusion and sent soft ripples through its water, but its chilling temperature was determined to dissuade any further embarkment. The cold was a shock to my system, but it did nothing more than encourage my limbs to stroke faster through the water.

So I swam on, journeying closer to the mouth of the cave. Once within the cavern's jaws, I trod water to assess the layout of the monsters' lair. Protruding just above the water's surface were many large nests constructed of grass, sticks, and mud. The oversized bird nests dotted the cave's interior, perching themselves atop the protrusions of rock formations within the water. Each lay dormant, making the likelihood of running into one of the monsters slim to none.

I paddled to the nest nearest to the entrance. My fingers latched onto the mixture of mud and grass as they began their search. I clawed the circumference of the nest before peeping into its center. Nothing. No glint of metal. No shard.

Moving to the next nest, the whole process repeated itself. Yet again, my fingers failed *to seek out the treasure. Nest after nest, I found nothing but mud caked to my fingernails.*

I'd find it. I had to.

But maybe my interpretation of the clue had been wrong. Was the monsters' lair really the lair of a monster, or was there a more philosophical meaning? Did needle in a haystack refer to an actual haystack, or was I right to assume it meant the near-identical array of nests?

I groaned in frustration and slapped the water's surface, sending a spray of droplets through the air. My elbows hooked behind the lip of the nest, and my head lulled back.

I squeezed my eyes shut against the falling shower of mist and sucked in a deep breath. Remain calm. Wrap my head around the situation. Worst case scenario, I was wrong to begin with. But if the shard couldn't be found within this cavern, I'd search somewhere else. Don't give up hope before searching each and every nest – twice if that was what it took. If even then the shard couldn't be found, I'd start over at square one. It was as simple as that. Problem solved.

With a shaky breath, my eyelids peeled back to stare at the dark ceiling of the cave. In the farthest depths of my peripheral vision, a small streak of light drew my attention. The little flicker reflected off the ceiling, pointing directly at a muddy bundle of grass and sticks nestled against the stone wall. The slant of hope disappeared within the protective center of the nest.

Propelling myself through the water, my arms extended with unnecessary force. My legs kicked me forward and gave me the last push to reach my goal. I grabbed hold of the nest's edge, and hefted myself into its center.

A piece of shimmering metal – barely the size of my pinky toe – lounged against the nest's raised edge, oblivious to the torment it inflicted mere moments earlier. My hand reached out, and my fingers gingerly curled around the jagged shard to encase the chill steel in warmth. Steadfast, I retreated to the water and hastily powered through the portentous liquid. When I reached the slick bank, I scrambled up the slope, slipping and sliding the entire way. The soft crunch of grass beneath bare feet welcomed my land arrival as I strode to my discarded garments.

After drying off the best I could, I clothed myself. I dropped the minute shard into the safety of my breast pocket before moving to Cobalt's side to rummage through the saddlebag. Retrieving the scroll, I pulled it from its confines and let it unroll within my grasp.

The pretentious ink that led me to this place morphed to form new letters, new words, and new hope. It proudly defined my next path to the second piece of my partner. Each boldly darkened stroke engraved itself within my memory before being delicately veiled and stored away.

As I mounted my steed, I spoke to him, "Let's go hide away my treasure." Cobalt took off, gliding low over the terrain to head directly north. Our destination stood solemnly across the clearing, each of its abandoned buildings struggling to endure their crumbling fate.

We rode through the desolate village by ground. Dust stirred between Cobalt's legs to leave a lingering trail in our wake that gradually spread to the decrepit boardwalks lining the street. The dust settled within the buildings, entering through the broken window panes and the doors left ajar. The majority of this forgotten village was unsafe to enter — let alone store my beloved treasure — but at the edge of the village limits stood the only viable, secure structure within a full day's journey.

The livery stable's sliding door rested upon the sun-bleached outer wall and allowed Cobalt to trot right in. We rode into the typical livery. Horse stalls lined the right while feed bags and tack storage were to the left. A pile of old, musty straw sat in the far left corner with a pitchfork leaning casually against the wall. The wooden rungs which led to the haymow were only an arm's length from the pitchfork.

I dismounted my pegasus and retrieved the scroll from the saddlebag before climbing the ladder to the mow. After stepping upon the platform, a stack of ancient hay bales greeted me. I untied my scarlet cape and gently wrapped the single shard and clue within its secure warmth.

I tossed a few bales to the side and set the scarlet bundle atop the others. "I'll be back," I promised before stacking bales around my very heart and soul to form a makeshift hideaway, praying to whomever was listening that they'd be protected.

My days shrouded in darkness wouldn't end until my scheduled execution, but even the knowledge of my impending death couldn't strike fear within me. It wasn't life that I was afraid of losing, but my very essence within this world. Had another person's life not been depending upon me, I would have released my grasp on this torn and bloodstained cloak centuries ago.

But that wasn't the case. William's future depended on my present. I had been so close to breaking the spell. In barely fifty years, I assembled just over half of the pristine longsword. It would have been a piece of cake to save Will in my allotted time, but I got careless. Like most deserters, my past actions caught up to me; and I made one mistake too many.

A hissing sizzle rang musically in my ears as ever familiar, brilliant green sparks danced along the fissure between the glistening pieces of steel. The crack slowly sealed, eliminating the only imperfection in the metal and making two pieces one. The work in progress was laid back within its nest of hay to rest upon the scarlet cape.

The scroll replaced the longsword in my grasp, and I unrolled it. Calligraphic script rested upon the parchment to read: Travel to the body of water made of sand. Hold your breath to find what you desire, or the surface may never greet you again.

Water made of sand. *That had to be Sandon Pond. I had to hold my breath, so the shard must be buried at the bottom of Sandon Pond.*

After rolling up the parchment, I dropped it beside the sword and camouflaged their pocket within the hay. I hastily crossed the mow's platform and climbed down the rickety rungs. Hopping atop my steed, I steered him out of the livery and immediately urged him to the sky.

We took off north of Lochville, heading straight for the Kitoc River. Flying over the rushing currents, treetops greeted us for as far as the eye could see. I directed Cobalt in a northeastern arc between Stratwood and Fort Brook to ensure a reasonable distance between both bustling cities.

It was early afternoon when Cobalt and I descended into the cover of the forest. A heavily traveled road was not far ahead, and the sound of a horse and carriage was enough for me to hide among the dense brush. With great stealth, Cobalt and I inched closer and closer to the dirt road until I spotted the carriage.

Its jet black base was outlined with a single strip of white. That same white ran along the borders of the door and each window. A family crest consisting of a white shield with the cross moline at its center proudly displayed itself on the door. An arrow shot diagonally through the cross while two bird claws mirrored each other on the cross's other diagonal. It was a peculiar crest — one I had never seen. Even more unusual was the lack of gold or silver. For a noble carriage to be naked of either precious metal was unheard of. Not only that, but what was a nobleman doing way out here? Fort Brook was never fond of outsiders, and Glosaston was a poor farming village. What would a nobleman want with either one of them?

Before I had the chance to delve any deeper into the noble carriage, it was out of sight. I took the opportunity to soar over the road and continue flying above the treetops. Cobalt flew straight to Sandon Pond, landing just within the boundary of trees adjacent to the water's eastern shore.

Staring out upon the large pond, I pushed back the hood of Will's cape to unveil my head. The warm, midsummer breeze blew against my cheeks as I deliberated my options. Dusk was nearing, so should I start my search or wait till the next day? It made logical sense to start now, find the shard within the night, and then move on to the next piece tomorrow morning. But would I be able to search after nightfall when darkness consumed the earth?

I huffed out a puff of air and pushed aside my inner dilemma. To save time, I would start my search now and look for as long as I had to even if the demons of darkness descended upon the water. Urging Cobalt out of the trees, he stepped the few strides required to stand at the pond's edge.

As I swung my leg over Cobalt's rump to dismount, a sharp and searing pain coursed through my right shoulder. Crying out, I lost my footing on the stirrup and fell shoulder first into the shallow water. The heat of one thousand fires burned through my muscles as I grasped at the flames' source in my shoulder. Air hissed past clenched teeth and exited my mouth in a flurry of moans and groans that softened to quiet whimpers.

"I never thought I'd actually catch you." The words were uttered incredulously and almost regretfully. "Please tell me you're not Dawn Lockwood."

Craning my neck, my eyes matched the man's freckled face with his voice. Messy, fiery red hair — almost orange — hung down his forehead to meet grayish blue eyes drowning in forlornness. Golden accents decorated the knight's armor, but my sight was drawn to a single star that rested above his collarbone. A shadow of a smile graced my

22

lips. *"Congratulations, Spencer. You've finally become a captain."*

"But at what cost?" Spencer questioned as he stared down at me pitifully. He extended his hand and pulled me to my feet. *"Sorry,"* he apologized when I winced, but I didn't know whether the apology was for capturing me or inflicting bodily damage.

"Hold still," he said before tearing the arrow – flesh and all – from my shoulder. Brows furrowed and teeth clenched as Spencer balled up the tail of my cloak and pressed it against the bleeding wound. A single hiss of pain escaped from my lips, and I instantly regretted it upon seeing the guilt it brought to my former subordinate.

"I'm so sorry," he said.

"Don't be. You're following orders. But if you want to do me a favor, take my belt and use it as a tourniquet."

Without hesitation, Spencer undid the buckle and pulled the leather from the belt loops of my jeans. He wrapped the belt around the pit of my arm and secured it tightly over my wound to keep pressure on it.

"I have to take you back," he said.

I stepped past Spencer to stand beside my steed. Gathering the reins in my left hand, I grasped the saddle horn and swung into the saddle. *"Let's go. I won't cause you any problems."*

Spencer's brow arched, but he didn't voice his questions until our flight to the castle was almost over. We had just flown over the sleeping Centrielle when he finally asked, *"Why would you voluntarily come back?"*

His question caught me off guard because I wasn't quite sure of the answer. Being taken to the king should have me fleeing in the opposite direction, not running toward him. I should've been terrified and quaking in my boots, but I wasn't. King Caldwell did not strike fear within me like he did to others. I had dedicated my life to protecting the king and queen – many times at the expense of my own morals and values – so what was the worst they would do?

Then there was Spencer. My former subordinate had been promoted to my old rank. His mission was to bring me back to the castle, and I'd hate to imagine what would happen if he failed. His career would be over, and he'd worked too hard to have his blood, sweat, and tears squandered over one mission. I couldn't allow him to lose his job over actions I brought upon myself, especially since he had a family to support. His wife and children needed to be fed, clothed, and sheltered. I refused to risk his family's wellbeing.

"You caught me fair and square. It would be dishonorable for me to run away now."

"Honor," he scoffed. *"Honor means nothing in this day and age."*

That was news to me. *"Since when?"*

"Since the raid on the castle half a century ago."

"What does that have to do with this country's honor?"

The tilt of his head revealed an unamused smirk that failed to touch his eyes. *"You'll see."* Spencer said no more on the subject and fell silent for the short remainder of our voyage.

A morning sunrise brightened the dreary atmosphere that surrounded the castle.

Spencer landed his deathly white pegasus, and I followed suit. The two of us waited patiently for the wrought iron gate to rise before crossing into the guardhouse.

"'Bout time you hauled her ass in!" one of the guards shouted.

Another chimed in, "What took you so long Captain Spencer?"

Spencer stared straight ahead, not even acknowledging the guards' insubordination. With confident authority in his tone, he instructed, "Inform King Caldwell and Queen Ember that Dawn Lockwood will be awaiting their judgement in the throne room." He didn't bother waiting for a snide reply and continued into the castle's outer yard.

Upon our immediate arrival, a young male servant ran to stand before Spencer. Head bowed, dusty blond locks veiled the boy's eyes as he quietly asked, "May I bed down your pegasus?"

Spencer swung out of the saddle and with a gentle smile, placed his reins in the boy's open palm. "Thanks, kid," he said as he ruffled the boy's hair.

The boy beamed at Spencer, and happiness radiated from his cheerful eyes and wide grin. He turned from Spencer and focused an expectant gaze on me. "I'll take your pegasus too, Ma'am."

Returning a warm smile, I dismounted and handed the reins to the child. After watching the boy lead the equines into the stable, Spencer and I walked into the inner courtyard, passing through a stone archway. We entered a huge, sparsely decorated hall and took an immediate right to climb a dark, twisted stairwell. Navigating the hallways, we made one more turn before entering a grand, golden room. Two enormous thrones, both adorned with jewels, sat atop a satin red platform. Each gigantic chair was unoccupied, but that soon changed.

From a second entryway of a solid stone door, King Caldwell and Queen Ember entered the throne room, both wearing expressionless masks. A heavy aura of authority fell upon the room as the royal patrons each sat themselves in their respective throne. The obvious display of wealth and power showcased in their expensive attire and gleaming hunks of gold atop their heads only added to the thickness of the air.

"Kneel," Caldwell curtly ordered.

I obliged, awkwardly dropping to my knees.

"It's about time you brought her back, although it is disappointing to see her breathing. Care to explain why you blatantly disobeyed orders?" The hostility in Queen Ember's snide tone sent a tremor down my spine.

Disobeyed orders? Spencer would never dream of doing so. He was the model of the ideal knight – obedient and strategic with the mindset of a brilliant leader. Even when he was the low man on the food chain, Spencer was quick on his toes and had a knack for analyzing his surroundings. He would never jeopardize his mission because of his personal ties.

Or so I thought.

Eyes downcast, Spencer sloppily saluted the queen. "Your Highness, it was upon my assessment of the situation that I deemed Miss Dawn Lockwood harmless and unarmed. It would go against every value I hold dear to murder a defenseless symbol of Siven in cold blood."

The king disagreed, "Your judgment seems to be mistaken, Sir Spencer, for the only symbols of Siven are seated before you."

Spencer's head rose, and he inhaled a deep breath as if it would be his last. "I beg your pardon, Your Majesty, but I believe it is you who is mistaken. Had I killed Miss Lockwood and the news of her death spread, there would've been an uproar amongst the citizens. I ask you to please keep in mind her former image and position within our society while you pass your judgment."

Caldwell's beady eyes narrowed, and his jaw clenched. He spoke through his teeth, "Know your place, Sir Spencer. There will be consequences if you speak out of turn. Do you understand?"

"Yes, Your Majesty."

"Good," he said flatly before turning a menacing glare to me. "You will rot away in the dungeon for a millennium and be publicly executed at a later date."

All my blood drained from my face, and I could only image how ghostly pale I must've looked. "Wait!" I jumped to my feet in protest. "What about William?" What had gone wrong? This wasn't how my meeting with the king and queen was supposed to play out.

"My concern does not lie with Sir William for his position has long since been filled. I am more interested to hear about your rendezvous with the rebel sorcerer. How did that fare?" Caldwell's tone turned terrifyingly pleasant, almost sweet as he asked the question.

William was not replacement. Humans were not replaceable.

"I cannot say."

An irritated sigh blew past his lips. All pleasantries forgotten, he snarled, "You have one last try. Care to change your answer?"

"Yes, I do. It's not that I can't say, but I won't say"

The king's temper flared, and the dam that held back his anger burst. "Sir Spencer!" he shouted. "Take this heathen out of my sight, and lock her traitorous self within the bowels of the west dungeon!"

Traitorous? Me? This wealthy pig who sits by while his people starve dared to call me a traitor! "Who's the real traitor here? You're betraying William! You're torturing your people! Siven is bound to crumble under your reign! You've taken a peaceful sanctuary and turned it into a blood thirsty kingdom! Of course the citizens would rebel against a dictator like you!"

Caldwell listened to my outburst, his face ever reddening. His breathing escalated as mine steadied to an even pace. Horrifyingly calm, he stood from his throne and stepped down from the satin platform. He came to stand before me, his eyes staring slightly up at mine. With his composure finally cracking, the king roughly grabbed the fabric of my shirt and jerked me down to his level. I winced from the flaring pain in my shoulder, but my reaction was ignored. "You can think what you want about me," he said with a sadistic grin splitting across his face. "The opinion of a dead person means nothing." The king released his grip on my shirt and shoved me into Spencer. "Take her away at once!"

Spencer hastily retreated from the throne room with me in tow. As he pulled me *under the stone archway, I shouted my last remark, "I'm not dead yet!"*

Eyes the shade of a stormy sky bulged in dumbfounded shock. "Are you trying to lose your life?" Spencer questioned.

"I can't lose what is already lost."

TRUST IN THE ENEMY

Four days passed in utter darkness. The luxury of light came at a fixed schedule when one of the many castle servants brought down miniscule scraps of food and water. Although I saw them every day, interaction with the servants was strictly forbidden. No matter how many times I tried striking up a conversation, they were tight-lipped – as if their mouths had been sewn shut.

That's why my attention pricked when fragments of a conversation floated down the stairwell. I strained to make out even the smallest of words or a single syllable; but all too soon, the quiet murmurs disappeared. My heart sank at the silence but lifted once more as the sound of boots clanking down the stairs drifted through the darkness. A sliver of light penetrated the blackness and grew to toss long shadows into my cell. A lone figure, lantern in hand, rounded the base of the stairs and came to stand mere millimeters from the floor to ceiling bars that separated the two of us.

Blinking my eyes against the burning light, my sight slowly adjusted. I shielded my eyes just enough to finally recognize my visitor.

"Mom."

My elation was short-lived, though, for my mother's face twisted in agony. The pain etched into her gentle, olive orbs dampened her eyes and slid down her cheeks. The normally serene smile that graced her lips was nowhere to be seen. Instead, her lips trembled in anguish, consuming her signature, genial grin.

Raven's reaction left me in a state of confusion, but then realization smacked me upside the head. I looked like the losing end of a street fight. Dark splotches of dried blood splattered the light tan of my button up shirt that was once a creamy white. The navy fabric bunched in my lap sported the same discolored patches, and let's not forget the lack of personal hygiene over the last few days.

"Mom," I breathed out softly as I stood to my feet. "I'm fine. It's not as bad as it looks, so stop your worrying."

"I'm your mother. It's my job to worry." Raven's words came out as quiet whispers, barely strong enough to reach my ears. Her hand tentatively passed through the gaps of the bars to gently press against the very edge of a large, dark splotch at the top of my right shoulder. Her expression visibly relaxed, softening the corners of her eyes when her hand came back clean with not a single smear of crimson.

A light sigh escaped her parted lips, and the mask of motherly concern was overshadowed by a foreign seriousness that demanded my attention. "Dawn, I need you

27

to listen and refrain from asking any unnecessary questions. Can you handle that?"

The first thing that popped into my head was Why?, but deeming that an unnecessary question, I simply nodded.

Raven went on to explain herself, "No matter what happens, you must not despair. Even if it takes centuries, I need you to believe in us. Don't give up on tomorrow because of today's darkness."

My eyes crinkled in confusion. "Us? Who is us?"

"You, me, your father, your daughter, William, the citizens of Siven," my mother listed. "It doesn't matter who us is. Just know that we're rooting for you. We won't abandon you. Please, promise me you won't give up hope in this world before help arrives."

Every ounce of curiosity I possessed screamed within my mind to ask about this help Raven spoke of, but my logic quelled that naive curiosity. "I promise."

With a single deep breath, the weight of the world lifted itself from her shoulders. Olive orbs lightened, and thin lips finally upturned ever so slightly. It was only a shadow of her normal jovial self, but it was a start.

Seeing my mother smile had me longing for the remainder of my family. It had been almost half a century since I'd seen them. "How are things back home?"

"We've all adjusted," my mother answered. "Rose misses you dearly, but Cam's doing a good job of keeping her busy. By the time you come back, Rose will be an expert in all things equine."

I smiled at the thought, remembering my own childhood with my father. I bet he took Rose riding over the treetops and through the meadow like he used to do with me. Some habits just don't change.

"What about you and Dad? How are you two doing?"

An exasperated sign blew from pursed lips. "We've been better considering the king terminated our contract. Cam has a meeting with him in a few weeks to try to convince him to reconsider."

Their contract was... terminated. No, that couldn't be. The deal to supply the castle with royal pegasi had been in my family for far too many generations to count. Breeding, raising, and training equine was the Lockwood way of life. It was my family's main source of income. Why would King Caldwell break that sacred trust between Siven and the Lockwood family?

It was because of me; it had to be. My selfish actions led to this. My wrongdoings shattered my family's only hope of survival. Without that precious income, what money would be used to buy food? Mom. Dad. Rose. They'll slowly starve, wasting away to skin and bones. It's as if I was the one denying them the very nutrients of life.

"Dawn," my mother called to me, dragging me from my horrid thoughts. "It's not your fault."

"But—"

Raven would hear none of my rebuttal. "We are family. Family stands by one another even if sacrifices must be made. A flimsy contract is not worth turning my back on my child."

"What about the money?"

"Don't waste precious time worrying about something as miniscule as a few gold coins," she brushed off my concern as if it was nothing. "We've gotten by before, and we'll get by now."

Before I could further voice my concerns, a loud rapping resounded down the stairs and echoed within my small confines. "That's my cue to leave," Raven said, her smile forlorn. She locked eyes with me, her free hand gripping my forearm. "Please remember what I told you. Don't lose hope." With those final words still hanging in the stale air, my mother left.

The darkness that she had cast aside quickly returned with a vengeance.

My eyes stared blankly at the cold stone floor, seeing nothing at all. The bleary gray was perfect – just as dull and meaningless as my life had become. The outside world meant nothing to me. Light and colors were foreign pleasures I knew little of. Human interaction was a delicacy I was forbidden to taste.

Hope – what a truly depressing concept. It was supposed to lift you up, make you want to live another day for the slim chance it will be better. But day in and day out, that dreadful concept did nothing but wave bait in front of my face. I reached out to it – trusted in it – but I was betrayed. The ideal that I sought was snatched away from me. My so-called hope was consumed, eaten away by the darkness. Hope failed, and there was no bright tomorrow to believe in.

So what would come next? With hope vanquished, all I had was despair; but despair was a more formidable foe than hope. Despair didn't sugarcoat. It gave me the cold, hard truth and emphasized every failure I committed, every promise I broke. I couldn't close my eyes without seeing it – the long list of people I let down. How disappointed would they be to see me now? I could picture it, their eyes refusing to look at me out of disgust.

I could no longer be called a human. No, I was an animal – one that had been caged and locked away. Unfit for human interaction, I was left in the darkness – trained to be a silent, obedient pet. I was that straggly stray cat – emaciated and broken – but no one paused to take a second glance. One stray among thousands, there was nothing special about me. Like any other nuisance, I had been stored away and conveniently forgotten.

Conveniently, but maybe not completely. The words of my mother rang within my mind, playing over and over again on repeat. The help she promised became my bait. It was the leverage hope used to lead me on, and it made me dearly wish she wouldn't have told me. If I had been oblivious, I could've wasted away to nothing and finally gave up on this world. That was my problem, though. I knew of that mysterious help, and I clung to it for dear life.

I clung to it – believed in it – for I don't know how long. The minutes ticked by and blended together into months, years, maybe even centuries. Without the help of day and night, the passing of time was lost. I tried to keep track of the days by the number of meals I received, but that schedule wavered after the first week. It became so irregular that it was painful to even contemplate.

So here I was, balled up against the stone wall. My legs drew up to my chest with my arms tightly wrapped around them. The stained navy cape draped over my still form, and I hadn't moved from that spot in what seemed like an eternity.

What would be the point in moving about? I had neither energy nor ambition. An empty, hollow being needed none of those. Emotions, thoughts, and memories were meaningless. It was easier not to feel, because I was sick of crying. I shed far more tears in the past few centuries than any person should ever shed in a lifetime. If I could choose, I'd abandon every last emotion in existence. It would make this torture far more tolerable.

I flinched when the resounding screech from the tower door echoed in the small space, but it received no other reaction from me. Even the clicks of boots descending the stairwell didn't make me so much as bat an eyelash. It wasn't until light penetrated the darkness that I finally moved, pulling the cape over my head to protect my over sensitive eyes.

"What a pity," a distinctly feminine voice said. "And here I thought I'd be rescuing a headstrong warrior, not a broken rag doll."

Rescue? What kind of sick joke was this woman playing?

I weakly glared at the audacious visitor.

"That's more like it," the woman praised my minute movement as if it was a great achievement. She curiously gazed at me, tilting her head slightly. "Hmm, maybe this will spark some life into you," she thought aloud.

A trio of soft clinks emanated from the bouncing of a golden pendant and chain against the stone floor. I contemplated the small, circular pendant and wondered about this woman's true intentions. What was the worst that could happen? I tentatively reached out to the pendant, and my fingers curled around its coin-like shape.

Engraved on one of its faces was a charm of good luck – a four leaf clover. Elegant cursive bordered the perimeter to read *May Good Luck Always Accompany The Bearer.* Flipping the pendant over, the name I found inscribed in gold brought silent tears to my formerly tearless eyes. I blinked against them, trying to savor every noble letter of a name so familiar it could've been my own.

William Bates.

My eyes lifted to the woman – finally seeing her clearly for the first time

– and all the pieces fell into place. Her body was clad in the crown's gold accented royal guard armor, but the bulky metal couldn't mask the resemblance of her fawn beige skin. Just a few shades lighter, her hair was neither dark as rich soil nor light as the coat of a dun horse. It was a happy medium, being rustic with the slightest hue of red. The long strands interwove down her right shoulder to form a messy braid. Bangs swept across her forehead, barely draping almond shaped eyes. Those pools of deep, earthy brown confirmed my suspicions.

I sat upright, staring at the mesmerizing orbs. "Sydney?" I asked hoarsely.

The woman responded with a single nod of her head. "It's been a long time, Dawn," she said warmly with a smile to match. "I'm sure you have a million questions to ask, but I'm afraid we don't have much time. Please trust us to get you out of here safely."

"Us?"

The word barely left my lips when I received a bone chilling answer. "Don't forget about me," the eerily familiar voice spoke with an impudent coolness.

A hazy transparency of a human figure appeared in the empty space beside Sydney. The lantern's dim light shone right through it, but the bright rays gradually halted against a solid body. I didn't have to see this person's wry smirk or golden blond locks to know who it was. He looked exactly as the last time I laid eyes on him – from his onyx cloak to the high ponytail tying his hair back. "Have you missed me?" he asked, quirking his eyebrow.

What was Kent doing here? He was the cause of this whole predicament, so why was he here? Why would he help me – someone who despised his very existence? Had his inflated ego overpowered whatever knowledgeable sanity he possessed? No conscious person would willingly stroll into the enemy's home base to offer even the slightest assistance to a neutral party. What did this man want from me? What did he hope to gain?

"What's with the suspicious glare?" he asked. "Can't I help someone out without expecting anything in return?"

Funny he should mention that, because I never accused him of wanting something. I didn't say a single word to him, let alone make accusations I have no proof to back up. The sorcerer's own guilty words confirmed what I knew to be true. He was only helping now so he'd be owed a favor in the future.

"Shut up, Kent," Sydney effectively shushed the man. She then addressed me, "Dawn, do you trust me?"

How could I not? Sydney was practically family, so I nodded my head.

"Then please understand that Kent is on our side. Trust him as you trust me."

As much as my blood boiled at the thought, I didn't have many options to choose from. It was either trusting the sorcerer or rotting away with the demons that dwelled in the dungeon. Too afraid of the latter, I chose the lesser of two evils. At least taking the path of the sorcerer would lead me back to my own rescue mission. "Alright," I conceded hoarsely. "Bygones will be bygones."

"Nice choice!" Kent exclaimed with childlike pride. "Now let's get you out of this hell hole!"

The sorcerer outstretched his arms to brush the pads of his fingertips against the metal bars that caged me for far too long. The pads of his fingers lingered on the bars before his hand slowly lowered. He descended their lengths until he crouched on the ground with both palms flat against the stone floor. Straightening to his full height, he casually flicked each bar. As the sorcerer's fingers touched the metal, the bars crumbled to fine dust and clouded the enclosed dungeon like a thin layer of smoke.

Sydney crossed through the new gap and stood over my still form. The smoky dust parted at her presence and swirled around her ankles. The subtle lantern light illuminated her extended palm and beckoned me to place my hand in her warmth. Her fingers closed securely and reassuringly around mine before she gently pulled me to stand on my own two feet. Like some almighty savior, she offered me a way out.

She nudged open my opposite hand and retrieved her welcoming gift. Sydney placed both her hands behind my neck to clasp the golden chain beneath my hair. "There," she said, stepping back to admire her work. "Now he'll always be beside your heart."

While the pendant wasn't needed to have William in my heart, it calmed my mind to have a piece of him still intact. It wasn't like his cape. The two were completely separate entities. I allowed the warmth of his cape to be sullied by my blood. I corrupted it, so it no longer held William's pureness but my failures. This golden pendant was different. Its essence was still innocent, untouched by the hands of despair. The embodiment of hope – I'd protect its righteousness with all my might.

The sorcerer cleared his throat. "As heartfelt as that was, I believe it would be in everybody's best interest to move on to phase two."

Sydney nodded in agreement. She then explained, "I will lead the two of you out of the castle. After that, you'll go with Kent, and he'll give you further instructions later. Okay?"

I nodded.

Sydney turned to the sorcerer, an expectant look upon her face as if to tell him it's his turn. He blinked once before raising his hand and snapping his fingers.

My body suddenly felt light as air, like I was a feather that would blow away in the slightest of breezes. Every last ounce of my flesh floated in this space. There was no heaviness atop my shoulders and no weight pressing down upon my knees. With a single step, I feared my feet would lose all contact with the ground permanently.

The look on my face must have been priceless because the sorcerer chuckled. "Don't fret. That's what it feels like to be invisible."

"We don't have time for any more explanations," Sydney said, turning her back to cross the dungeon floor. "Let's go." Sydney grabbed the lantern from the ground and led the way up the twisting stairs. The sorcerer and I followed close behind. When we reached the door at the top, it screeched open. Sydney stepped aside, letting Kent and I exit into the light of day first.

Despite the weightless invisibility, my skin soaked up the warmth of the sun. Every bone I couldn't feel was replenished, anchoring me to the ground like the roots of a great oak. Heat spread to every recess of my body, blanketing me in a bright embrace. My very soul drank up the essence of life as the warm afternoon rays chased away the demons of darkness.

A firm grip on my wrist tugged me from my appreciation of the sun. I shook off the sorcerer's hand but followed close behind him nonetheless. We casually strolled through the castle grounds and crossed the outer court. As much as I wanted to sprint through the gatehouse and flee as far as I humanly could, I put my trust in Sydney. Plus, I doubted my body in its weakened state would even make it a quarter mile.

Upon reaching the gatehouse, a royal pegasus was tacked and waiting. A guard handed it over to Sydney, wishing her a safe journey. He stared straight at the sorcerer and me, but his dark orbs held neither contempt nor alarm. His eyes may have been looking in my direction, but they saw right through me. The stiffness in my airy muscles dissipated as the guard turned his sight to the rising gate.

I followed Sydney and Kent through the gatehouse, finally setting foot on free soil. Sydney immediately took to the sky, riding south over the road to Centrielle. She left me – confused and slightly frightened – in the care of a man I barely knew.

"Uh," I muttered, trying to find words to voice my concerns.

The sorcerer brought his pointer finger to his lips to shush me. He turned east, walking across the manicured grass which bordered the fortress's towering walls. Pausing, he looked over his shoulder and motioned for me to follow.

I trusted Sydney, and Sydney trusted the sorcerer. Out of respect for Sydney's judgment, I followed a few paces behind the man. He led me across the remainder of the trimmed grass and forged a path through the untamed underbrush once we entered the forest. We trudged through long grass, stepping around trees and crunching over fallen leaves. Once the image of the castle was completely engulfed by the intertwining branches, the sorcerer and I came to a halt.

A long, low whistle slipped from the sorcerer's lips to resound through the trees. All was quiet for a moment before a loud, menacing neigh broke through the layers of foliage in response. The thundering of hooves pounded against the earth, and the ground seemed to tremble under the pressure. Bursting through the branches, a colossal equine slid to an abrupt stop, leaves swirling at its hooves. Dark as the night, the beast snorted and pawed at the earth. It locked eyes with the sorcerer and submissively bowed its head until its pointed horn grazed the forest floor.

"Meet Demon," the sorcerer said as the equine raised its head to tower a foot above its master. "He will be your transportation to Halbrook."

"Halbrook?" I questioned. "What's in Halbrook?"

The sorcerer shrugged his shoulders. "Not a clue," he answered, rubbing his equine's cheek. "Sydney wants you to wait for her in an abandoned storehouse. It's about a mile outside the village, and Demon will get you there safely."

"Is that all?"

Kent nodded. He motioned to his steed, simply pointing to the ground. Without a second of hesitation, the unicorn bowed and folded its legs beneath its massive body. "Your ride awaits."

I hopped on the equine's broad back, sliding into place. My fingers twisted in the beast's dark mane as it rose to its feet. "What about the invisibility spell?" I asked.

"It'll wear off in a few hours."

It would last long enough to make it to Halbrook. Satisfied with the knowledge, I directed Demon east, fully prepared to depart.

"Wait a moment!" the sorcerer called as he cut in front of the equine's path. "How many pieces of the sword have you found?"

I quirked an eyebrow at the man's sudden inquiry but answered nonetheless. "Six hundred fifteen."

"Have you spoken to him yet?"

My blood boiled at the sorcerer's insolence, and my palm twitched. If the man was a step closer, I'd slap him across the face. "How the hell would I?" I snapped. This man was the reason for William's disappearance, and he dared to make a humorless joke at Will's expense.

The sorcerer recoiled – astonishment bright in wide, icy eyes. "I apologize," he said, bowing his head slightly. "It seems I jumped ahead of the situation. The time is obviously not right; but one day, you'll understand. Good luck with the remaining two centuries to complete the sword. Please pardon my abruptness, but I'll be taking my leave." The man backed into the trees, and vanished in a blink of the eye.

A SECOND CHANCE

The sorcerer left me dazed and confused, failing to unravel the deeper meaning to his words. He was hiding something. That I knew, but exactly what he hid was a mystery to me. It grated on my mind, because what did it have to do with William? Was there more to the conditions of his spell than he originally told me?

I pushed the endless thoughts to the recesses of my mind, filing them away for a sleepless night. My journey across the countryside of Siven was far more mesmerizing and required less conscious thought to appreciate. It engrossed me, all the colors and sounds overwhelming after centuries of darkness. It was the little, unappreciated happenings of everyday that I often took for granted that had me wondering at the vastness of life and endless possibilities this world had to offer.

Freedom after centuries of being bound and caged gave me a whole new gratefulness of my surrounding world. The caressing wind wrapped its wispy arms around my body and ran its delicate fingers through my free flowing auburn locks. Birds chirped in the treetops, their melodies drifting to my ears to soothe a weary soul. Each tiny blade of grass stood proudly beside another and formed an endless sea that stretched for miles. The sun's rays penetrated through the crevices between the branches and leaves overhead to cast light even on the forest's darkest nooks and crannies.

This was a world of beauty. Its cruelties could almost be overlooked, overpowered by its natural charm; but humanity's morbid prejudices, injustices, and animosity could not be forgotten or pushed aside by alluring words and images. The sins of humans could not be erased by the serenity of nature for it was not nature that sinned. It was not the fawn that killed its mother or the butterfly that attacked the pansy. The wolf did not bite the waning moon, and the great oak did not massacre its siblings. Humans brought cruelty to an instinctual world, and it was a burden the whole human race had to shoulder.

But if nature was not cruel, then why did the wolf eat the doe? It was to survive to see the sun of tomorrow, but humans had no such excuse for the injustices they willingly placed upon each other. That wolf ended the doe's life to extend its own, but humanity had evolved to abandon the concept of survival of the strongest. Humans had developed consciences to determine right from wrong, but some seemed to have a skewed sense of morality. The differences and so-called abnormalities of mankind were seen as weaknesses when, in reality, they were the exact opposite. Those very aberrancies were the roots of humanity's beauty – setting humans apart from any other species.

If that was true, then why was Siven on the brink of destroying itself? What gave Caldwell and Ember the right to abandon ethicality in favor of creating their twisted version of a perfect world? Why were the refugees from the five surrounding countries being persecuted – hunted down for the cards life dealt them? What was the difference between my family and William's? Did the few thousand year difference of gaining citizenship make the Lockwood family any better than the Bates family? No, it did not, so why was that contorted logic applied to every other citizen?

"What if I wasn't here? What path would you take then?" William's words echoed in the confines of my mind. So many centuries ago, I couldn't give him a definite answer, but my choice was as clear as a summer day. To protect the remnants of humanity's beauty, I would fight against the crown. I would save William; and then together, we'd defend the rights of every resident of Siven, citizenship or no citizenship.

Demon's steady canter slowed to a smooth jog. The equine's fluid strides carried me through a deer trail that opened up to a tiny clearing surrounding a decrepit, rotting building. Sliding barn doors were tied against the building with rope while its accompanying entrance was left ajar. Each of its many windows was smashed, the broken glass still scattered beneath the sills.

Demon stilled and stood before the open door. I slid from his back and patted his thick neck in appreciation. The unicorn promptly turned tail and departed in the direction from which we came.

I entered the empty storehouse, leaving boot prints in the layer of dust settled on the floorboards. The building was bare, having no shelves left to reflect its former use. The light of dusk shone through the broken windows to cast long shadows that masked the vast emptiness. With the darkness of night fast approaching, I leaned my weight on the wall and slid to the floor. I sat within a patch of dimming light, holding tightly to its remaining warmth as my heavy eyelids fell over my eyes.

The following morning, a gentle shake to my good shoulder jostled me to consciousness. Sydney, bright and cheery eyed so early in the day, crouched in front of me. She spoke softly and quietly, "We have to leave soon."

Rubbing at my eyes, I wiped away my weariness and managed to push myself to my feet. The very tip of the sun barely peeked over the horizon and tossed orange rays of light upon the awakening earth. The light shone into the storehouse to illuminate a more welcoming environment. It might have been the two tacked horses munching on hay in the corner or the wide open barn doors allowing a cool morning breeze to brush against my cheeks; but above all, it was the cordial smile of Sydney that blanketed me in an impregnable sense of security. This person's mere presence put my mind at ease, silencing my unrelenting nerves.

Sydney retrieved the horses, leading them to the open doors. "Where is the next shard?" she asked as she waited in the doorway for me.

Even after centuries of imprisonment, I couldn't forget that clue. The thick ink engraved into my mind flashed before my eyes as if the worn parchment had unraveled within my grasp. I could recite the words as if they were the names of my family and friends, but I kept the answer short and sweet. "At the bottom of Sandon Pond."

Sydney nodded in acknowledgment and handed a pair of reins to me. After taking the reins, I followed Sydney out of the storehouse, and we mounted our equines. "Let's go," she said as she urged her horse south.

We rode into the dense forest with Sydney forging a path for me to follow. We were silent, not that it bothered either of us. I was used to traveling alone, and the stillness of isolation had become my only ally. Sydney may have been family; but even with her, I knew my voice would fail me. It was rusty after centuries of collecting dust on a shelf, and I wasn't exactly into spring cleaning.

With the comfortable silence being broken only by the occasional chirp of a bird, Sydney and I made record time in reaching Sandon Pond. The sun hung low in the sky, leaving only an hour or two of daylight left.

I followed Sydney out of the trees. Lightly pulling back on the reins, the equine beneath me ceased its forward movements. I swung from the saddle and stared at the still water.

So serene and quiet, the pond was the very image of eerie peace – like the calm before the storm. The blades of grass swayed with the breeze just as they had centuries ago. The trees, standing tall and proud, masked any creatures it could be hiding in thick, twisting shadows. Each rustle of a branch had those shadows reaching out, arms clawing and grasping at any victim willing to be pulled into the forest's clutches to be consumed by the darkness.

But I could see it. Sinister orbs of amber stared at me. An arrow pierced through the air, and unlike last time, the sharp tip dealt a fatal blow. Blood stained the grass, seeping into the earth to forever taint this once pure ground. Hefted onto the back of a crown's pegasus, a body lay limp and lifeless. Dark auburn hair fell listlessly to conceal the body's face, but its identity was no mystery.

That was my body.

Firm but gentle hands fell upon my shoulders, and their support stilled the small tremors coursing through me. "Dawn," Sydney called softly, "you are safe. No one is going to hurt you." She repeated those few words over and over again until the sharp gasps I didn't realize I was taking evened out to slow, deep breaths. She held onto me for a moment longer before letting her arms fall to her side. "Are you okay?"

There was no conviction to my answer, but I said, "I'm fine."

Sydney's eyebrow raised skeptically, but she didn't push the subject. Instead, she patted my back and said, "I'll keep watch." It was only a statement, one of simple action, but it was exactly what I needed to hear.

I stripped to my undergarments and stepped into the chill water. Dropping to my knees, my hands began their tedious search of the pond's muddy bottom. They raked through every square inch of mud as I crawled from one side of the pond to the other. I came up empty-handed, only finding rocks, twigs, and the occasional crayfish. Daylight was starting to fade, and I covered barely half the pond.

I waded in the middle of the water - my feet barely touching the bottom - when my toes brushed against a smooth object. It felt foreign, unlike the countless rocks I uncovered. I inhaled a deep gulp of air and dove into the water. Blindly, my arm extended to cut a path through the murky water until it bumped against the pond's bottom. My fingers frantically sought for that foreign object as they slid through a thin layer of mud and coarse stones. Bubbles of air escaped my mouth until no air remained, and I was forced to the surface.

I dove down again. Both of my hands joined the search even as my right shoulder protested its involvement. The dull ache wasn't enough to stop me. Even as it turned into a wincing throb, my hands continued to dig through the mud. I spun in a circle, hands sweeping all around, as my air once again left me. Ready to depart, my fingertip brushed against the bottom one final time, and I felt it – the shard that eluded me for nearly seven centuries. With burning lungs, I freed the piece of metal from its mud encasement and scurried to the surface.

My head burst through the water's surface, sputtering for breath. I vaguely heard Sydney calling my name; and upon opening my eyes, I spotted her worried gaze. "Are you okay?" she called.

This time I could respond with certainty, because I was more than okay. I hadn't lost again. I came out victorious, holding my prize proudly over my head.

I didn't say a single word, but Sydney knew. As I stepped ashore with water dripping off me, she wrapped her arms around me in a tight embrace. She effectively soaked herself from both her own tears and me. "Hope," she choked out after a sob. "There's hope. We can still save him."

A concept I once abandoned, I now clung to. It beat and bruised me, but at the end of the day, it was the only thing pushing me to live, to wake up again and face the world. Maybe I was wrong about hope. It hadn't hurt me; I hurt me. My own utter despair clouded my senses, and I mistook futility for hope. I had been wrong. Hope didn't abandon me. I abandoned hope.

Encased in Sydney's warmth, it was hard for me to deny that she was right. We could save William, and we would. We'd hold on to that hope, nurture it through despair, and let it blossom into the brightest, most beautiful of all flowers.

After a night of bedding down in the forest with the two of us huddled together, Sydney and I departed bright and early. "Where to?" she asked as she mounted her mare.

"Locheville," I yawned. "The sword and the clue are hidden in its livery."

Sydney nodded and took the lead. We circled Sandon Pond to steer clear of Kerrigan before riding south. Once again, we embarked on a silent journey. The silence only broke after we safely crossed the road to Centrielle and were well on our way to the Kitoc River.

"Hey, Dawn," Sydney called over her shoulder as she slowed her horse and made room on the little forest path for me to ride by her side. She averted her gaze, choosing to stare into the tangles of tree branches. She was quiet for a brief moment before her voice – less confident that usual – finally spoke up. "How was William doing before this whole situation happened?"

I couldn't say that I was caught off guard, because I knew this conversation was eventually going to take place. Even so, I didn't expect the question so soon. "Well, I can't speak for him," I started, "but he seems to have finally moved on and come to terms with it. Ever since Rose came into our lives, he seems to have a new reason to smile."

Sydney's eyes were bright and shining, damp with too many emotions. "That's great. He deserves happiness." She wiped at her face, clearing away the tears before they could stain her cheeks. "Are you worried about him?"

To an outsider, that question would be deemed unnecessary, because the simple answer was evident. Who wouldn't be worried about their partner, their lover? I was, but not for the obvious reasons.

"I wish I could say no and tell you I wholeheartedly believe in him, but he doesn't respond well to isolation. When he has too much time to think, his mind wanders to places that should be left undisturbed in the past. But even that is assuming Will is conscious and knows what is going on. There are just too many unknowns for me to believe that he is one hundred percent okay, no matter how much I want to."

"I get it," Sydney said softly. "He's strong, but he's only human."

Sydney and I let the topic rest in favor of more lighthearted conversation. We spoke of our families, of the unforgettable memories forged within our pasts. We laughed at each other's childhood shenanigans, simply forgetting about the world's injustices for a while. In that moment, it was only Sydney and me in our own peaceful little slice of Siven. Although the serenity wouldn't last forever, it was a welcome distraction for the time being.

It wasn't long before Sydney and I were riding through the water of the Kitoc and the abandoned Locheville came into sight in the distance. My eyes zeroed in on the decrepit buildings, and I swore I spotted shadowy figures slinking between the alleys. We rode closer, and I could finally make out the dark shadows.

The gigantic reptile – about a story and a half tall – stood in the middle of the street. Its elongated head, much like a horse's, stared in the opposite direction. Smooth scales of copper and amber glistened under the sun's rays. With webbed feet, the beast paced back and forth across the dirt road as defined muscles rippled beneath the layer of scales. A thick, enormous tail dragged on the ground and stirred up a constant cloud of dust.

"We may have a problem," I said as I pointed at the beast.

Sydney peered in the pointed direction, and her eyes bulged, nearly popping out of their sockets. "That would be a big problem," she agreed. She sighed before a light smile graced her lips. "The hoops we have to jump through for my little brother are starting to pile up."

MEMORIES TO BELIEVE IN

"What should we do?" Sydney asked after we backtracked to the safety of the river. "There's no way we can ride down the main street and waltz right pass that monster."

Sydney was right. The oversized lizard was not a creature to mess with, and I was in no mood to become its next meal. "Our best bet would be to leave the horses here and sneak around the back. Then we can enter the livery through the side door."

"Alright, let's go then," Sydney said.

We left the horses to roam on the other side of the river before running at top speed to reach the outer buildings of Locheville. It took only a few hurried strides before my chest heaved painfully with each fast-paced step, and I was once again reminded how my physique had dwindled. Sydney adjusted her own pace to match mine, and by the time we reached the back walls of the buildings, both of us were hunched over and gasping for breath.

Once we recovered, we stuck close to the buildings and cautiously maneuvered through the narrow alleyways. Wide enough for only one person at a time, I followed Sydney and paused when she peeked her head into the street.

"It's clear. We can cut across to the opposite alley, and it should lead us to the livery."

I nodded, and Sydney took a final glance into the street. She dashed from the alley, and I quickly followed. After a few long bounds, the two of us were once more hidden within a claustrophobic alley. We snuck slowly through cobwebs and random clutter. Reaching a narrow corner, we squeezed through the tight opening and finally found the right alley.

Halfway down the building was a single door. Sydney reached it first and grabbed the knob. Jiggling it, she tried turning it but to no prevail. Before I could suggest anything, Sydney backed against the opposite building and rammed her shoulder into the door.

"That's not going to—"

The door flung violently open as Sydney crashed into it. As I stared at her – awestruck – she rubbed her shoulder and smirked, quite smug with her success.

I laughed lightly before shutting the door and stepping around Sydney. I climbed the rungs to the haymow – exactly seven evenly spaced boards. The wood creaked as I stepped onto the platform, and the melody was beauty to my ears. Zoning in on the stack of bales, my heart raced in my chest.

They were right there – the embodiments of William. I hefted a single bale to the floor and brushed away a layer of loose hay. My breath stilled in my lungs as gleaming metal showed its bright face against deep, scarlet red. I reached for it, sliding my hands beneath the fabric to gently lift both the sword and the clue from their burrow within the hay. I cradled them in my grasp and refused to look away from the shiny metal. The sword's golden pattern wove up the hilt, entwined itself around the guard, and broke halfway up the blade, coming to an abrupt stop at the blade's jagged edge – incomplete and yet intricately beautiful.

Digging for the shard in my pant pocket, I carefully matched it to its respective place at the blade's end. I nudged the shard in its crevice, and a quiet sizzle resounded through the silence. The two pieces fused into one. The fault line between the separate pieces turned golden to add to the labyrinth-like pattern, but the blade looked no longer than it was mere seconds prior. Even so, that tiny shard – insignificant on its own – was a step closer to completing the sword. It was a small step, but a step nonetheless.

I gently set the cape and sword atop a bale of hay. With the scroll in my grasp, I unrolled it; and the bold, prideful calligraphy welcomed me back. I read it aloud, *"The shard you seek can be found at the base of the highest peak where two creeks meet."*

Warm breath tickled my neck as Sydney stood behind me, curiously peering over my shoulder. She tilted her head, and confusion clouded her vibrant orbs. Staring at the scroll, her eyes scrutinized the parchment before speculative orbs turned to me. "Are you pulling my leg?" she asked.

"Huh? What are you talking about?"

Sydney gaped at me. "The parchment is blank."

Blank? The parchment was far from blank. Each word, each letter, was as clear as a midsummer sky. The thick ink – dark like the night – contrasted against the creamy parchment, making the words as visible as the nose on my face. "You can't see it?"

"There's nothing for me to see," Sydney replied, staring at the scroll. Her eyes squinted at it as she desperately searched for the prideful words. Frustration soon took over, and she gave up with an irritated sigh.

"You have got to believe me, Sydney," I said, slightly amused. "I'm not insane. There really are words here."

Sydney quirked her eyebrow and questioningly peered at my face. She held it for barely a second before the mask fell. "You're not insane. Maybe crazy but not insane," she laughed lightheartedly. "I'll have to take your word for it."

"Crazy," I tested the word, laughing along with Sydney. "Fair enough. I'll give you that one, but—"

In the midst of the serenity, my words failed me, my voice refusing to come out. My vision wavered and blurred to only smudges of color before going completely and utterly black.

My eyes blinked open, trying to refocus my vision. I stood upright, but there was nothing beneath my feet. In fact, there was not a thing in sight. All around me was a vast nothingness – a white void for as far as the eye could see. No matter which direction I looked, all I saw was white. There was no blue sky above and no solid earth below.

This was not where I was supposed to be. What happened to Sydney? What happened to the livery? Where was this place, and how could I escape it?

I had to get out.

Staying put wouldn't help, so I picked a direction and hesitantly took the first step. I expected my foot to fall through the void - unable to find steady ground – but it connected with some sort of force field to send soft ripples endlessly through the vast sea of white. Step after step, I aimlessly wandered. But soon I became unsure of where I had already been. It felt like I walked in an endless circle, but there was no way to know for certain. Without a single landmark, I carelessly ambled and lost sight of my original purpose of finding an exit.

I trudged through the void for I don't know how long; but after what felt like an eternity, I began to hear quiet noises. They were barely audible, and I thought maybe my mind played tricks with my ears. Maybe the static clouding my head pounded in my ear canals loud enough for me to mistake it for external noise. It could have been nothing; but then again, it could be something or maybe someone.

I closed my eyes and focused on the unknown sounds. Listening intently, I stepped slowly in their direction, stopping every few feet to refocus on the noises. As they grew louder – more profound – I realized they weren't in my head, weren't a figment of my imagination. The pitch and tone were distinct, and I knew exactly what they were.

Sobs.

An ominous foreboding settled within my mind. Those weren't just anyone's sobs. They were familiar and yet foreign. Laced with a despairing anguish, they sounded heartwrenching as they cried out for help. It had been tens of centuries since I last heard them, and I honestly thought I'd never hear them again.

I broke into a dead sprint like my life depended on it, but it wasn't my wellbeing I feared for. I ran as fast as my straining legs would take me, and pushed the burning desire for more air to the back of my mind. My eyes scoured for him – darting left, right, and back again. My heart almost leapt out of my chest when I spotted a lone figure in the distance. Seeing him only made me run faster, pushing harder against the force field beneath my feet.

On his knees, his elbows dug into his thighs and his head burrowed into his hands. His body trembled, shaking with every sob that fell from his lips. His skin not covered by a light blue button up and dark trousers was pale, lacking its beautiful olive undertone. The tears he shed pooled between his knees, and they slowly seeped through the force field. The droplets fell beneath his hunched form and continued to fall into oblivion.

When I finally reached him, I dropped to my knees behind him and threw my arms around his chest. I pulled him close, refusing to let go anytime soon. "William," I breathed his name as I leaned my head on his shoulder. My hand slid up his neck to rest on his slick cheek, my thumb rubbing rhythmically against the tear-stained skin.

His trepidation ceased as each of his limbs froze. A broken sob died in his throat. His fingers trembled as his hand tentatively hovered over mine. When his palm finally rested over my knuckles, his touch was soft, barely tangible. His fingers curled to entwine with mine, and he gently squeezed them.

William leaned into my touch as his earthy brown orbs sought after mine. When they finally met, the hope I had for his wellbeing crashed and burned.

There were so many emotions held within his two orbs. They were the gateway to his soul, and his soul had given up. The pain, the longing, and the resignation were etched into the swirling irises. Centuries of believing, of holding onto optimistic naivety, told their tale of being consumed by a great abyss. It was not a quick and easy process – far from it actually. There were scars of a horrendously brutal battle from the blade of inner demons known as guilt and regret. He fended them off with the pride of a warrior, but even a warrior had limited strength. Beat down again and again; his strength dwindled, abandoning him with his naked vulnerabilities. All that remained was a shattered man, broken but not beyond repair.

"Dawn," he choked out hoarsely, the lonely sadness seeping into his cracking voice. "Is this really you? Are you really here, because if you're not, this is the cruelest joke my mind has conjured up." William begged, pleaded for this moment to be true – to be more than a figment of his imagination – as his lower lip quivered between the bite of his teeth.

I nodded, tears pricking in the corners of my eyes. "I'm here. I'm right here," I told him. "This is my hand caressing your cheek, my voice sounding in your ears, and my body pressed against yours. I'm right next to you. Trust in your senses. I know you can feel me because I can feel you too."

William cracked. He twisted within my grasp to wrap trembling arms around my back. Burying his face in the crook of my neck, his tears renewed as he clung to me. His breath came in sharp, ragged gasps that he couldn't hide no matter how hard he tried.

There were no words I could utter to take away the pain that plagued him. All I could do was hold tight and let him know I was here. Humming a soft melody in his ear, my left hand entangled in chocolate locks while my other kneaded the tension from his shoulders. We kneeled like that long after my legs tingled with numbness, and eventually, his sobs silenced. Tears stopped spilling down puffy cheeks, and his erratic pants calmed to even, deep breaths. The tight, white knuckle grip he held on the fabric of my shirt eased until his palm pressed gently between my shoulder blades.

William's next breath was shaky as he turned his face away from my view. Barely audible, he whispered, "I'm sorry. You shouldn't have to see this."

No words had ever cut so deep. I leaned back, placing my hand on William's cheek to ease his face back to me. As I held his head between my hands, I came face to face with remorse ridden, red-rimmed orbs. "William, there is no need to apologize. This isn't the first time I've seen this, and it's okay if it's not the last. We work through our problems together. We always have, and we always will."

His eyelids veiled the mirrors to his soul. "But I am the problem."

It happened all over again, parallel to the decades after his parents' deaths. This time, though, I would be by his side to protect him from himself. "You're wrong," I said with the conviction of one thousand victorious knights.

William's eyes snapped open, impervious and disbelieving, but wanting nothing more than to trust in those few, short words.

I continued, "There is not a single human in any city, of any country, that is a problem. Problems are not the lives of living beings. They are unjust actions, biting words, and uncontrollable disasters, but your existence is not one of them. We may cause problems, but our existences are not included in that category."

William stared at me for a brief second before a shadow of his crooked grin crinkled the corners of his eyes. He laughed, albeit humorlessly, but the sound tumbled from his lips. "Have I ever told you I love you?"

I sighed in relief. "Indeed you have."

"Then please indulge me while I say it again. Dawn Elizabeth Lockwood –" his voice wrapped tenderly around each name, my name "– you are the breath of air that graces me with the sustenance of life and the glue that bonds each shattered piece of my being together."

William, always over dramatic, did not give credit where credit was due. As touching and heartwarming as the sentiment was, I was not the one to deserve such praise. He had fought his inner battles, not me. I was mere moral support on the sidelines while he went toe-to-toe with the enemy. If anyone deserved such flattering admiration, it was William. But I would not say that and ruin Will's moment, for I did not believe in undermining such words of love.

No more words passed between us in quite some time. We resituated ourselves to more comfortable positions other than our knees and faced each other. The silence lingered, but it did not hang over us in a curtain of unease. On the contrary, it was a soothing silence – one that allowed us to gaze upon the other with new eyes, as if long lost friends had reunited. And in a sense, that was true. I wanted to commemorate every feature, no matter how flawed or imperfect, to the deepest niche within my mind where it would forever be protected against forgetfulness. And by the warm, heartfelt glimmer in his eyes, William thought the same thing.

Chocolate locks, cropped short on both sides of his head, swept in a wild array to drape a couple inches from their roots to William's right. Short bangs that had the slightest touch of curl fell unorderly down his forehead to barely tickle thin eyebrows. Although red-rimmed and shining bright with the remnants of tears, vivid orbs were as deep and clear as the most lavish gem and contained as many specks and swirling spirals as there were shades of brown. His flat nose, complete with a rounded tip, was just as red and puffy as his eyes; and pale, dusty lips no longer trembled. His jawline, strong with a soft touch of roundness, was set in deep concentration. Broad shoulders supported his neck, and muscles were well defined beneath the fabric of his clothes.

This was William, or at least, it was his surface. Much like a geode, the outer casing was mere protection – a false front that concealed the inner crystals. As much as I enjoyed William's aesthetic beauty, it wasn't his physical attractiveness I fell in love with. There was so much more to him that managed to capture my heart, like how he blushed at the slightest compliment and fumbled for words when flustered. He had the nervous habit of rubbing the back of his neck and would vehemently deny it when pointed out. He had a major sweet tooth, his favorite being strawberry hard candy, and it was a miracle his pearly whites hadn't rotted away by now. He pouted like a child when he didn't get his way but was quick to move on from the disappointment. When asked by our daughter to participate in a stuffed animal tea party, Will was always ecstatic and radiated more glee than the child who asked. All these were simple little quirks, not entirely uncommon, but they warmed my heart each and every time.

William's hand reached out, gently caressing my cheek. He leaned forward to close the small gap between us and pressed soft lips against mine. There was no rush, no desperation. It was just William and me as we moved our lips against the other. Will pulled back, taking a light breath of air, before saying, "I've missed you so much."

"Me too," I said. "Me too."

In that moment, I realized something. It had been near eight centuries since our last encounter, since that fateful day. "Do you know what's going on?"

He shook his head. "Not a clue."

"It was a spell from the rebel sorcerer. One second you were there, and the next you were gone." I shuddered at the memory as it resurfaced.

"Then where am I now, and how did you get here?"

I shrugged my shoulders.

William huffed out a sigh. "What a disgusting mess," he mumbled. "Leave it to me to screw everything up."

Where had that come from? What even gave him the slightest idea that he was to blame? "None of this is your fault," I said.

William diverted his eyes, choosing to stare at his lap. "Someone's to blame. The universe didn't wake up one day and decide to go on a rampage."

"That doesn't mean you have to shoulder a burden that isn't yours to carry."

"Then who's to blame?" he questioned, daring me to list off names. When I said nothing, he continued, "The poor maybe? They sit back and take it. Or maybe the nobles since they keep quiet. Might as well blame the knights for failing in their duties to protect. No, let's aim higher. It all falls upon the king and queen for their duty is to the people, is it not?" He stared at me, chest heaving from the outburst, as he waited for my reply – for me to tell him that he was wrong.

But I couldn't. "You're right," I said. "Every last one of us has played a role in this mess, no matter how small. The citizens, both rich and poor, didn't rise up until it affected each individually. They put themselves first. And yes, the knights failed to protect the citizens while striving to please the king and queen, but the king and queen were the first drops in the sea. The ripples spread and are continuing to grow exponentially. So, you see, the blame is not yours to carry alone."

"What will we do?" he asked. *What if I wasn't here? What path would you take then?*"

"We'll fight."

"It's gotten that bad?"

I nodded. "It's been quite a few centuries."

"How many is *quite a few?*"

47

"Eight."

"That long?" he asked, and I nodded again. "How have you been?"

If there ever was a more loaded question, I had never heard it. Even so, I started from the beginning. The sorcerer and how to break the spell, Rose staying with my parents, my capture and imprisonment – I told it all. "The last thing I remember was being with Sydney in Locheville's livery. We were talking about the next clue and joking a bit, but then I woke up here," I said. "What about you?"

"My tale lacks excitement and adventure, so it's not nearly as interesting to hear as yours," Will said with a crooked grin. "I've been lost in this godawful place with nothing to do."

He might have been smiling, but the grin did not reach his eyes. There was more to his tale than he was letting on. "Are you sure that's all?"

William cocked his head, rubbing at the nape of his neck. "Of course. What else would there be?"

"I know you, William, and I know how much it takes for you to break." William's hand froze on his neck. "I just want to know if you're okay."

He blinked, keeping his eyes closed for a few seconds. When he finally looked at me, he took a deep breath and shook his head. "I'm not okay, but I'm better. To be honest, I thought I'd rot away in this place, but even without food or water, I never die. I can't even sleep, no matter how long I lie with the intentions of fading away. It's like I don't even exist. I'm afraid I've gone into a state of oblivion."

"That's impossible," I told him. "You aren't forgotten – far from it. I remember you. Sydney, Rose, and even that sorcerer do too. You're still a part of our lives."

"I know that. It's just–" he paused. "It's hard not to question my existence when I'm surrounded by nothing. There isn't anything to prove that I'm real or that I ever was. I mean, you're here now, but what about when you're gone?" His voice cracked, and his hands reached for mine. He enclosed my right hand between both of his. "You're the only proof I have."

"Do you remember when Rose called you daddy for the first time or when I first introduced you to my parents?"

He nodded tentatively, curiosity shining in walnut orbs.

"You still have all your memories. Trust in the moments of sheer joy and even the ones of insurmountable pain. The emotions that well up inside of you are all the proof you need, because those are your connections to the people that you love."

William smiled, and it was genuine this time. He released my hand only to wrap me in a tight embrace. "Thank you," he whispered.

"Any time," I told him, "but if you still want a tangible reminder, I think I have something that will work."

I wiggled out of his grip and reached to unfasten the chain around my neck. I pulled the pendant from beneath my shirt and beckoned William to lean forward. After he did, I clasped the necklace in place.

He stared at the pendant for a mere moment before his orbs grew bright with elation. Wide, childlike eyes met mine, and innocent pleasure dominated his tone. "I'm the luckiest man alive."

"That you are," I agreed.

William threw his arms around my torso and held me. Tilting his head, he leaned in to press soft lips against mine. My arms wrapped around his neck, pulling him ever closer as our breaths mingled. He cupped the back of my head, his fingers stroking through the strands of hair. Our lips moving as one, we fitted together, so familiar with the other that it was second nature. There was no over thinking that led to awkward clashes of teeth. It was just William and me reclaiming each other after too long of a forced separation.

The warmth of his lips dimmed, and William's gentle touch was barely perceptible, too soft even for him. The sudden loss of contact had my eyes snapping open, and I was met with speechless anguish.

William's arms were wrapped around me. I could see them, but their touch was intangible. His mouth formed words that my ears were deaf to, but I didn't need to hear to know what he was begging and pleading.

I reached out to him, caressing his cheek. My thumb wiped at the silent tears pooling in the corners of his eyes as my own arm began to dissipate. "I'll be back," I promised.

William nodded and forced his lips to form a fictitious smile. I couldn't hear him, but somehow, he heard me.

BROTHERS

My upper back and head rested upon itchy hay as I looked up at the moonlit boards of the roof, being met with a display of cobwebs. I stirred, sitting up and brushing pieces of hay from my hair.

"How are you feeling?" Sydney's voice startled me before I spotted her slumped against the opposite wall.

"I'm fine, but you'll never believe what happened."

Sydney rubbed the drowsiness from her eyes and sat up straighter. "You saw William."

Was that an unnaturally accurate guess? "How did—"

"Kent filled me in on the spell's specifics."

How thoughtful of the sorcerer! He happened to leave out that detail when talking to me but openly shared it with Sydney.

"Is... is he okay?" Sydney asked.

I nodded. "For the most part, he needed a morale booster." I touched my neck. My mind froze when my fingers felt chill metal. The pendant still hung on its golden chain. "I hope I was able to supply one."

"I'm sure you did," Sydney said with a yawn. She glanced to her side, peering through a lone opening in the wall that had a pulley system of ropes hanging in front of it. "We still have a few more hours before sunrise. I recommend using them to catch some shut eye."

We both took that advice. It wasn't until the early rays of the sun poured into the mow that the two of us awoke. We got ready quickly. Sydney scouted an escape route while I wrapped the incomplete sword in the scarlet cape.

"Do you have any ideas as to where we should start our search?" Sydney asked, standing near the alley door as I climbed down the ladder.

"Not one," I admitted as I followed Sydney into the alley, "but I know a person who might."

Sydney accepted the vague information with a nod as we squeezed out of the alley. We exited Locheville behind the decrepit buildings and briskly jogged across the clearing. After sloshing through biting water, we found the horses grazing upstream. We mounted the equines and took off into the forest.

A few short minutes of silence were broken by Sydney's curiosity. "So who's this person that can help us?"

A smile tugged at the corner of my lips, and my heart rejoiced at the mere thought. Images of whitewashed pasture fences and a cozy family home nestled in its own meadow flashed before my eyes. High above the clouds, I would look down and giggle, squirming in a pair of strong, gentle arms. Vibrant green gazed down upon me as his hand swept through short, sandy locks centuries before the strands had been touched by gray. "My father may know."

Sydney peered over her shoulder to stare at me momentarily before returning her gaze to the dense brush ahead. "Are you sure you can bear the consequences that may arise from involving your family?"

Her concern was well placed, but I could've gone without the reminder. It was selfish of me to even consider, but my family were the only ones I could trust at the moment. "I am, but I will do everything in my power to minimize any negative outcomes."

"And how do you propose we do that?" Sydney asked.

I thought for a moment and then answered, "We'll wait till after dark to get in, ask for directions, and get out."

"No heartwarming reunions?"

I didn't want to say it, but a head shake wouldn't suffice. "There won't be time." The only reply was a barely visible nod of acknowledgment, and then the two of us fell silent.

Our silence did not mean all was silent. The little pitter patter of rodents scurrying over fallen leaves and crisp grass echoed as if they were pounding hooves. A red squirrel rapidly dug at the base of an oak tree. Its head twisted from side to side before it dropped a single acorn into the hole. After quickly concealing its treasure, the squirrel darted into the underbrush. A single woodpecker perched on a tree and pecked at the bark in short, rapid continuation. Between the pecks, the squawking and cawing of the forest's other bird inhabitants rang through the trees. When combined, all these noises produced an odd tune, but the sound of nature couldn't have been more comforting.

With nature singing, I crossed a dirt road in confidence. It was a familiar path that marked a near-end to our cross-country trip, but we couldn't beat the setting sun.

Crickets chirped, and a wolf occasionally cried to a waning moon by the time a looming darkness opened up to a stable yard lit by escaping kitchen light. The crunch of hooves signaled our arrival as the front door creaked open just far enough for a head to peak out. A pair of olive orbs squinted at us as Sydney and I tied the horses to the hitching post. When we stepped into the seeping light, the figure gasped before running a few feet to throw her arms around the two of us. She pulled us into a tight bear hug and kissed each of us on the cheek.

"You're alive!" she cried as she pulled Sydney and me into the house. "Cam!" she called before mumbling to herself, "I've got to wake Rose."

"Mom, stop." I grabbed her wrist before she could run into the family room.

Raven froze midstep and stared at my hand around her slim wrist. Her eyes slowly rose to meet mine, and all jubilant excitement vanished. Shoulders slumped, and her arm went limp in my grasp.

I released my grip as my father sleepily trudged into the kitchen, scratching at the tip of his crooked nose. His complexion was pale, lacking its usual luster, and his cheeks were unnaturally hollow. Graying and receding hair stuck up every which way, and dark bags beneath his half-lidded eyes were hard to miss. He stifled a yawn as he began to ask, "What's the–" Sleep deprived orbs landed on me, and all speech was forgotten. He stumbled the few steps to reach me as if he was a much older man than his age suggested. When his arms wrapped around me, his embrace was weak. His body – not long ago in pique condition – was frail and fragile within my returned embrace.

"Are you okay?" I asked as I gingerly hugged my father.

With a smile big enough to crinkle the corners of his eyes, he said, "Don't worry about me. I'll be fine in no time. I'm just so happy you're back." He squeezed me gently, and the light embrace was more than enough to emphasize his sheer joy.

But I had to shatter it. I wiggled free of my father's embrace. "I didn't come to stay," I said, and as much as Cameron tried to veil his disappointment, he didn't hide it fast enough. "I need a little help."

It wasn't even a heartbeat later when my father asked, "What do you need?"

"I need your knowledge of the mountains to help decipher a clue." My father nodded and waited for me to say, "The clue is – *The shard you seek can be found at the base of the highest peak where two creeks meet.*"

"Hmm." He rubbed his stubbly chin as he thought. "If I recall correctly, the creek that runs behind Charlie's cabin crosses another crick. That's probably the place you're looking for. Do you remember how to get to Charlie's place?"

I shook my head.

"That's fine. It's not that hard. Just travel northeast from here, and once you cross the road to Fort Caldwell, keep an eye out for a broken path through the tundra. You'll find it eventually if you keep riding straight. Follow it north, and it'll take you right to Charlie's front door. I'm sure he'll gladly show you two to the creek," my father said.

I thanked him. "We'll be off now."

"Not in that," my mother scolded as she raised her brow skeptically at the light clothing Sydney and I wore. "You're going into the tundra for heaven's sake. Bundle up while I tack some pegasi for you." Raven hurried out the door.

Cameron helped Sydney and I raid the closet for more appropriate attire. By the time we had the supplies stuffed into old saddlebags and walked out into the stable yard, my mother was waiting with a pair of ghostly white pegasi.

I hugged my parents goodbye before swinging into the saddle. Right before I departed, I asked them not to tell Rose I had been back. It would be easier and safer if she didn't know.

Sydney and I took to the sky, soaring well above the shadowy treetops as the light of a crescent moon and twinkling stars shined the way. We hurriedly put miles between us and my family before descending into the forest for the night.

Bundled in heavy trench coats, hats, and gloves; Sydney and I departed as the sun rose above the horizon. Before the warming rays were directly overhead, the two of us crossed the fort-bound road. The temperature fell steadily as we rode over the frost speckled earth. The ground was barren save for the occasional wiry tree and patch of cotton grass. A beaten path of dirt twisted through the hardy grass, and we followed it.

The farther north we traveled, the more natural life vanished beneath a layer of powdery snow. A howling wind bit at my cheeks, sending flurries of flakes through the air to hide the path below. Sydney and I grounded the pegasi and slowly worked our way closer to the mountains. The slope of the land gradually increased. As we climbed higher, the wind broke against towering fir trees, their branches swaying with the mighty breeze.

It was midafternoon when Sydney and I happened upon a cozy little log cabin nestled between two giant firs. Only a few yards from the cabin stood a small stable big enough for only a few head of stock. Both modest buildings were strewed with snow, and the flakes piled up to reach the bottom of the window sills. The entrances were shoveled free, but the falling snow slowly built back up.

The cabin's door creaked open as an older man shrugged into a wool jacket. He wore a gentle smile as he crunched through the snow. "Well, if it ain't Cam's little squirt," the man's booming voice welcomed. He stood before my pegasus and ran a hand through his mussed, gray hair. "What brings you to my neck of the woods?"

"I need a guide into the mountains," I told my uncle.

"Any particular place in mind?" Charlie questioned.

"The base of the highest peak where two creeks meet," I said.

"That's quite specific." His hazel orbs stared at me quizzically as he rubbed the nape of his neck. "Are you going to fill me in?"

Of course, he knew. Charlie led an off-the-grid kind of life, but news traveled to all corners of the country. "Can I fill you in on the way?"

After a moment of contemplation, Charlie nodded. "Give me a few minutes, and we'll head out," he said before disappearing back into his cabin. When he emerged, he had donned a fur hat and a thick pair of gloves. He made a beeline for the stable and shoved the swinging door through the snow.

A few moments later, Charlie led a dapple gray stallion out of the barn. He pushed the door shut before hopping atop the pegasus' bare back. "Follow me," my uncle said. His steed pranced in place, unfolding his wings with a few quick flutters. With one mighty flap, the stud hovered above the layers of fallen snow.

I followed suit with Sydney right behind. My uncle fell back in line with us and said, "Start talking."

I told my tale from the beginning – from the invasion so many centuries ago to the late night stop at my parents' house. I willingly spilled all the details knowing full well that I was giving him every reason to back out before it was too late. My uncle had every right to turn back before I dragged him in too far. If he did, I wouldn't hold it against him. After all, it's easier to walk away than to keep fighting, and I'd give him the opportunity to run.

When I finished, Charlie sighed. "Squirt, you're a spittin' image of Cam. You're both stubborn mules. You should've come to me sooner. I would've torn that damn castle apart stone by stone and burned it to smithereens."

A heavy weight lifted from my shoulders, and the dull ache diminished. Although he scolded my inability to seek assistance, his words comforted me like a blanket did a child. There was no doubt in my mind that Charlie would've stormed the castle, but that would've gotten him killed. No gain would come from his death, only more loss.

"Oh, well," Charlie continued. "What's done is done, and we can't change that. We'll just have to fight back and hope for the best." His speech ceased only to point out our final destination. "There it is – the crossing point of the creeks."

The water was clear and crisp as spiraled clouds of steam rolled across the surface to rise into the sky. The farther creek hugged the base of the mountain before parting to unite with the second creek to form a tiny reservoir. The water split once more, tumbling down a series of smooth rocks. Through the mist of water vapor, the rays of the evening sun glimmered in the flowing ripples. One ray – brighter than the others – shone down upon a group of protruding rocks, and a resulting glare bounced back.

Fresh snow crunched beneath my boots as I jumped from my steed's back. The water of the hot springs sloshed with each step I took. When I reached the cluster of stones, I precariously balanced on the slippery surface. I bent down slowly, reached into the crevice between two rocks, and retrieved what I knew to be there. A single droplet of water slid down the metal's smooth edge, hesitating at the point before plummeting to the creek below. I held the shard tightly as I stepped back to the snowy bank, the snow melting beneath my feet.

"Is that what you're looking for?" Charlie asked from atop his mount, still hovering above the earth.

"It is," I answered as I hopped back on my pegasus.

"Then let's head back to the cabin and see what I can do about that shoulder of yours," my uncle said. He steered his stallion back the way we came and took the lead.

Sydney and I followed right behind. "There's no need. It doesn't bother me much anymore," I said.

"Don't give me that crap. That's a load of—"

Sydney cut Charlie off with an alarmed *shh*. Earthy orbs grew wide with apprehension. "Did you hear that?" she asked.

VOICE OF REASON

I listened intently but heard nothing. "Hear what?"

"I don't know," Sydney whispered. "Just listen."

We all fell silent, eyeing each other for any sort of movement that could explain whatever it was that Sydney heard. The creek babbled, and each pegasus' wings fluttered. No other sound could be heard, and none of us moved the slightest inch.

Charlie broke the silence, "It could've been a rabbit."

Sydney looked all around, twisting in the saddle to peer behind herself. She shrugged. "Maybe you're right," she said quietly, "or maybe I was hearing things. I guess we should get going."

We started riding again, and I pulled up alongside Sydney. I put my hand on her shoulder and squeezed gently. "Don't worry about it. It's better to be safe than sorry."

"Dawn."

My hand froze. I stared at Sydney, and she stared right back. Her lips hadn't moved, and the quiet, muffled voice didn't belong to my uncle. "Did you hear that?"

With wide eyes, she nodded.

"It sounded like it was right beside us," I said.

The three of us held still, holding our breaths for fear of making the slightest noise. The wind stirred the powdery snow, but its whistle couldn't drown out the voice.

"Dawn." It was louder this time, and I swore the source of the voice was there with us. My name rang again, louder still.

I knew that voice – its velvety tone and the way it caressed my name. It resounded again, becoming more of a stifled cry. Recognition burned bright in Sydney's eyes, and the same name tumbled from our lips.

"William."

Time seemed to stand still as we waited for the voice – his voice – to speak again. Tails swishing and wings flapping grew irritatingly loud. Each murmur of the breeze threatened to drown out any reply as did the pounding in my ears. My own breath, light as it may have been, reverberated loud and clear.

But he spoke, and I heard him. "Sydney, Dawn, can you hear me?"

"Yes!" Sydney cried, twisting in every possible way to search for her brother. "Where are you?"

His muffled voice answered, "The pendant."

Pendant? What pen–

My hand tore at the top button of my jacket, fumbling fervently to push it through the slit. It popped open, and my fingers sought the golden chain wrapped around my neck. I clutched it and pulled it from beneath my shirt. Hanging at the end, a circular pendant proudly shined.

I held the pendant in my palm, the engraving of William's name face up. "Will, are you okay?"

His answer was loud and clear, no longer muffled beneath layers of fabric. "I'm fine," he assured. "It's just that... your voice and Sydney's. I could hear them."

"For how long?" I asked.

"There was the sound of water at first, and then a man's voice before I heard you. It took me a bit to figure out where your voice was coming from. Heck, I thought I was crazy at first when you couldn't hear me." He paused. "It's all thanks to Sydney."

My eyes left the pendant and fell upon Sydney's face. Earthy orbs shined bright with tears on the verge of spilling. She bit her bottom lip and squeezed her eyes shut but to no prevail. No matter how many times she blinked, the threat of tears didn't subside. She rubbed at her eyes with the back of a gloved hand, and her hand stayed there. "Tell me you're okay. Tell me you're not hurt, that you're safe and sound."

William's voice resounded softly, reassuringly, and comfortingly. "Everything is okay. I'm fit as a fiddle."

"You sure?"

"One hundred percent."

Sydney released a slow, unsteady breath. Her hand retreated from her eyes to rest on her thigh. When lids opened over brown orbs, they were rimmed in red. Even so, a smile danced upon her lips, giving her eyes a sheen of pure happiness.

"How have you been Sydney?" William asked.

And that's all it took for Sydney to calm down, to jump head first into conversation with the little brother who disappeared all those years ago. As we rode back to the cabin, the air was filled with jovial laughter. Stories were tossed back and forth, mainly between the siblings, but the enjoyment was for all.

Even though the wind was biting and the air was cold, it felt warm to me. William's booming laughter echoed as if he was physically beside me. Hearty chuckles shook my uncle's shoulders, and Sydney's smile was childlike – pure and innocent. Being surrounded by the ones I love, even if only in spirit, warmed every inch of me. In a situation such as this – a fading moment destined to be an everlasting memory – it was impossible to feel cold.

"That didn't happen!" William whined.

"You bet it did," Sydney insisted. "You cried like a baby when the dog chewed up that old teddy bear."

"Alright, alright," he sighed. "I admit it, but that bear slept with me every night since I was in diapers."

"You were already 2,500 years old – an adolescent for goodness sake."

"A man is never too old to have a teddy bear," William said. "Plus, anyone would cry if they saw their friend torn to pieces."

We all laughed as Sydney said, "It was a stuffed animal, and Dad even got you a new one."

"And I loved that one too, but it wasn't the same. Friends can't be replaced."

When we got back to the cabin, Charlie bedded down the pegasi in the stable. Sydney and I sat at a small table in the kitchen, occupying the two chairs as we went through the contents of our saddlebags.

From within my bag's depths, I withdrew the unfinished sword, still wrapped in scarlet. I set it on the table and delicately unfolded the cloak until the gleaming steel showed its marked face. Digging in my coat pocket, my fingers curled around the latest shard and set it beside its larger counterpart. I stared at them, almost unwilling to unite the pieces.

"Let's just test it now. There's no need to drag this out any longer. This way, we'll know for sure" William's voice echoed in the quaint kitchen.

He was right. I couldn't confirm my theory if we never tested it. There was no time to waste, because I couldn't get closer to my goal without connecting the pieces. I needed the next clue to continue. If that meant saying goodbye to William for the time being, then so be it. I'd rather break his spell sooner than risk dragging it out days, months, or centuries that only added up to the time limit.

I nudged the pieces of steel closer together. "Goodbye, Will," I said.

Sydney intently watched the pieces inch closer and closer as she said, "See you later, little brother."

The reply came as the metal began its fusion. His words rang above the sizzling and bubbling of melting steel. Even after the golden labyrinth extended to fully meld the pieces into one, William's words hung in the air to repeat over and over again within the confines of my mind.

"Until next time."

But that's all it was. The words were only remnants of the original – mere echoes that resounded in my ears. When the echoes died down, only silence remained. Neither his booming laughter nor his soft whisper could be heard. The connection that carried his voice through the oblivion of the void all the way to this world had been broken.

The shard and the pendant – two halves of one key – couldn't unlock that door without the other. Once unlocked, both halves were needed to keep the connection open. But if the door was left ajar to allow communication, the next clue wouldn't appear. The key had to be broken, used as two separate parts in order to continue. The connection had to be severed. I knew that, but it still pained me to let go.

Charlie walked through the door. He paused under the threshold, his eyes peering at the sword on the table. As he latched the door, he asked, "Is he gone?"

I nodded at the same time Sydney said, "Yeah."

Charlie pulled the hat off his head, tossed it on the wooden counter top, and shrugged out of his jacket. He hung the coat on a hook by the door. As he turned to face Sydney and me, he cracked his knuckles. "Alright," he said with a thunderous clap that made me jump, "let's fix that shoulder of yours."

My breath stilled in my lungs, and the hairs on the back of my neck stood tall. Defensively, my hands flew up to wave my uncle off. "It's fine. It honestly doesn't bother me anymore."

Charlie quirked an eyebrow. "Oh really?" he said. He took a few steps closer to me, and the knowing gleam in his eyes sent a chill down my spine. His hand fell upon my right shoulder, and he squeezed, digging his fingers into my flesh.

Fire shot from the pads of his fingers and blazed its way through my entire shoulder. The slice of knives scorched muscle, and clenching teeth did nothing to distract from the icy burn. "Point taken," I hissed.

My uncle's grip eased, and the fire slowly extinguished, leaving only resilient embers among the ashes. I huffed out a breath of air in defeat and met Charlie's almost apologetic gaze. "Turn around," he said.

I did as instructed and rested my arms on the back of the chair. My head dropped to lean against my crossed forearms as a gentle, yet firm pair of hands pressed against my shoulder. With a tone of softness, Charlie warned, "It's going to sting."

That was the understatement of the century. As he applied pressure to the old wound, it started out with a warm heat emitting from my uncle's calloused hands. The warmth was quickly overshadowed by a numb tingling, but the numbness was short-lived. My muscles were being torn, forcibly ripped from each other. It was like a parasite burrowing deep within me as it ate its way through my flesh.

"How's your old man?" Charlie asked.

I focused through the pain, trying to organize my jumbled thoughts. "He could probably use your services more than me."

"Why? What's wrong with him?"

I squeezed my eyes shut. "I'm not exactly sure. He just... he looks ill. He says he's fine, but I'm not convinced." The unnaturally pale complexion of my father clouded my mind.

"He's such a stubborn mule," Charlie commented. "All he had to do was ask, and I would have dropped everything to go see him."

Sydney interjected, "But there's a ban on sorcery, even when used for medicinal purposes."

"Oh, well, it's too bad I couldn't care less about such a dumb decision that risks the health of thousands of innocent people. Such a shame. Whatever would an old man like me do without a ruler to screw up everything I've ever worked toward?" He huffed out an irritated breath, and his fingers flexed against my shoulder blade. "Some laws were made to be broken."

As much as his mockery made me want to laugh, I couldn't help but agree. Not only my father, but an entire country of people was put at risk – near eight million lives. They could seek a general doctor – that was if they could find one. But even if they did manage to find the diamond in the rough, natural medicine had its limits and a hefty price to go with it. Mixtures of herbs and native plants could only do so much. They couldn't fuse together the fragments of a broken bone in a matter of minutes or extract a toxin from the bloodstream before the poison had its chance to kill.

Even sorcery had its limits, but it was a far better option than relying upon an overpriced and almost extinct practice of old-fashioned medicine. To outlaw the practice of sorcery – especially medicinal sorcery – was a crime befitting a dictatorship, not a kingdom.

Charlie's fingers kneaded my flesh as he continued, "The consequence doesn't matter. I'd break millions of laws if it meant helping my kin."

"That mindset will get you executed," Sydney said.

"Oh, yeah? So it's gotten to the point where the king and queen are killing citizens for the smallest of infractions?" my uncle asked.

"It's worse than that."

I tilted my head to peer at Sydney. Her eyes downcast, she kept rubbing at her hands beneath the table. She blinked rapidly as if trying to stall the formation of tears, unwilling to let even a single one fall from her eyes.

Charlie voiced the question I couldn't bring myself to ask, "How bad is it then?"

A shaky breath blew past Sydney's lips as she stared at her hands in her lap. When she finally found the will to answer, her voice was that of a frightened child. "Women, children, the elderly, not a single one of them is spared. If you're not carrying your citizenship papers, you'll be executed on the spot – no questions asked. You could be minding your own business, and a knight will accuse you of being a refugee. The knight becomes the judge, jury, and executioner all in one."

"That can't be!" I burst out, sitting bolt upright. "I've known most of those knights for centuries!" A speckled face adorned with fiery red hair flashed before my eyes. "They would never—"

A sharp smack to the side of my head silenced me. "Quit your squirming," my uncle scolded harshly, but his tone did not match his words, the punishment not matching the deed.

Charlie softened, speaking warmly to Sydney, "It does seem a little far-fetched that the knights would obey such orders so mindlessly. What is keeping them from rising up?"

"Fear," Sydney answered quietly.

Charlie prodded further, "What are they afraid of?"

Sydney finally looked up from her lap. All emotion was wiped clean – her face a hard slate of stone, like she had forced a shut down in order to protect herself from the truth that only she could tell. "There's a quota that must be met each month – a quota of lives that is. If it isn't met, it's the knights and their families that pay with their lives instead."

"Has that ever happened before?"

She slowly nodded. "Shortly after the quota was instated, Captain Spencer McCadden refused to acknowledge it. When the month ended, and he hadn't taken a single life, Spencer was publicly executed in the town square of Centrielle. His wife and two of his three daughters were killed while trying to flee."

Spencer was... dead. No, that couldn't be. He was a bright young man. It wasn't long ago when he was a quiet rookie just transferred into my squad, even shorter when he was a captain trying to find his footing. If he had played his cards right, he could've made it to the top to be known as king. A Siven under his rule would be a Siven I'd gladly call home.

"What about the third daughter?" I asked.

Sydney said, "Kent and his boyfriend are taking care of her."

I may not have liked the sorcerer, but at least the child was safe and in capable hands.

"What about the economics?" Charlie thankfully changed the touchy subject. "Are the poor still getting poorer while the rich are getting richer?"

Sydney shook her head, some of the color returning to her cheeks. "Everyone is in the same boat. Nobles are losing their fortunes while the poor are living in squalor. The high class is dwindling, and the middle class has disappeared altogether. The only ones prospering are the king, queen, and their guard dogs.

"But it's not just the economy that's in trouble. International relations have taken a hit as well ever since King Caldwell banned all trade with our neighboring countries." A burning fire grew bright in Sydney's eyes, a mixture of both pain and searing hatred. "Tensions are rising, and King Caldwell is gambling with the lives of millions of people. He is on the brink of self-destruction and will take Siven down with him."

This man, the king William risked his life to protect, needed to be stopped. It was a mistake to serve under him, but hindsight only came after the decision was made. According to Sydney, Caldwell had the citizens of Siven on a short leash – so short that fear was running rampant and replaced the feeling of security in one's life. With fear binding the citizens like invisible shackles, they had victimized themselves to allow the king to string them up like puppets.

Even so, they weren't to blame. A single citizen could not be pinpointed and told that all the world's problems were their fault. Yet, someone had to be held responsible for this mess, and if anyone, shouldn't it be the ruler whom allowed it to happen?

It really wasn't that hard. In whose mind was prejudice and discrimination deemed okay? What screw was loose in Caldwell's head that made him believe a person's place of origin determined that person's worth to society? Just because a person had more pigment to their skin, brighter hair color, or smaller eyes didn't make them any less of a human being; yet Caldwell believed they were below him – not good enough to kiss the ground he walked on.

I took great offense to that viewpoint, not for myself but for William and Sydney. Life had dealt me a relatively easy hand, but the Bates family originated from Arkaynai and was forced to jump through countless hoops to even be considered for Siven citizenship. Will's parents were forced to give up their way of life, their culture, and even their names. Bates was not their original surname. Long before Sydney and Will were even born, the family name had been changed from Okabe to Bates in order to conform to Caldwell's twisted image of Siven. That alone was a large price to pay for a family whose culture held great pride and honor in their family name.

For William, Sydney, and people like them, someone had to stand up against the injustice with the power to provoke the passion of the masses – the everyday, hardworking citizen. Spencer's sacrifice and the many sacrifices of nameless martyrs couldn't be in vain. The rebellion needed to be revived – to rise from its ashes like a phoenix – and for once, the young sorcerer would be seen as the hero instead of the villain. It was a cause I knew I would join once my own problems were solved.

"We'll just have to fight back," Charlie said as he removed his hands from my back and patted my freshly healed shoulder. "It's time we raise some hell."

"We?" I asked, spinning around to face my uncle.

"Well, sure," Charlie said, "I can't let my only niece go out on a dangerous journey all by her lonesome."

I quirked an eyebrow and rolled my eyes. "I think you missed your true calling as the king's jester."

"You're right. I would've skewered him on a sword a long time ago."

Sydney chimed in, "It's never too late."

As we all laughed, we worked together to prepare a small but relatively decent meal of meat and potatoes. A few nicks and an accidental finger cut later, the three of us were seated around the little oaken table eating a warm meal. We talked away the rest of the evening as Sydney cleared the table, I washed the dishes, and Charlie stacked them in the cupboards.

When the cleanup was done, Charlie said, "We better turn in for the night. We've got an early morning and a two-day journey ahead of us."

Charlie set out a thick bundle of blankets on the living room's floor. The room was so snug and cozy that the blankets easily touched each wall. He stoked the fireplace, adding a couple pieces of wood to the crackling pile. We said our good nights before Sydney and I bunkered down on the floor, the warmth of the fire rocking us to a deep sleep.

HAD TO BE WRONG

After two and a half days of almost continuous riding, we made it to the next destination. Three sets of hooves touched down on lush, slightly overgrown grass; but not one of us moved to dismount.

"The clue was quite vague," my uncle commented, and Sydney and I nodded in agreement.

Before us lay the bridge that crossed over the Kitoc River hundreds of miles upstream from where the river split in two, or better known as the hiding place for the next shard. Its ruddy red and burnt orange bricks were bleached by the sun. Many were chipped or missing altogether, but the bridge's foundation stood solid. Two thick pillars rooted into opposite sides of the riverbank and connected together with a flowing arch of bricks. Vines snaked along the bridge's sides to hang above the rushing waters below. Surrounding the bridge was a vast sea of swaying grass – the largest clearing in all of Siven.

"It's somewhere in the vicinity," I said. "We may as well start looking." I swung out of the saddle and loosely wrapped the reins around the saddle horn. "I'll take the bridge if you two take the grass." We each went our own way. Sydney searched the clearing on the right side of the bridge, Charlie was on the left, and I was in the middle.

I walked to the beginning of the bridge where brick met dirt road. My eyes scoured the brick and swept across the entire bridge, but my hope of an easy find was squashed. With a heavy sigh, I began my search.

Hardened clay was rough and rigid beneath my fingers as they skimmed over the bricks. Running along the grooves, they dipped into each crack and crevice, feeling for even the slightest sharp bite of steel. It was a monotonous task – my fingers trailing straight across before sliding down to back track and rise again to the beginning point. I outlined each brick one by one and slowly inched my way along one side of the bridge.

A brick jiggled and rocked beneath my touch. My breath stilled in my lungs as my fingers curled around the hunk of clay. I carefully extracted it, dislodging it millimeter by slow millimeter. It rested on the edge until I finally pulled it free. I reached into the opening and felt my way through miniscule grains of silt. The pads of my fingers grazed each corner and clawed at the farthest recesses, trying to desperately find more space to search.

But there was nothing. The late home of the brick was empty.

I slammed the brick against the opening but repeatedly failed to line it up right. Smashing it into the bridge, little chunks broke off and crumbled to fine dust that swirled in the breeze. The brick crashed against the bridge over and over with a rhythmic pang each time. It dwindled away until the majority of it was strewed by my boots, merely broken chunks and fine powder.

How dare the brick have raised my hopes! It was the only full brick that was loose – not chipped or dented, not already missing – but a fully intact brick. Where else would the shard be? In the grass? That was the most unlikely place. The shards have never been just lying around waiting to be picked up by any passerby. Maybe the shard was encased in this clay brick? How convenient that would be! If I demolished the brick, would it be there? If I tore down the whole damn bridge, would I even find it?

A trickle of blood smudged the burnt orange, and the remaining lump of brick fell from my grasp. I stared at my fingers, yet the scraped skin of the joints didn't register in my mind. The sting of the pain did not release me from my trance, but the smear of crimson that flashed in my view was enough to snap me back to the task at hand.

I abandoned the lump of clay, begrudgingly moving on to the next row of bricks. The imperfections grew greater in number the longer I examined each nook and cranny, but none housed my elusive treasure. My vision went out of focus, seeing only the blur of reds and oranges, but I couldn't be bothered to adjust the view. There was no point. The bricks were all the same, each a conspirator with the first perpetrator. They all mocked me, silently laughing as they concealed the single piece of steel.

It wasn't here. The clue was too vague, and I wasted precious time at the wrong location. There were countless bridges in Siven, and I was stupid to believe it was this one. What made me think I was right? This was the largest bridge, but the clue said nothing about the size. It said very little at all. Some help that was!

I raced off the bridge, my legs moving faster than necessary for the short distance to the pegasi. The ghostly white steed's head shot up at my arrival, but it stood perfectly still for me to swing into the saddle. I called out to Sydney and Charlie. "We've got to go!"

Both looked up, wide eyed, from opposite sides of the bridge. "Why? What's wrong?" Sydney yelled back. As she did so, she jogged through the shin-high grass. She reached me first with Charlie soon after, and both their chests heaved for breath.

"It's not here. We need to search somewhere else." My words jumbled together, quick as they raced through my mind at a mile a minute. My pulse beat rapidly and pounded against my head, and I couldn't get my hands to hold still – to stop trembling.

Sydney's hand gently covered both of mine, and one by one, she eased my fingers open. The reins fell from my grasp as her hand retreated to her side. "Take a breath and think," she said.

I inhaled deeply, filling my lungs to their capacity before blowing the air out through my mouth.

"Think like the captain you once were. What would you have your squad do in this situation?" Sydney asked. She held the left rein between her fingers and cautiously eyed my face.

I stared down at her, fearing the pity she must have felt for this shell of a former captain, but there was none. I met orbs of swirling dust, like a tornado ravaging the earth and throwing up a vortex of rich soil. They were on edge – sharp and precise – but beneath that initial caution was a patient confidence, one that trusted in me to find the right answer on my own.

But could I? That captain was long gone, died centuries ago when William was stolen from this world. I had gone so far as to abandon the very ideals a captain would protect. I walked out on the king and queen. My subordinates were left behind with the promise of death if they followed in my footsteps. Spencer was a prime example, and look where that got him – six feet under. Then there were the people I was supposed to protect. I wasn't doing too hot in that area either.

And Sydney and Charlie weren't my squad members. They weren't a rank below me, and all three of us had abandoned the military and its martial law. We were partners – equal in every decision, every choice made – and they were letting me choose. Two pairs of trusting eyes looked upon me and put their faith in the decision I made. I wasn't their captain, and they weren't my subordinates. We were one and the same – three people that put their trust in each other.

Looking out upon the bridge and the rushing water of the Kitoc, I knew that's what I would do. Sydney and Charlie trusted me in picking this destination, so I needed to believe in them by believing I deserved their trust. I had to wrestle with my own doubts, because they were wrong. We hadn't searched everywhere. There was still the riverbank, and the shards seemed to be attracted to water.

I huffed out a slow, deep breath and held Sydney's earthy gaze. Swinging from the saddle, my feet planted in the grass as I said, "We stay here and continue searching."

Sydney smiled. "Let's take a break to eat so you can calm down a bit."

Charlie and I nodded in agreement, so the three of us settled down in the rolling clearing. Our lunch consisted of a jerky sandwich and water. Not exactly appetizing, but it was something to eat. I gnawed through the chewy jerky and scarfed it down like there was no tomorrow. It hit my stomach like a rock, and a chug of water followed it down.

I was supposed to calm down, but I couldn't. I needed to be doing something. My hands had to be busy, or my mind would start overthinking everything again. That was the last thing I needed right now.

"I'm going back to searching," I said as I stood.

I bypassed the bridge, eyeing the crumbled mass of clay lumps, in favor of sliding down the riverbank. A mixture of sand and tiny rocks soon overcame the soft grass. Dotting the river's flowing water were smooth stones that seemed to float on the surface and held their own against the crash of the river.

I stepped into the lapping, shallow water against the riverbank and dropped to my knees. As my pants soaked up water, I ignored the added weight and sifted through wet sand. Any stone large enough to conceal the shard was overturned. Mud caked beneath my fingernails as they raked through the dirt, hoping to scratch against metal.

As I crawled along the bank, I continued to come up empty-handed. When I reached the pillar of the bridge, I stood to my full height and wiped my hands on my pants. I wasn't having any luck on this side of the river, so I might as well try on the other.

I took a single step up the riverbank but paused. Glancing over my shoulder, I eyed the path of stones poking up through the water. It was the quicker route, and I really wanted to find the shard and move on.

My boots squished and squeaked as I stepped in the mud, my feet sinking about an inch. It released with a soft pop and gurgle of water filling the imprint. My foot landed on the first stone, but slipped with the shift of weight. The view of the river was replaced with the underside of the bridge as I fell, landing hard on my butt with a loud splash.

I hissed in pain as I rubbed at my lower back. Allowing my upper body to fall into the water as well, I lay with my eyes closed, breathing deeply.

I should've seen that coming. How hard would it have been to walk around? But, no, I just had to try my hand at hopping across stones. Oh, well. Lesson learned – go around next time.

My eyes blinked open, and I began to push myself to my feet. I froze, my vision locked on the chipping bricks of the bridge's underbelly. A relieved smile crept onto my face as I sucked in a light breath of air. Lodged between rustic red and charred orange was shining silver.

It was worth the fall, and I would gladly do it again.

I hopped to my feet with renewed energy, as if I hadn't just bruised my backside. The shard shined right above me, but my adrenaline-fueled excitement wouldn't magically grab the little piece of steel from many feet out of my reach. I eyed the shard before my vision traced down the support pillar. My palm pressed flat against the brick, its rough surface scratching my skin.

Hopefully, my luck would hold out for ten more minutes.

Lifting my foot, I dug the toe of my boot into the biggest crevice – barely enough to get a foothold – and tested my weight. With no other option, it would have to do. My fingers clawed for leverage, and I scaled up the pillar inch by painful inch. Skin scraped off my fingertips to leave smudges of crimson in my wake. My feet climbed slowly, calculating each miniscule movement, as possible footholds became few and far apart. I precariously balanced my weight on the toes of my right foot while my left nudged along the rows of bricks. When it found a precise foothold, I pushed my body upward, latching onto a chipped brick.

My head was a few inches from brushing against the bridge's underside, and the shard was so close. I pressed myself flush against the pillar before my left hand eased its bloody grip on the bricks. Stretching to its fullest, my arm extended as my fingers grabbed at the shard. The very tips of my fingers feathered along the steel's jagged edge, but it was just barely out of my reach.

There went the last remnants of my good luck.

I eyed the shard and glanced at the rushing river below. I was an idiot. There was no doubt about that.

I propelled myself off the pillar, leaping for the shard. My hand enclosed around it, and the steel cut into my palm.

And then I fell.

It wasn't one of those slow motion falls. No, this was hard and fast. I crashed through the water's surface, my breath being knocked from my lungs on impact. Piercing cold water filled my mouth and scorched its way down my throat. It hit my lungs hard, and I vehemently coughed for air but only swallowed more of the river.

I struggled for the surface, wanting nothing more than to break through it, but no matter how hard I grasped at it, it was out of my reach. I could see it though. The light of day penetrated the river, illuminating a large, fiery ball as the current flowed recklessly past it. It swayed on the surface as it smiled down upon me. The sun could be a rueful ass sometimes, gloating with all its glory in a sky filled with air.

My time ran out. The burning in my chest became an unbearable truth to that fact, but all I needed was a minute more. I could grab hold of that boastful sun if only I had an ounce of breath left. I kicked violently at the currents and clawed through the raging water, but the light didn't get any closer. If anything, it got farther away.

My back crashed into a hard surface. A single bubble of breath escaped my lips, and my last chance to reach the light died with it. A rough grip wrapped around my wrist as water yielded to my body. The surface broke around me as I was dragged onto a cold, unnatural formation in the middle of the river.

"Dawn!"

Violent coughs racked my body. Spitting up water, my lungs begged for air, heaving harshly in my chest. I panted and gulped down breath after breath.

"You damn fool! What were you thinking?" Charlie exclaimed almost hysterically. Eyes wide and unblinking, his face contorted with a mixture of anger and worry. He kneeled in front of me – his hand still wrapped around my wrist – and hauled both of us to our feet. My soaked boots slipped and slid beneath me, but Charlie held tight to my arm.

I stared at my feet to see solid water supporting my weight. It glistened beneath the rays of the sun and stretched to the riverbank. The ice bridge dammed half the river, forcing the rushing water to reroute around the obstruction.

"Dawn, are you okay? What's going on?" the panicked voice resounded from the pendant hanging from my neck.

"I'm fine," I panted out. "I got it." I held my hand out, palm up. My bloody, scraped fingers unclenched to reveal the jagged little shard.

As Charlie and I carefully stepped from the ice to the grassy riverbank, Sydney met us with an exasperated sigh. "Really?" she questioned, tilting her head and staring at my open palm. "You're hands are covered in blood, and you almost drowned! Yet, you're more worried about the shard!"

I gave her a small smile in return.

Sydney shook her head in disbelief, her palm pressed to her forehead. "You're an odd one."

I shrugged it off. "If protecting what I love is odd, then I'll happily be an oddball."

"What good will that be if you die trying? If you're dead, you can't protect anyone," Sydney said.

William's concerned voice chimed in, "Please be careful. Don't put yourself in unnecessary danger for me."

"Yeah, yeah, I'm sorry. It won't happen again."

"I'm not convinced," my uncle said as he crossed his arms over his chest.

"Alright," I conceded. "I make no guarantees. I'm sorry for this time, but it'll probably happen again. I apologize in advance for any future incidents that may occur."

Charlie's hand fell upon my shoulder and patted my back. "I'm proud of you. The first step of recovery is admitting you have a problem. Good job."

I sidestepped, moving just out of his reach. "You think you're funny, don't you?"

Charlie rubbed his stubbly chin in thought for a long moment. "Just a bit, yes."

The three of us stood around talking with William for a short while. It was the typical *hello*'s, *how's it going*'s, and *goodbye*'s. I fused the shard in its rightful place at the sword's jagged end before replacing the sword in my grasp for the scroll.

I unrolled it and read it aloud. *"Freshly dug, freshly filled, and freshly covered. A deathbed of a father, it's hidden within the shadow of his name."*

My stomach dropped, and I feared I'd see my lunch for a second time. As I stored the scroll in the saddlebag, my fingers fumbled with the ties. When I went to mount the pegasus, my foot missed the stirrup, forcing a shaking hand to hold the leather. My foot slipped in, and I swung into the saddle. Before my butt hit the seat, I urged the equine to take flight. My head pounded against the wind, and my heart raced in my chest, almost drowning out the voices of my companions.

"Dawn, wait! You don't know it's him!" my uncle shouted, his voice far off – distant, but not in the form of feet or miles.

I couldn't wait. I couldn't let this lingering, gut-wrenching feeling be right. It was wrong, and I had to prove it. He was okay. He said he was fine – in tiptop shape – and I believed him, left his pale, fragile form without so much as a hug goodbye. I'd hurry back, be greeted by his smiling face, and we'd all laugh about my jumping to a wrong conclusion. Because that's what it was, what it had to be. Wrong.

He wasn't dead, wasn't buried beneath six feet of cold, hard ground. It wasn't his time. He still had multiple millennia left on his clock. There was so much life he had left to live, so many experiences yet undiscovered. He had to see his 10,000th birthday, attend the surprise party that's been planned since his 9,500th year. He had yet to reach retirement where he'd spend his days hiking in the mountains with Charlie or fishing on the Kitoc with Raven. There was a trip planned for the following spring to the northwestern country of Ezmarin to look at a new bloodline of pegasi that he wanted to import. He went through hell and high water to get the permits centuries ago. There was no way he'd miss that trip.

But most of all, there were people that needed him. Raven needed her husband, and Charlie needed his baby brother. He was Rose's grandpa and as close to a dad as William had. His chess buddies needed someone to lose to and buy a round of drinks afterward. The Kingsberry livery needed him to trim and shod hooves. There was no one who took more pride and care in their work than he did. Both his four-legged and two-legged clients appreciated that. He was a man that was needed in the community, one that made Siven the tiniest bit brighter.

I needed my father.

Hot tears stung my eyes. They burned under the rub of my fingers and blinked against the wind. My sight was blurry, merely blobs and smudges that shined through the tears. Wet trails ran down my cheeks, and I could taste the bitter saltiness.

I had meant to go home, to ride into the stable yard and jump from the pegasus' back before its hooves collided with dirt. I would sprint to the front door, knock once, and then go right it. I'd find Cam, Raven, and Rose sitting around the kitchen table enjoying their dinner. They'd look up at the sudden intrusion and smile after seeing it was only me. Rose would slide from her chair and dash to wrap her arms around my waist. Raven would welcome me home while Cam insisted I grab a plate and join them.

But that's not where I went. I dismounted my pegasus in a small, man-made clearing. Trees hand planted millennia ago neatly lined the meadow, and rose bushes grew in front of them. They were planted in a color pattern of red, white, pink, white and repeated all the way around to complete a short wall of roses. Lined in precise rows and columns were headstones protruding from the earth. The farther back the headstone, the more sun bleached and chipped it was. In the first row on the far left, a pristine headstone stood upon the earth, immaculate carvings of wrapping vines and flower petals adorning its arched top. It cast a dark shadow atop freshly turned sod, so fresh that new blades of grass had yet to sprout.

I mechanically shuffled forward, my feet moving without thought. Step after slow, deliberate step, I inched closer to the grave as I held my breath. My eyes closed; and with one last step, my boot sunk the slightest millimeter as the fresh dirt gave way beneath me. Slowly opening my eyes, I stared down at the headstone.

This world was a cruel place.

My breath came out as a broken, strangled sob; and my knees buckled. I fell, my fingers clawing the dirt. One hand rose, gingerly touched the cold stone, and traced each letter engraved upon the surface.

Cameron Thomas Lockwood
Beloved Husband, Father, Grandfather, and Brother

PAINT AN UMBRELLA

It wasn't fair. None of this was fair. Three days ago, he was fine – alive and breathing the air of this world. Three days. Merely seventy-two hours. Was he ill? Yes, but he was far from his deathbed. He looked like he had a cold or maybe the flu, neither of which should have strangled the last breath from his chest. It didn't make sense. What did my father do to deserve this? Why was a good man stolen from this world when malicious people were allowed to walk upon the earth long after their time should have expired?

My fingers slid down the cold stone, lingering on his name before falling to the dirt. He was beneath me, buried under suffocating earth. So far away and yet this was the closest I'd ever be. There would be no more bear hugs, no more warm clasps to a shoulder or pat on the back. His booming voice would never again resound through the house, and echoing laughter wouldn't linger in the halls. Calloused hands could no longer tame a frightened equine or mend stall doors. A toothy grin couldn't brighten the darkness, and the spark in lively green eyes wouldn't rekindle.

My hand grazed the shard sticking up through the dirt. It was hidden within the headstone's shadow, and for the first time, I loathed the shard. It had no right to be here, to be embedded in my father's grave. It was a scar, an imperfection on his last place of rest. Unforgivable. Of every last square inch of this world, it decided to disgrace my father's name. It dared to make a mockery of his death by dragging it into this spellbound treasure hunt.

I snatched the shard from my father's grave and shakily stood. Wiping at my eyes with the collar of my shirt, I willed away the tears as I retraced slow steps back to the pegasus. I reached for the wrapped blade tied securely to the saddle, hanging flush from the saddle horn.

"Dawn?" a hesitant, questioning voice resounded from the pendant.

I didn't want to talk, not to him, not to anyone. What was there to say – to tell him my father died, and I just found out? I didn't want anyone's pity. All the *I'm so sorry for your loss*'s and *how are you coping*'s would break me. What was I supposed to say to that? I wasn't the one buried six feet under, so why did it feel like I couldn't breathe? How was I supposed to explain a

72

feeling even I didn't understand?

So I didn't even try. I unwrapped the blade just enough to expose its jagged end and touched the two pieces of steel together. The crackling sizzle blew past my ears until only silence remained. William's voice did not resound again.

But my uncle's did. He called my name as powerful flaps eased him to the earth, Sydney right beside him. Charlie froze atop the pegasus, his shoulders tense, as his eyes moved from me to the freshly dug grave. Hazel orbs drained of any hope, and his head bowed. Shoulders rose with a jerky breath before he raised his head. His eyes were dead, void of even the slightest emotion – merely a hardened mask. "Dawn, I'm so—"

Those were the exact words I didn't want to hear. "Don't," I tersely warned, more bite to my tone than necessary. I mounted my equine, and spurred out of the clearing as fast as I could.

This wasn't what I wanted. I pushed them away; but I wanted nothing more than to collapse into their arms, scream my lungs out, and shed every stinging tear held behind stubborn dams. I needed my walls to crumble, my heart to stop aching.

But I didn't turn back or even glance over my shoulder. I rode on with the soft drone of my name echoing in my head, and it wouldn't stop. No matter how fast I pushed the pegasus, I couldn't outrun the voice – no voices. It was William, morphed to Charlie, before permanently becoming a deep, throaty baritone. A memory – a mere remnant of the past – his voice could only be heard in my head, a soft calling of my name I'd never hear again.

It was a short ride but one that couldn't end soon enough. Even so, when my feet hit the dusty ground of the stable yard, I found myself unwillingly to enter the house. I stalled, going so far as to bed down the pegasus. Dragging my feet, I trudged from the barn, across the yard, and up three exterior stairs to stand in front of the house's front door. My hand rose, poised to knock, but only fell limply to my side. I grasped the knob and slowly turned it. Pushing the door in, I stepped across the threshold.

The kitchen was empty, dark without the curtains drawn or a single lamp lit. I inched across the wood floorboards, and they creaked beneath my weight. My hand ran across the smooth back of a dining chair as I passed it. I paused when the family room came into view.

The evening light of the sky settled upon the room in a soft orange glow. It gave the room a warm, comforting aura but one of false security. There was nothing comforting about the dreadful ache of the rocking chair or the empty tobacco pipe hanging from limp fingers. Her back to me, my mother sat in Cam's chair, staring out the window. One hand draped onto the window sill, pipe between her index and middle fingers, while the other cradled a head of strawberry blonde locks to her chest.

I crossed the room to stand in front of my mother, but neither of us looked at the other. I knelt down, and my hand reached out to my sleeping daughter. Rosy cheeks were delicately soft beneath my touch, but the faint trail of dried tears couldn't go unnoticed. I held her hand as my head fell to rest on my mother's knee. When I finally found my voice, it was barely a whisper. "How?"

Raven sucked in a breath of air as her fingers curled tightly around the tobacco pipe. Her answer was calm, steady as if it had been rehearsed countless times. "The morning after you left, he collapsed. His health took a sudden turn for the worst, and by the time I got back with the doctor, he was gone. The doctor's not sure what caused it. She said it may have been something he ingested, and it didn't seem contagious." She didn't look away from the window once.

There were no answers. No one knew what happened, but how could I be satisfied with that? My father was gone, and I didn't know how or why. Where was my closure? How could I accept this worldly injustice without knowing what stole his life?

But I nodded at the information nonetheless. Even so, I couldn't stay here, not with his picture smiling at me from the mantle atop the fireplace and my mother trying with all her might to hold herself together. It wasn't fair to either of us, to stay together acting like we were okay when both of us wanted to break down behind our own walls.

So I left, dashing through the front door and passing the entrance of Sydney and Charlie. A hand brushed my forearm, but that's all it was. She didn't try to stop me, and I was grateful for that.

I wandered into the middle stable, down the aisle to the very last stall before the tack room. Unlatching its door, I stepped inside the stall, and the soft rustle of hay was a welcomed comfort. A shadow of a melancholic smile found its way to my lips when large brown eyes looked up at me in recognition. The equine made no move to stand, so I met him on the ground and leaned against his side, draping an arm over his neck. He craned his neck to nudge my shoulder with a speckled muzzle. My hand ran from the cowlick at the base of his forelock all the way down his long face. Holding his head in my hand, feeling the warmth of his flesh and velvety coat, I couldn't support the walls anymore; and the dams burst, overflowing with body racking sobs.

I played in the yard, skipping in zigzagging lines and scattering chicken feed as I went. About fifteen hens pecked at my trail with a handful of chicks scurrying behind. The rooster perched on the hitching post near the house and routinely wailed his feathers when I passed him. He hopped down, gobbled up the sprinkled feed, and returned to his perch before the hens caught up to my trail.

I plopped down on the dusty ground, content in watching the chickens. A little puff of feathers on bright orange legs scuttled up to me. A high pitched chirp erupted from such a tiny body. I reached out to it, hand extended palm up with the back of my hand resting on the ground. The chick didn't hesitate to hop into my open hand, and I cupped it gently within my grasp. I hunched over, keeping the baby bird close to the ground in case it hopped from my hand, and lightly brushed its feathers with my finger.

"Hey, Buckaroo!" a deep, lively voice called from within the stable. "Are you done feeding the chickens?"

"Yes, Papa!" I answered.

"Then come in here. I have a surprise for you!"

I kissed the chick on its sunny head before setting it down and springing to my feet. I dashed to the middle stable as fast as my little legs would take me. Pausing in the doorway, I spotted my father standing halfway down the aisle, peering tenderly into the stall. "Papa!" I called before running up to him.

Cam greeted me with open arms, picked me up, and twirled me in the air. Giddy giggles and throaty chuckles filled the barn. With a wide, gleeful grin plastered to his face, my father held me to his chest and peered over his shoulder. "I've got something to show you," he said with as much excitement as a child on their birthday. I clung to my father's neck as he flicked the latch on the stall. He left the door cracked behind us after he carried me in.

A dark chestnut mare met Cam and me at the door. Ears pricked forward, the mare nudged my father and nickered. "It's nice to see you, too," Cam cooed softly, patting the pegasus' neck, "but where's your little guy hiding?"

A tiny head peeked out from behind the mare. "Ah, there you are," my father said, kneeling down. Outstretching his hand, he tempted the foal closer. "Come on, Cobalt. It's time to meet your new owner."

Hesitantly, the young colt took an awkward step in our direction on onyx-tipped legs. He planted himself to the ground, stretched his neck as far as it would go, and sniffed at my father's hand. Big brown eyes stared at us in cautious wonder before all caution was thrown to the wind. He stepped right up to us.

"That's it," Cam softly reassured the foal. Placing me on the ground, my father moved between the mare and me. "He's your pegasus, Buckaroo. Go and say hi."

I held my hand out like my father had, patiently waiting for Cobalt to acknowledge it. The spotted foal brushed his speckled muzzle against my hand. I gently rubbed Cobalt's nose, and he leaned into my touch. A high-pitched whinny echoed in the stall as the colt pranced in place, his feathery wings fluttering at his side.

"He likes you," my father chuckled, beaming down at me. "Now you have a one-of-a-kind pegasus all to yourself."

"One of a kind?" I asked, running my fingers through Cobalt's curly mane.

"Yep," Cam grinned. "I had his momma sent out to Ezmarin, and she came back with little Cobalt in her tummy. You won't find another spotted pegasus like him in all of Siven."

I turned from my new companion and threw my arms around my father's neck. A quiet gasp blew past Cam's lips before strong, gentle arms wrapped around my shoulders.

"Thank you, Papa. He's perfect."

My father smiled at me warmly, an affectionate pride bright in shining green orbs. "You're welcome, Buckaroo."

"Dawn... Dawn, are you okay? Can you hear me?"

My eyes slowly blinked open, but they weren't met with the wooden boards of Cobalt's stall. Light blue, nearly pastel in color, flooded half my vision while a white nothingness consumed the rest. The fuzzy softness of Cobalt's coat against my cheek was replaced with the smooth, woven threads of cotton fabric. Brown eyes, as dark and rich as pure cocoa, held my own reflection within their swirling depths, not even a single speck of gold breaking my image.

"Are you okay?"

I shook my head, biting my lip and squeezing my eyes shut. My fingers clenched at the back of Will's shirt as I buried my face in the crook of his neck. I couldn't hold it in anymore. I had neither the strength nor the willpower to, so I let go of every barrier I hid behind. Weeping sobs tore their way out of my lungs, and the cries muffled against William's collarbone.

His arms tightened around me, one hand cupping the back of my head and his fingers rubbing through the long strands. Voice tender and soft-hearted, he asked, "What's wrong?"

I tilted my head, not enough for him to see my face but enough to choke out an answer. "My dad's dead."

From head to toe, William's entire body went rigid. Fingers froze in my hair, and arms stiffened around my shoulders. A shaky, unsteady breath breezed by my ear. His embrace tightened even more with a hand splayed between my shoulder blades. William clung to me as much as I held on to him.

This was what I wanted – someone who understood my pain, someone who wouldn't pity me. Not a single *I'm sorry* or *it wasn't his time* was uttered. William knew what it meant to lose a father – two of them now – and he knew there was no combination of letters or syllables that would ease the sting of loss. It wasn't possible. The comfort of inspirational words could distract the mind for a mere moment, but grief demanded to be heard. It ate away at its victim, engulfing them in a world of gray – one without happiness or sadness, simply an existence without clear meaning.

But as humans, we longed to hear those words no matter how simple or superficial they may have been. If they were uttered from the right person – someone special or maybe even a stranger with the same sheen to their eyes – then those words could transform the gray, desolate existence to a world of color. It wouldn't be overnight. Color couldn't paint a masterpiece in a matter of hours. It took time. One day there would be a splash of tranquil blue, and the next would be the warmth of yellow. The wisdom of purple and passion of red would dot the canvas. Splattered in the mix were the acceptance of green and the flamboyancy of orange. Amidst all that color would be the base of white, of purity.

But I was in the gray, and it was a result of my own doing. Words only helped if they were willingly heard and allowed to be spoken. It was a mistake I often made and would probably continue to make; but right now, I wanted those inspirational words of color, not the generic *I'm sorry*'s. Those only added to the smudge of gray when I desired a splash of color, even if only a tiny dot in size.

I sniffed and rubbed my teary eyes against the fabric on my shoulder. Inhaling deeply, I tried to steady my breathing, to stop my cries. It took a few deep, slow breaths, but my sobs did cease. I turned my head and finally showed my face to William.

He stared at me as his hand moved to caress my cheek. He wore a smile, small and bittersweet yet tenderly compassionate. Red-rimmed eyes shined bright from fresh tears, but his own grief and sorrow were pushed to the deepest depths of his pupils, giving foreground to emotions that a single word could not explain. In irises like a wind-blown desert, with ripples upon ripples of swirling rings, was held the look of love in its most innocent form. He peered at me as if I was the center of his world, as if having me by his side was the greatest blessing he had ever received. It was like a clear evening sky where only a single star walked among the heavens, and a person couldn't resist gazing upon that star in wonder and amazement. That was the same gaze William aimed at me.

Underneath that gaze's stare, I felt safe and secure. "Can I ask you something?" I inquired softly.

"Anything."

"How... how did you deal with it?"

"I didn't," he admitted as he brushed his fingers through his bangs and pushed them to the side. "I ran from it, and it consumed me. You've seen the aftermath of that choice, and I wouldn't recommend it."

"Then what do I do?"

"Weather the storm, and continue living. The rain will lighten up eventually. The sun will shine again, but there will always be sprinkles every now and then. You just have to find an umbrella," he said.

"An umbrella, huh?"

He nodded. "Yeah. Like you. You're my umbrella."

William painted my gray canvas white, giving the base it needed to add color to my world.

LESSON LEARNED

My time with William was even shorter than the last, but it was enough for me to rein my emotions in. I awoke in Cobalt's stall, still lying against his side, and I knew what I had to do. Leaving my steed, I retrieved my saddlebags and the sword from the tack room. I dropped the saddlebags beside Cobalt's stall before carrying the sword out the back door.

The evening moon and millions of twinkling stars lit up the sky and glowed upon the slumbering earth. The wind was calm, only a gentle breeze that danced through blades of grass and leaves on tree branches. It was the perfect night to do this, being so serene and peaceful, quiet and undisturbing.

The blade of the uncompleted longsword shined under the luminosity of the moon as it rose to pause only centimeters from my neck. Eyelids veiled my orbs, and a deep breath filled my lungs. I gathered my long, auburn locks in my left hand and collected each strand into a manageable bundle. The blade's biting edge lined up just right, and with a swift flick of my wrist, it cut effortlessly through every last strand.

My hand stretched out in front of me, and my fingers opened up. Strand by thin strand, the whispering wind carried away all my past regrets, every decision made, every word spoken, every promise broken. I watched them soar, some only a few feet and others out of sight, but they all eventually fell. I turned my back, abandoning my past to fully focus on the present and future.

I walked back into the stable and headed straight for the tack room. I didn't have to light the kerosene lamp to find what I sought. It was always in the same spot – his spot. Covered beneath a blanket was Cam's saddle, cinch still attached with the matching headstall hanging from a nail on the wall.

The set was a sight to be held in the light of day. The saddle's skirt was a rich, oiled brown and was intricately inlaid with branches, leaves, and flower blossoms the color of sand. The seat was the same sandy tan with its edge lined with silver plating. The horn and gullet were accented in silver with an identical plantlike design. A matching sword sheath hung diagonally from the saddle horn. The accompanying headstall sported the same design with silver conchos at each side of the browband.

I sheathed my blade, and it fit perfectly. Draping the headstall and reins over my shoulder, I hefted my father's saddle from its stand and carried it to Cobalt's stall. It took a little fancy maneuvering to unlatch the door, but I nudged it open with the tip of my boot. I tacked my stallion with ease, secured the saddlebags behind the saddle, and led Cobalt into the yard. I tied him to the hitching post and eyed the house.

Dim light seeping through the kitchen curtains pulled me in, and I entered my family home without second thought. A single lamp sat in the middle of the dining table, casting a soft glow throughout the room. The rest of the house was pitch black, to the point where I couldn't even make out the back of the sage settee I knew to be there. Sydney and Charlie sat across from each other, both pausing a conversation to stare at me with wide eyes.

"Are you ready to go?" I asked.

Sydney gaped at me, brown orbs scanning my face. "Go where?"

"Wherever the next shard takes us."

Sydney was silent for a moment, quirking an eyebrow at me. She exchanged a quick glance with Charlie before nodding her head. "Give me a few minutes to tack up," she said. The chair screeched against the wood floor as Sydney stood. She disappeared out the door, quietly pulling it shut behind her.

"Why don't you have a seat?" my uncle suggested, gesturing to the now vacant chair across from him.

"I'd rather not."

Charlie sighed as his fingers rubbed at his temple. He looked as if the last few hours had added centuries to his age. "Look, Squirt," he started, "I won't be coming with you. Raven and Rose are going to need someone here for support."

"Where are they?" I asked.

"In bed," Charlie said. "We didn't tell Rose you were here."

"It's better that way. She doesn't need a mother who shows up and disappears in the same day."

"Are you sure about that?"

I nodded. "She needs me to bring William back and stay. It wouldn't be fair to her to keep showing up and then leaving. Plus, this is dangerous. The more I'm here, the more all of your lives are at risk."

"That doesn't mean we don't want you here."

"I'm painfully aware of that, but your lives are precious to me," I said.

The door swung open, and Sydney stood beneath the threshold. She turned to me. "I'm ready whenever you are."

"Let's go then." I took a single step to follow Sydney into the yard but stopped. I peered at my uncle, and he stared right back. I didn't want to say goodbye, but the last time I failed to, I never saw him again.

"Get out of here," Charlie said, shooing me to the door with a wave of his hands. "We'll all be here when you return."

I gratefully smiled and whispered out a *thank you* before joining Sydney at the hitching post. We mounted our pegasi in silence and stared at each other. It was a look of mutual understanding, both of us wordlessly agreeing not to speak of the last few hours.

"Where are we going?" Sydney asked.

I twisted in the seat of my father's saddle and dug in the saddlebag. Grabbing the scroll, I pulled it from the bag and unrolled it. I leaned toward the seeping kitchen light and read the clue aloud, "*Hidden among red fruit, it can be found within the berry of a king.*"

"So in Kingsberry?"

I nodded. "Sounds like the marketplace."

"That's about an hour ride by pegasus so we should set up camp outside the city and enter on foot in the morning," Sydney said.

"Let's head out then."

Kingsberry was an old, vintage city of grandeur – second only to Centrielle. There were rows upon rows of brick buildings, most two stories, but the occasional extra story reached for the sky. The outskirts of the city consisted of small, quaint family homes while more extravagant dwellings resided near the center. The centerpiece of the grand city was a long, rectangular pavilion. Its support pillars were carved to look like trees with their branches twisting and climbing to hold the lattice roof above their heads. The festival building was surrounded in a clearing of cobblestone that matched the narrow streets. From the pavilion, a brief stroll in any direction led to various family-owned shops – anything from bakeries to barber shops. Our destination – the largest marketplace in all of Siven – was found on the south side of Kingsberry after immediately stepping from dirt to cobblestone.

But the city of grandeur that I fondly remembered was no more. Shrouded in an inconspicuous brown cloak, I entered the city and couldn't help but feel lost, as if I was in the wrong town. The street was nearly empty, and it was far too quiet. Doors and windows were boarded up, the many buildings' tenants being long gone. The grandeur had disappeared along with Kingsberry's pride. The city was dirty, unhygienic with garbage scattered everywhere and an overabundance of swarming flies.

I stopped dead in my tracks when I left the backstreet to enter the marketplace. This was wrong. Where were all the people? Nobles who once frequented the market were nowhere to be seen. Over half the stalls were empty, and the occupied ones were rather pitiful. What happened to the fine silk and satin? Where were the livestock brokers and the plentiful fresh produce? What happened to the customers? People from all corners of Siven would travel days to buy in Kingsberry. Crowds used to be so packed that a person couldn't shift their weight without bumping shoulders with someone else. Children would hold tight to their mothers' hands for fear of otherwise being swept away in the barely controlled chaos.

It was the exact opposite now. Except for the few dealers, only a handful of people wandered around. With only a single carriage tied, all of the hitching posts were vacant. The once deafening roar of the crowd had faded to only the occasional murmur. This was a disaster, not only for Kingsberry but for Siven as a whole.

"Sydney," I said, keeping my voice low, "what happened here?"

Sydney gestured to the prideless buildings and vacant stalls. "This is what happens when the crown dictates every little detail in our lives." she stated disdainfully. "They took away our very right to live and, for many, their very will to. Look down any alley, and you'll find one of two things – the homeless and poor struggling to live or the dried blood of those that have given up."

She had warned me back at Charlie's place, but I wasn't prepared for this. I naively held on to the hope that Sydney had told the tale of the few select extremes, but that tiny flame of faith was snuffed out. This wasn't a case of one in every ten thousand. It was the everyday hell that the majority were forced to endure, to suffer and struggle to barely sustain life. What did I expect? Spencer wouldn't have given his life for a meaningless cause so, of course, the crown had fallen so far as to sleep with the very demons its people feared.

"Open your eyes and truly look at these people. Study their emotions. On the surface, you'll find despair, hatred, and fear; but on a closer look, you'll also discover hope lying dormant deep within. They're waiting for their heroes to return and ignite the passion they've been desperately holding on to," Sydney said.

Her words seeped through every pore as I looked around. The few merchants, while making almost no sales, smiled kindly and chatted with those passing by. The handful of would-be customers stared longingly at unaffordable goods but held no contempt for the seller.

"Who are their heroes?" I asked.

Sydney's head tilted in speculative questioning. Beady eyes bored holes right through me. Instead of answering my question, she fired one back at me. "When did this all start?"

I assumed she meant the decline of the king and queen's human decency. "Just after the border war with Guthris."

"Not that," she said. "When did it start to escalate so quickly?"

I shrugged.

"Then how about this one. Why do you think we've survived on the run this long in such a small country?"

That had never before crossed my mind. I normally avoided cities like the plague, but I often crossed heavily traveled roads. I soared through the sky and was probably visible for many miles. Thinking back, it was a miracle Spencer hadn't caught me sooner.

"Trust me when I say this," Sydney said. "It's not because we were careful or unseen. It's because we have the people's support. All of this –" she gestured to the surrounding city "– didn't happen until you and William left the crown's side. Somehow, the two of you held the extent of their villainous reign in check. The heroes the people of Siven are waiting for are Kent, William, and you."

"What? Why? I've done nothing to deserve such a title. I can't even call myself a knight anymore."

"But you are. You abandoned the crown, something the citizens are too afraid to do. You've done so without destructive force. You have proven yourself."

I didn't walk away from my former life for the wellbeing of Siven. I was trying to save William, to protect my family. The citizens – the people who put their trust in me – were only an afterthought, one that still didn't have my full attention. And it wouldn't, not until my own family was whole again. It was selfish. Even I knew that.

"Heroes die."

"Everyone dies eventually. Heroes die for a just cause and sacrifice themselves to protect others."

I was no hero. "And that's how you want to go?" I questioned.

Sydney shook her head. "No, I'd rather die alone."

"And why's that?"

Earthy orbs diverted to the ground as Sydney slowly walked off. Her answer was barely a murmur, and I wasn't sure I was meant to hear it. "I don't want my death to be someone's last memory of me."

I followed her and kept quiet. She didn't look back at me once. Instead, she scanned each and every stall, empty ones too. I followed suit.

Produce as a whole was scarce. We passed small potatoes and withered peas, but fruit was hard to come by. It wasn't like in the past. There used to be a whole banquet of imported fruits from mangos to kumquats and everything in between. Now a person was lucky to find a golden ear of corn.

I peered down a side street, remembering how the market stretched through the city, but there wasn't a single vendor. The street was occupied with a group of five children. While being scrawny and clothed in rags, they still giggled and smiled as they played a makeshift game of marbles. Instead of the colorful balls, the children had stones laid out in a chalk drawn circle. A little girl with hair as dark as her skin kneeled on the cobblestone as she lined up her shot. She didn't knock a stone from the circle so a tall boy with bronzed skin took his turn.

The game went on with each child taking a turn. It was an innocent game, but the king and queen could learn a thing or two from these smiling children. Three of the five were sons and a daughter of parents not native to Siven. A brother and a sister, both dark in comparison to the others, were treated as friends by the children of a country that condemned them. The third boy – one that shared William's heritage – smiled brighter and laughed louder than any other. The remaining two girls, one small in stature with pale blonde hair and the other tall with freckles dotting her cheeks, chatted enthusiastically with their friends. Not one of these children held animosity for the others. They didn't condemn their differences but accepted them as unique features of each friend. It was a simple lesson that seemed like common sense to many, but the king and queen needed schooling in this subject.

The girl with pale blonde hair stared longingly at the building the group played next to. Her freckled friend tossed an arm around the her shoulders and gestured to the circle of stones. The bronze skinned boy handed her the shooter stone with a smile, and the girl took her turn.

I eyed the same building. The top story was the typical brick, but the ground level had large glass panels to showcase the inside. A sign hung on the window declaring the shop to be open, and thick white letters were painted upon the brick to read *Sion's Bakery*.

"Sydney," I said as I tapped her shoulder. "You keep looking. I'll be right back." She nodded in acknowledgment before continuing down the street.

I walked toward the bakery, and the five children paused their game to smile at me. I waved to them before entering the little bake shop.

The ring of a bell announced my arrival, and a young woman dropped her dust rag at the unexpected noise. She spun around with mild surprise lighting up rosy cheeks. "Oh, good morning," she welcomed me before hurrying behind the counter and disappearing into the back.

I stepped across the squeaky floorboards and picked up the fallen rag. The woman's excited call in the back carried into the front shop. "Garrett! Honey, we have a customer!" I set the dust rag on the counter top and glanced at the glass showcase. Over half of it was empty, but the various cookies and breads that were present looked freshly made, probably baked earlier in the morning.

"Good morning. What can I help you with?" a man no more than a century or two older than me asked with a wide grin. He wiped flour covered hands on an equally flour covered beige apron as he stood before me on the opposite side of the counter.

"Could I get a loaf of the cinnamon swirl and five sugar cookies?"

Chestnut colored orbs brightened instantly, and the baker answered, "Of course." He reached for the pile of white paper bags and grabbed two of them. After bagging the bread and rolling the top down, he placed the first bag on the counter top.

I reached in the front pocket of my pants and pulled out a single gold coin. I set it on the counter just as the baker finished counting out the five cookies. He was rolling the top like the first bag when he noticed the coin and nearly dropped the cookies. Fumbling with the bag, he managed to set it on the counter top before gaping at me.

I grabbed the two bags and said, "Keep the change." Then I walked for the door.

"Wait!" the man called as he dashed around the counter, coin in hand. He held it out to me. "I can't accept this. This could buy my entire stock for a month. It's way too much."

I gently closed his fingers around the coin. "Keep it," I said again. "It will do more good for an expecting young couple than it would for me."

His eyes shined brightly with added moisture, a single tear trailing down his tanned cheek. He wiped at them with the collar of his shirt. "Thank you so much."

"You're welcome," I said just before walking back into the street.

Before the door fully closed behind me, I had five pairs of eyes staring at me. Their game forgotten, the children had inched closer to the bakery but were far enough away to stay out of any customer's path. Wide eyes longed for the bags in my hands and followed each movement of the paper. It was like they didn't even see me. To them, the sweet smell of baked goods was too overpowering, and they only focused on the bags like a dog begging for scraps of meat.

I walked over to them and crouched down to their eye level. Each of the children reluctantly turned their attention from the bags to my face. I said, "If you guys can share, you can have these. Do you think you can do that?"

Each head nodded enthusiastically, and they squirmed in anticipation. I offered them the bags, and the freckled girl snatched both of them. She dashed back to the chalk circle with the other four right on her tail and plopped down on the cobblestone. The bags couldn't be passed around fast enough as too many hands grabbed at the contents.

As I turned to leave, a chorus of voices shouted, "Thank you, Lady!" I waved and then ventured back to the main street of the market.

"You're such a softie." The quiet, unexpected voice had me almost leaping from my skin. My heart pounded angrily before my mind sorted through the sudden adrenaline rush. Sydney had found the shard.

"How long have you been listening?" I whispered.

"Since *keep it*," Will replied just as quietly.

"You would've done the same thing."

"I'm not denying that."

I smiled, knowing it to be true. The image of William helping the baker and those children kept the grin plastered to my face. "See, I was right. Now hush until we get out of Kingsberry."

Spotting Sydney was far easier than it should have been, but without the normal crowds, every person present stood out like a sore thumb. She walked toward me, glancing down every street she passed. When she saw me, she waved the shard for me to see, two ripe apples in her other hand. We met in the middle. Sydney gave me the shard as we ducked into a back alley.

I eyed the apples she held and poked at them. "Who are those for?" I asked.

"The pegasi," she said, tossing one in my direction.

Scrambling to catch it, my arms flailed miserably. It slipped from my grasp once, twice, three times before being pinned against my chest. "Warn me next time!" I huffed.

"Sure, sure," Sydney chuckled. "Let's go get the pegasi before someone sees them."

CLOSE YOUR EYES

"Please tell me we're going somewhere less wet," Sydney whined. Droplets of water dripped from her unbraided hair as she wrung it as dry as she could. Dexterous fingers rewove the three bundles of hair and banded the end before wringing her shirt.

"The water isn't very warm this time of year, is it?" I commented, fighting the face splitting grin that threatened to conquer my lips. Sydney's eyes darted to me as booming laughter echoed from the pendant. If looks could kill, my head would've been bitten off. In a final attempt to defend my still attached head, I said, "I offered to do it, so you can't blame me."

Sydney was not amused in the slightest. Moments prior, she slipped on a rock and fell not so gracefully into the chill, autumn water of the Kitoc's shore. But on the bright side, she retrieved the shard.

"Here," she grumbled, thrusting the shard into my stomach. "If we have to go to another body of water, you'll be the one taking the plunge."

I decided to push my luck a little further with the teasing. "I'm not afraid to get a little wet."

Cackling laughter erupted again as Sydney's face deadpanned. Her arm shot out, and I flinched. The expected smack never stung my shoulder, but the shard was pried from my fingers. I stared at her, dumbfounded, watching her retreating back. She stopped beside Cobalt and swiftly drew the sword from its sheath. Holding it parallel to the ground, she confidently moved the shard toward the jagged edge. "You two are done," she said with a smirk.

"Oh, come on," I complained. "I'm sorry."

William chimed in, "It was a joke, Sydney."

"No," Sydney shook her head. "You two are annoyingly in sync and always messing around. It's getting hard to listen to every day so say goodbye until tomorrow."

"What if the next shard takes more than one day?"

William chuckled at my sarcastic humor, much to Sydney's distaste. "That's it," she said as she pressed the two pieces of steel together.

"Bye, Dawn. Love you," Will said, complete with an overdramatic smooch. "You too, Sydney."

The older sibling rolled earthy orbs at the younger's parting words as the sizzle of bubbling metal died down. She sheathed the sword, stepped around Cobalt to her pegasus, and swung into the saddle. "I hope there's water this time," she said with a devilish smirk that seemed out of place on a normally angelic face.

I walked to Cobalt's side and mounted my equine before retrieving the scroll. Quickly scanning the prideful words, I laughed. Luck was on my side. "No water this time," I gloated with a toothy grin.

"Just read it."

"The floating lights of this festive day will illuminate what you seek."

Sydney sighed in disgust as her hand scratched at the nape of her neck. "I'd rather swim with the Locheville monsters than attend the Fall Festival."

"Come on, Sydney," I pestered. "The Fall Festival is the best event of the year. There are fun games, delicious food, great music, and a night of fireworks. How can you not love the festival?"

Sydney quirked an eyebrow in disbelief. "When was the last time you actually attended the festival?"

"Will and I took Rose every year. Why?"

Sydney brushed it off. "It's nothing, but don't expect the same jolly event you remember."

The two of us bantered back and forth, but no matter how many questions I fired at her, Sydney refused to answer them. Despite my constant and rather obnoxious begging and pleading, this *new* Fall Festival was nothing more than fodder for my imagination. What could have possibly changed? The festival was an event of celebration, of renewed hope even after the darkest of years. It was almost sacred, and the crown wouldn't dare defile it, for that would be blasphemy – a wad of spit in the face of every man, woman, and child ever to attend it.

"Why won't you tell me?" I asked for the umpteenth time.

Eyes glues forward, Sydney ignored me. Not a single muscle twitched. She was as still as a marble statue atop the pegasus, only allowing an exasperated sigh to blow through parted lips.

"Talk to me, Sydney. What's going on?" Sydney normally jabbered away, talking nonstop about anything and everything. This role – the one of patient prier – belonged to Sydney, not me. Why was she so tight-lipped now?

"Centrielle isn't far. We should leave the pegasi here," she said.

"That's not what I meant by talking," I mumbled.

We tied the pegasi in the cover of thick brush, absolute silence lingering between us. Deafeningly quiet, the uneasy calm before the storm sent shivers down my spine. I itched to scream and shout, to yell at the top of my lungs just to hear some form of noise. Even a whisper would suffice. Anything. The tiniest cough or the almost inaudible ruffle of fabric. Her voice, even if only to spout directions, warded off the memories, but it went unheard now.

I stuck close to Sydney like glue, never falling more than three steps behind her. The thick forest gave way to an overly crowded road; and before treading one foot on the dirt, I pulled up the hood of my cloak. I fell in line with Sydney, and we followed the mass of people and carriages into Centrielle, situating ourselves in the middle of the many bodies. Heads down, we passed the knights on guard at the city limits without incident.

All at once, or maybe slowly assimilated but unnoticed till then, every sense was assaulted. Quick-tempoed, upbeat music echoed down the streets, running around corners and squeezing through the crowds. A loud chorus of conversations piled atop one another until it became a constant drone of voices. The tangy, sweet smell of roasted pork caressed my nostrils, and my mouth watered at the scent of fresh bread. Flower petals, soft pink in color, strewed the cobblestone streets; and rainbow ribbons adorned buildings, hitching posts, and picnic tables. Equally spaced on both sides of every street, a bundle of smooth stones anchored paper lanterns to the ground, preventing their sky escape.

"Sydney," I said, "what's so bad about this?"

Her head snapped to me, piercing orbs threateningly dark before draining of any fight. "Forget it. Just find the shard." She quickened her pace and slunk through the crowded bodies like a leaf gracefully floating on air.

I didn't follow her. Instead, I wandered in the opposite direction, eyeing each sky lantern I passed. Each flame's bright glow illuminated the paper, and the shadows swayed with the music. They danced to the beat, wispy fingers climbing the paper as if begging to be released, to be free to leisurely float among the reddening orange and pale blue. Even so, the flames' shadows failed to outline a single jagged edge. The lines swayed with slight curves but rough peaks and valleys were nowhere to be seen.

As I meandered closer to the town square, the crowd grew larger and the music louder. Smooth, satin red twirled beside raggedy tan with partners in crisp, tuxedo black and button up beige. Two opposite life styles danced side by side, caring only of the placement of their feet. Apologetic smiles and shy giggles passed between partners when flats nicked muddy boots or heels stabbed polished leather. The same actions, so innocent and domestic, mirrored each other almost identically. With each successful twist and turn or clumsy misstep, smiles widened to touch joyful orbs; and for one night of the year, all their worries were forgotten, left at home until the following morning.

I left the dancing to those with partners and ducked down a side street. Rows of picnic tables sat orderly atop cobblestone, and kerosene lanterns hung from steel posts to assist the floating lights in chasing away the shadows of the evening sky. A few families gathered around the nearest tables, plates piled high with an assortment of meats, breads, and even fruits, while the farther tables were vacant.

I followed the path of sky lanterns, walking through the rows of tables and eyeing both sides of the street. The flames danced to the beat of their own drums, but that's all they were – flames. Continuing down the road, I debated turning back to the city square, but the final floating light on my left drew me in. My eyes squinted to make out a single dip with a rough incline contorting the swaying shadow. I hurried to the floating lantern, my pace on the verge of running. My heart pounded rapidly in my chest as I stood before it, my eyes following each step of the shadowy dance. Peering behind the paper, I smiled and reached for the base of the flame. A burning heat brushed my fingers, but the momentary pain was worth curling my grip around the metal shard.

"Will, are you there?"

Barely a heartbeat later, he replied, "Always am."

"Of course," I laughed. "Where else would you be?"

"Wherever you are."

"Then that would be the Fall Festival."

"What? That's not fair," William whined. "We've always gone together."

"We technically are together."

"You're right," he said, and I could hear the warm, tender smile in his voice, "but this time, you have to be my eyes."

"It's a date then," I said, slowly wandering back to the city square. "Where do you want to start?"

"Hmm," he thought. "How about tonight's menu?"

I zigged and zagged through the bodies of people, cutting across the city square's corner to avoid bumping into the dancing couples. Spotting the crowded banquet table, I edged my way close enough to see the long tables of silver trays piled high. I glanced at all the options before mentally picking out William's favorites. "For an appetizer, you have stuffed mushrooms with a cheesy dip, and your main course is pork fresh off the spit with mashed potatoes and gravy. Oh, and grilled asparagus. You finish off the meal with an unnecessary amount of strawberries and chocolate chip cookies."

"Are the cookies still warm?"

"Fresh from the crown's kitchen," I said.

William groaned. "No more. It's too painful. We have to move on. How about a dance?"

"Will," I said, shaking my head at the thought. "I am not dancing here alone."

"Close your eyes."

"William."

"Please," he begged. "You don't have to move a muscle. Just close your eyes." The music slowed, the ring of piano keys ripping through the air. "See. The universe is rooting for me."

Eyelids veiled my orbs, and a single breath blew through my lips. "Okay. They're closed."

"Good, now listen to my voice. Visualize what I say. Okay?"

I nodded but right after realized he couldn't see me. "Okay."

When he spoke, Will's voice was confident and soft, sweet and composed. "I take your right hand in my left, and our fingers lace together. Your hand falls upon my shoulder, and I pull you close by your waist. Our first step is slow, hesitant because I have two left feet. Even so, you let me take the lead and are content in swaying back and forth in the same path. My foot steps on yours multiple times, but you laugh it off, squeezing my shoulder at every misstep."

"And your face turns beet red, all the way to your ears," I interjected.

William chuckled. "Most likely," he agreed. "You point out my flushed cheeks, and I deny the ever present color. To prove your point, the back of your hand rests against my heated cheeks, and you giggle. The sound is music to my ears, and your smile is a work of art. I can't stop the urge to kiss you so I don't even try. I abandon the concept of dancing and place one hand at the back of your neck with the other flat against the small of your back. Bodies flush against each other, I press my lips to yours."

I felt him – all of him. His hand splayed firmly across my back, and his chest pressed against mine. My hand tightened on his shoulder before it slid around his neck. Noses rubbed against each other as breaths mingled. An unseen spark jumped from one pair of lips to the other, crisscrossing from flesh to flesh. His eyes, swirling vortexes of burning cedar, blazed with uncaged passion.

Longing to see the fiery orbs, my eyes blinked open. Their image dissipated, vanishing with each flutter of an eyelid until disappearing altogether. I sighed, but smiled nonetheless. As if reading within the depths of my mind, the music morphed its pace to more of a lively jive – one much too complicated for Will or me to leisurely sway to.

"Take my hand and go for a walk?" William offered.

"If only," I breathed, barely loud enough for even myself to hear.

William asked, "Where are we going? What are we seeing?"

"We're at the town square, at the very edge of dancers far more skilled than us."

"I've got skill!" Will butted in.

"No interrupting. It's my turn to plan our date," I said, and I heard the childish pout in his sigh. "As I was saying, we leave the dancing to the dancers and stroll farther down the street. You stop at every game and insist on playing them all. You nearly rip my arm from its socket to drag me along to bob for apples. I watch from a safe distance as you dunk your head in the water. It takes about three tries of splashing around before you come up with a crisp, red apple between your teeth. You smirk around it and try talking, but your words are merely jumbled syllables that make no sense. After taking a juicy bite, the apple drops to your hand, and we move on to yet another game. You challenge me to a round of bean bag toss, and let's just say you're better at dancing."

William begged to differ. "If I recall correctly, I kicked your butt the last time we played."

"Shall we call it a tie, then?" I asked, passing behind a pair of children playing the very game we were in our heads.

"Isn't that over-exaggerating your skill?"

"I'm not that bad," I argued.

William snorted with laughter. "Sure, and I'm good at dancing."

"There's no need to lie."

"And who's the one lying?"

"Fine, I'll admit it. You're great at throwing bags of sand, but you suck at dancing."

"And you suck at *throwing bags of sand*," he mocked my voice. I was about to retort when he said, "But I love you and your horrible aim."

"You're such a smooth talker."

"I know," he said with pride, and I could image the goofy grin plastered on his face. "Since I won at bean bags, where are we now?"

I glanced around. I had failed to notice the street's slow incline, but the many people passing both behind and below me did not. Their pace was quick, hurried like it was superstitious just to step upon the stone, but the vastly colored and overabundant ribbons said otherwise. They climbed the supports and sprawled across the curving arch, braiding together to form a display of artificial rainbows. Single strands fluttered down to look out upon the city square where soft pink flower petals danced between the waltzing feet to create choreography of their own. It was almost too much, as if the cheery brightness hid some dark evil.

"Dawn," William gently called my name. "Is something wrong?"

My eyes fell to my feet, and all bright distractions failed to mask the darkened smears on the cobblestone. Once a dripping crimson, the liquid plopped on stone, pooling on the surface before seeping through the cracks and margins. The evidence wasn't washed away, and why would it? The act wasn't considered murder. Under martial law, it was the swift and just execution of a traitor, but the dried blood – some of which was probably Spencer's – could never be considered traitorous.

SOMEONE'S DAUGHTER

It was like rust, only stones didn't deteriorate under the elements in such a way. Rocks didn't bleed when it rained, nor did they drain of life under the trampling of feet. It wasn't the rocks' last breaths showcased upon the arched bridge that looked down upon the city square. It wasn't their final words or dying gasps. The stones were merely the messengers, the eternal resting place of people deemed dangerous to society by the most venomous rulers of all. They were the people – the victims – of a government gone wrong, one obsessed with tyrannical dictatorship. Their innocent lives were lost where my feet now stood.

I stumbled backward and stared at the stains before eyeing the surrounding crowds of people. With the waning light, the number of bodies had thinned, and those that remained were either preparing to leave or passed out drunk in the streets. It was odd. Normally, the crowds would gather around the city square to watch the fireworks, but that wasn't the case.

Maybe Sydney was right. The festival wasn't what it used to be, not now at least. In the early evening, children laughed and played with friends, and families gathered for picnics. But now, they left. What happened after the sun set to cause this change?

I searched for Sydney, scanning the city square. As soon as I spotted the single braid hung over her right shoulder, I hightailed it from the bridge and darted across the almost vacant dance floor. Sydney's head shot up to spot me, and she met me half way.

"Did you find it?" she asked.

"Yes, I'm here," Will said. "What's going on?"

Sydney grabbed my forearm and tugged me toward a back alley. "Let's get out of here."

"Wait, Sydney." I shook my arm free from her grip. "What is this? What happened here?"

Her face void of any emotion and her voice far too steady, Sydney said, "You don't want to know. You will see it every time you close your eyes. You will never sleep peacefully again, and your whole view of the world will change." She grabbed at my arm again. "We need to leave *now*."

I sidestepped out of her reach. "I'm not leaving until you tell me."

She stepped closer and extended her arm to me again. "Let's go before it's too late."

I shook my head. "Tell me."

"Please, Sydney, we can handle it," William said.

Her arm paused halfway between us. Fingers curled into a loose fist, and both arm and face fell. She turned her back as if to leave but stood eerily still. Her voice was hushed, quiet and raspy, "The closing event isn't a fireworks display anymore. It's a blood bath of executions."

I thought I could handle it, because in all honesty, that shouldn't have surprised me. What did I expect? What else would have caused the rusty stains upon stone? This wasn't some new, isolated case either. The citizens knew this morbid secret but ignored the taboo like some foul word that offended but did not harm, only an execution did more than harm. It killed. The blood lost could not be returned, and life drained away could not be reborn. Yet, everyone turned a blind eye, hurrying away to protect their own innocence. Given the opportunity of fight or flight, they fled.

Sydney grabbed my hand and tugged with all her might. She dragged me only a few steps before my feet pulled their own weight. I could blame it on the adrenaline coursing through my veins, but that was a lie. It wasn't a mad rush of hormones that propelled my legs to motion. No, I wanted to protect my naive innocence like everyone else, wanted to believe the world – no humanity – wasn't so cruel as to murder each other. After all, if I didn't see it, it wasn't real. I could pretend not to notice the sickened, scowling faces of the royal guards on post, of those forced to face the merciless reality that was Siven.

Their cold, emotionless eyes stared at cobblestone, but orbs weren't always void of feelings. They were veterans to this homicidal fiasco, trained to shut down, to forget this night and erase it from memory. Having made the mistake before, each knight refused to look up, many gluing their eyes shut. The rookies flinched when the first shrill cry rang throughout the city, and hands shot up to seal out the noise. Hearing it was as bad as seeing it, because the human mind was one of imagination. It supplied imagines far more gruesome and horrific than the act itself.

But I didn't have to pretend or imagine.

We couldn't dart down the alley fast enough before the long line of victims was led out. Male and female, infant and elderly, rich and poor, black and white and everyone in between, no one was spared. Each was presented, shackled and restrained. A hooded executioner – sword drawn and gleaming – stood tall and proud upon the arched bridge. Dragged before the god of death, the first victim whimpered out sniffling cries.

Tears streaked down rosy cheeks, and eyes were so puffy that their color was obscured. Locks of blonde toned with golden red draped over slender shoulders. Lips quivered, and the young girl's petite body shook with tremors.

My whole body froze, and my muscles refused to budge even a millimeter. It couldn't be. There was no way. She was safe back at home. He had promised they'd all be there when I came back. I trusted him to protect her so why was she here?

The executioner's blade, high in the darkened sky, mocked me. Smooth and glistening, it was like a deadly serpent, ready to sink its fangs into its prey. It coiled and waited for the precise moment to strike. Air parted way, rushing past the blade's sharpened edge. With one swift swing, it ended with an echoing thud as it connected with the thick block of crimson stained wood.

"Dawn! Will! Welcome back!" the jubilant voice rang through the outer courtyard. Little feet trampled on the ground and barely managed not to trip over each other. She came to a sliding stop and rocked on her heels with her hands clasped together behind her back. "How was your trip?" she chirped, a beaming smile showing off pearly whites.

"Same old boring nonsense it always is," William said as he hopped to the ground. Reins grasped in one hand, the other invited Rose closer, and Will picked her up, holding her to his chest. "I would have rather spent the day drinking tea with you and Sir Beary."

Rosy cheeks puffed out as lips pouted. "You owe Sir Beary. He was really sad when you canceled, and he wouldn't talk to me all day."

William playfully gasped in mock surprise. "How dare he! Who does that bear think he is? I guess he won't get to meet the friend we brought back for our dear little Rose."

Ochre orbs sparkled with anticipation, and her lithe body squirmed in William's embrace. Planting her hands atop his shoulder, she pushed with all her might to peek behind William. She patted his armor before peering at the pegasus, but orbs quickly fell upon Will's face to skeptically eye him. "It's not the pegasus, is it?" she asked.

I laughed as I came to stand beside the two, gift hidden safely beneath my cloak. "That's not ours to give away."

"Then what is it?" Rose asked.

I said, "You better tell Sir Beary to be nice, or his new friend may not like him." I pulled a teddy bear with a pale purple bow tied around its neck from beneath my cloak and offered the plush to Rose.

She reached for it, and once within her grasp, she hugged it to her chest. "Thank you!" she exclaimed, tossing one arm around my neck and the other around William. She squeezed tightly before letting go and wiggling free of William's hold. Her feet plopped on the ground as she bounced in place. "We should go introduce Sir Teddy to Sir Beary!"

The enthusiastic excitement was hard to say no to, but today's work wasn't quite done. If it was up to William, he'd skip his duties in a heartbeat. I, on the other hand, didn't enjoy answering to a red-faced king waiting to explode with anger, but my heart wavered. Two pairs of strikingly similar eyes pleaded, begging like spoiled puppies.

"You two go ahead," I gave in.

"Positive?" William asked, his eyes lighting up so brightly that I couldn't say no.

I nodded. "Don't worry. It's only a report to the king and queen."

"Good luck." William placed a swift peck on my cheek and slipped a second pair of reins into his hand. He led the pair of pegasi to the stables with Rose at his heel and a brilliant smile gracing his lips.

I reported the outcome of our mission to the king and queen, but what should have been a quick briefing turned into an intense interrogation. Every miniscule detail was discussed as if questioning both Will's and my judgments.

"Our sources had reason to believe the rebellion wouldn't settle so easily," King Caldwell interrupted me yet again. "Am I honestly supposed to believe not a single drop of blood was shed? Do I look like I was born last century?"

There was no correct answer to the last question so I ignored it all together. "And would that source be Drake?" I questioned.

"Irrelevant," Queen Ember said.

I shook my head. "No, I believe that is a key point in this blatant waste of time. He is the reason William and I were dispatched to the village. Is he not?"

"Watch your tongue!" the king warned.

"I will not. He caused this mess with uncalled for violence. That poor excuse of a knight attacked an innocent woman which led to a bloody brawl between his men and the residents of Colerich. He is unfit to protect your people, and yet he is in charge of dozens of knights."

The king's tilted gaze peered at me as he quirked his eyebrow. "I thought you said not a drop of blood was shed."

My pulse pounded through my veins, and my palm twitched at my side. "Drake drew blood. William and I got the situation under control after we ordered Drake and his squad back to the castle."

"And how did you do that?" King Caldwell rested his elbow on the arm of a bejeweled throne, his open palm holding his head up.

This was the third time I recounted the same event to the king and queen. They were old but far from being deaf. After all, both crowns jumped at the chance to defend their pet serpent. "As I said before, William and I drove Drake from the village. We sheathed our weapons and calmed the crowd. I attended to the woman, who is both physically and mentally scarred because of Drake, while William took testimonies and dispersed the crowd. The woman—"

Queen Ember cut me off, "Where are these testimonies?"

I huffed out a reply, "They will be handed in with the written report tomorrow morning. Now as I was saying, the woman and her girlfriend have filed an official complaint against Drake and four of his subordinates. An investigating team will have to look over the testimonies as well."

"Once I've read over the complaint, I will determine whether or not to investigate this matter further," the king said.

"Your Majesty, I highly recommend suspending Drake for the—"

"You are dismissed," he ordered.

My lips sealed tightly as I bowed my head. Curling my fingers into a fist, my hand pressed over my heart in a farewell salute before I turned on my heels and left the golden throne room.

I walked down dimly lit halls, the candle light doing little to illuminate the barbaric stone. After descending the twisting stairs, I passed through the first arched entry on the right that led to the castle's left wing. The empty passages were easily maneuvered, and I stopped before the middle door of the farthest hall. The door moaned and groaned – its hinges aching as the heavy wood was pushed in and again when shut behind me.

A pile of discarded armor met me by the door, the numerous plates and joints having been haphazardly tossed to the side. Only a few feet from the armor, William lay on a fluffy beige rug, and a flowery blanket draped over his back, not big enough to cover his flailed out limbs. Chocolate-colored bangs fell upon closed eyelids, and parted lips sung a soft melody of snores. Tucked safely under the grown man's arm, a teddy bear hugged William's chest.

Warm endearment bubbled within my heart as I stared down at the man. I quietly laughed, "What in the world happened here?"

"Will and Sir Beary were really tired," Rose answered from atop the bed nestled against the opposite wall. She held a worn out pencil and scribbled across a piece of thin parchment. Drowsy eyes glanced up occasionally, gazed at Sir Teddy tucked under the blanket beside her, and zeroed in on the paper again.

I disappeared into the adjacent room and quickly slipped out of my armor. When I returned to the main chamber, I tiptoed over Will's sleeping body, careful not to step on an arm or a leg. "What do you have there?" I asked Rose as I climbed in beside her.

Rose sidled to my side, pulling Sir Teddy along with her. She held the paper up proudly. "It's you, me, and Will," she said.

I gazed at the drawing. A tall figure composed of a circle for a head and straight lines for its body, limbs, and even appendages stood on the right. Squiggly lines of locks fell to the figure's mid back. A similar figure stood on the left, but this one towered slightly over the other and had coiled strokes of hair atop its head. Situated between the two, a shorter stick person reached up to slip small fingers into longer ones. On each face, smiles stretched from ear to ear, and large bug eyes stared at the viewer.

"Do you like it?" Rose asked quietly, peering between her drawing and me.

"Of course, I do," I genuinely said. "We'll have to show it to Will in the morning, but for now, let's go to bed."

Rose handed me the drawing and the pencil, and I set the two on the nightstand. Crawling atop the covers, Rose glanced over the edge of the bed and pointed to William. "What about Will?"

I smirked at the snoring man. "He looks comfortable where he is so you'll have to keep me company instead."

"Really?" Rose asked as a burst of excitement lit up ochre orbs.

"Of course," I smiled, patting the mattress beside me. I pulled back the covers as Rose crawled beneath them. "You are my little Rose after all."

Her name tumbled from my lips, but the strangled cry was useless. The name fell upon deaf ears of a decapitated head. The crimson tipped blade ignored the cry and rose to the dark sky. I reached for it, begging the space between it and my hand to vanish. It had to be crushed, shattered into a million pieces, a trillion specks of dust.

Sydney grabbed my upper arm and hauled me like a rag doll down the alley, the bridge and murderous blade cowardly hiding behind a building's brick wall. Her fingers clawed into my skin with a vice-like grip, but it was merely a prick in comparison. The silent buildings, the empty shells cloaked in armor, the trees escaping to the sky – they all passed in a blur, each one a fragment of despair. Sharp gasps and laborious pants burned my chest as Sydney and I fled into the thick forest.

The death grip on my arm loosened, leaving the stamp of fingers upon my skin. "That wasn't Rose," Sydney breathed heavily. "It wasn't her so snap out of it. We need to go." I stared blankly at her. She grabbed my shoulders, shook me lightly, and said it again before her words finally sunk in.

My limbs trembled, and a shaky breath exhaled through my lips. I had been wrong. She was okay. That was a personal victory, but even within the thicket of leaves and branches, the ear splitting shrieks banged against my eardrums, demanding the victims' final cries to be heard.

"Rose is alive and breathing. That wasn't your daughter."

The screams pounded at the walls of my mind. Their faces, scared and cowering, clouded my vision, and pleas of help clogged my ears. That pretentious, crimson-stained blade swung through air and flesh all the same, smiling with pride after each slice. It stared at me, a single drop of blood sliding down its pointed tip. Life after life was consumed with each victim's memories, thoughts, and emotions floating into oblivion.

"But that was someone's daughter!"

Sydney stepped back, releasing my quivering shoulders. "There's nothing we can do," she said quietly.

"She is a child. What could she have done wrong?"

"She was a child. It's too late."

"What sin could she have committed?"

William spoke up softly, "Dawn, calm down. We can't do anything right now."

"She is an innocent little girl."

A piercing smack resounded around us, and my hand rose to cup my cheek. "Open your eyes!" Sydney snapped. "Siven is ready to break out in

97

a civil war! Human decency does not apply to war! Sacrifices will be made, and you are powerless to stop them!"

"Sydney–" Will started.

"Is that what you really think – that all this has been for nothing, that all we're fighting for will amount to nothing?" I questioned, an eerie calm to my voice.

Fiery anger flashed in her dark orbs. Her voice was just as calm – daring – when she said, "You were locked up. All you're doing is trying to save William. It's not like you're fighting to save this country's people."

Will butted in, "Come on, you two. Stop this."

"No, you're right," I said. "I'm fighting to regain my family, but my family is part of this country, no matter how small a part. I will protect my family at any cost even if that means doing it alone."

"And how did that work out for you the first time?"

My eyes went wide, and my breath caught in my throat. The looming darkness encased me. Cold stone chilled my skin, and musky air tickled my nostrils. The throbbing ache, one that had been healed, burned in my shoulder. The dull thud of boots echoed down the stairwell with the great screech of the door.

I shook free from the demons of the past and brushed by Sydney. My boot pressed into the silver-plated stirrup, and I swung into the saddle. Clicking my tongue, I urged Cobalt to take flight. His hooves lifted from soft sod, and we rose above the treetops.

CHECKMATE

Tepid, honey-colored liquid swished in the glass between my hands. The glass rocked against the bar top with a rhythmic *tap, tap, tap.* Its contents sloshed against its sides, but not a single drop splattered the wood of the bar. The burning liquid stared me down, begging to scorch its way down my throat, but neither of us won the staring contest.

What was I doing sulking in the corner of a small-town tavern? The rolled parchment and uncompleted blade called me, but I ignored them, unwilling to face the cold reality of the world in which I lived. But was this any better? Could I live in my own little world of denial, hold on to the hope that I was dreaming – stuck in a nightmare? Was that all this world had to offer? Between the choices of a cruel reality or a whimsical delusion, I wanted neither.

Reality shouldn't be cruel. I shouldn't wake up in the morning to a clear sky but only see the clouds. The sweet melody of birds shouldn't be heard as earsplitting cries of those meeting their maker. I shouldn't feel the piercing eyes of demons staring from the shadows when riding on a bright forest trail. My first instinct upon running into another person on the street shouldn't be fear. I was afraid. We all were afraid, but of what? This crippling fear came from living, from experiencing the world's cruelties. That was reality. Reality was fear.

But a delusion should not be more whimsical than reality. No matter how great the imagination of the mind may be, it could not duplicate the physical feelings felt when interacting with the surrounding world and its inhabitants. I could image William taking my hand in his; but the warmth, the comfort, and the security that came with it could not be replicated. The jolt in my chest upon seeing Rose's giggling face light up with the brightest smile I had ever seen was not reproducible without seeing it in person. The tears shed for my father racked my body, and they were far too real to be only a figment of my imagination.

Choosing between delusion and reality, I chose reality. Even with all the cruelty, the injustice, and the fear; reality overpowered delusion because in reality, people fought for each other. The bonds forged between us gave us the willpower to protect the ones we loved. Because of our fear, we sought solace in each other to make us stronger, to hold each other together even if it meant giving up ourselves. That was reality. Reality was believing we could better the world by protecting each other.

But that was easier said than done. Reality had a loophole, and ironically enough, it was each other. People had to agree, to see eye to eye or at least consider the other's point of view, but that rarely happened. That was where the two worlds clashed. Without accepting each other, hatred led to fear, and fear led to broken bonds.

The stool beside me screeched against the floor and squeaked under added weight. "Why has the great Dawn Lockwood graced my domain with her presence?" Icy blue orbs peered intently at me. Strands of gold – draping from a high ponytail – tickled the bar top, and an elbow planted against the bar supported a tilted head.

I eyed him warily, but after remembering all he had done, I breathed out a sigh. "There was a shard by the well," I muttered.

He smirked dryly. "Then why are you sitting in a tavern? Shouldn't you be hunting down the next shard?" A long finger tapped the rim of my glass. "Or maybe you're drinking away your sorrow. Who knows?"

"What are you doing here, Kent?" I asked.

"It doesn't look like you've had much."

I looked down at the alcohol and uncurled my fingers from around the glass. Crossing my arms over my chest, I said, "I never was much of a drinker."

Kent chuckled softly as he sat up straight and snatched the glass from the bar top. The rim reached his lips, and the pungent liquid flowed into his mouth. He downed the alcohol in a few quick gulps, and icy orbs squeezed shut. After a few shakes of his head, he slowly set the glass back on the bar. "That crap's nasty. I hope you weren't planning to actually drink it."

"What are you doing here?" I asked again.

The sorcerer swiveled on the stool, spinning to face the tables of people. His arms swept out to indicate our surroundings. "Brestone is my kingdom – the base of the rebels so to speak. I notice when a stranger walks in, especially one that's not so strange to me. I wouldn't feel safe calling this home if I didn't."

"This is your home?" I asked.

He nodded. "It's got everything I wish to protect." His gaze fell upon the occupants of the tavern, hesitating at each person with the softest of smiles playing on his lips. Then his eyes traveled along the bar and locked on a closed door nestled in the opposite corner.

A flash of fiery red and star-like specks crossed my mind. "I heard you took in Spencer McCadden's daughter. Is she here?"

With icy orbs refusing to leave that door, Kent nodded. "She's with

Darrel. Would you like to see her?"

"I would," I said.

Kent slid from the stool. His back to me, he raised his hand and wiggled his pointer finger for me to follow. He led the way around the bar, straight to the very oaken door he had stared at. Twisting the rickety knob, he pulled the door open to a dark stairwell. Instead of lighting any of the numerous lanterns mounted on either side of the walls, the sorcerer snapped his fingers, resulting in a bright flame sparking from the pads. The light floated above his hand, cupped within his palm, and produced a soft blue glow bright enough to illuminate the cramped space.

I followed him up the stairs, a dull creak sounding every few steps. At the top of the stairs was another door, and we passed through it into a small hallway. An option between three doors presented itself – one at the end of the hall to the right and two side by side in front of us. Kent strode a few steps to the right, opened the door, and extinguished his makeshift light before stepping inside.

The room was half lit by the rays of the sun. A refreshingly cool breeze flowed in from the open window on the right whereas the left one was locked tight, its curtains drawn. Two twin beds hugged opposite walls, and the one beneath the ruffled curtains had a pair of figures occupying it. A tall man with rich russet skin sat at the foot of the bed. His feet hung over the edge, and his head lolled back against the wall. An open book lay abandoned in the man's lap.

As the door squeaked shut behind me, the man's eyes blinked open. His hand rubbed at reluctantly opened brown orbs before running over his short, shaved hair. He breathed out a heavy sigh through his nose as his eyes drooped shut again.

"Darrel," Kent softly called the man's name as he stepped to the bedside.

Dark bay eyes snapped open. For the split second before consciousness fully sunk in, they held an almost angry surprise – that of a person desperate for undisturbed sleep but rudely awakened far too early – but after falling upon Kent, they softened. The neutral line of lips brightened to an affectionate smile, like a person wore upon receiving the gift they most wanted for their birthday. His hand reached for Kent, cupping the sorcerer's cheek; and he leaned up to kiss him softly, eyes fluttering shut.

A flush settled upon Kent cheeks, nose, and even the tips of his ears; but he still kissed back. It was only when Darrel tried to deepen the kiss, his tongue darting out, that Kent cleared his throat with a grunt and patted his hand against Darrel's cheek. "Later," he said, playfully pushing his boyfriend's head away. "Right now we have a guest."

Darrel craned his neck to peer around Kent. When he spotted me, he said, "Oh, it's you."

"It's... me."

"Ah, sorry," he said, carefully sliding from the foot of the bed and setting the book down in his wake so as not to disturb its sleeping occupant. He closed the space between us in two long strides, and he towered over me with a cheery smile. Extending his hand, I shook it as he said, "We haven't formally met, but I'm Darrel. It's a pleasure."

"Nice to meet you, too."

"She wanted to see Fallon," Kent informed.

Darrel turned back to the bed. "I finally got her down for a nap in her own bed. It took reading the same story four times, but she finally fell asleep."

I stepped beside Darrel and stared down at the slumbering child. Pulled up to her neck, an old quilt tucked in her small frame. Tight curls of blazing red – almost orange – draped her rounded face. A sprinkle of freckles dotted her cheeks and crossed the bridge of a button nose. Her mouth hung open, rhythmic breaths causing her chest to rise and fall, with her thumb lazily dangling between her lips.

Out of his three daughters, Fallon was the only one that was a spitting image of her father.

"She'll be treated as our own until it is safe to find her next of kin, and even then, we'll protect her," Darrel said, peering at Fallon's peaceful face.

The three of us stood in silence, each mesmerized by the child's innocence, but the quiet peace did not last. "Where's Sydney?"

My breath froze in my chest, and I stared at Kent only to find him watching my every move. Icy orbs bored into me, and I adverted my gaze to the floorboards. I shuffled back, inching my way to the exit.

"What happened?"

My retreat ceased. "Nothing," I muttered.

Kent cocked his head. "Then why don't I believe you?'

"What makes you think something happened?"

"Hmm... let's see," the sorcerer mused. "You were glowering at a glass of rum instead of continuing an all-important search, and we can't forget the fact that one half of your rescue team is uncharacteristically absent. Does that sound about right?"

Tight-lipped, I continued to stare at my feet, but a low grunt had my eyes snapping to the duo before me. Kent rubbed the side of his torso as a smug looking Darrel had his elbow cocked, his hand on his hip. "Be nice," he berated. Kent merely scoffed and rolled his eyes.

"I apologize for my boyfriend's lack of manners," Darrel spoke, peering at Kent from the corner of his eyes. He then looked at me with his expression soft. "I know we're probably the last people you want to confide in, but we're all ears."

"It's a long story."

"We're not going anywhere," Darrel said.

I glanced between the two, and even Kent had embraced a more comforting smile, having ditched his snarky grin. With a huff of air, I reluctantly began, "It was the Fall Festival." Realization crossed the duo's faces and any form of positivity was swept away. "Sydney knew, but I didn't. She tried to get us out of there, but I refused to leave. I wanted to know what she was hiding. I just... never expected it to be that."

Smudges of crimson stained strawberry blonde locks, dying them with gruesome death. A shriek rang out, long and continuous – the last cry before the god of death descended upon a frail neck. It glistened and gleamed under the first glance of a mournful moon, its sharpened edge not the least bit remorseful. His morbid grin couldn't be hidden behind a cowardly mask.

A firm hand fell upon my shoulder. "What happened between you and Sydney?" Darrel prompted.

I swallowed the lump in my throat. "A child was executed, and I... I can't accept it. Sydney said it was a necessary sacrifice, and we argued. It got heated, so I ran off on my own."

Darrel gently squeezed my shoulder before crossing his arms over his chest. "You know, as much as it hurts to admit, Sydney is right. She could've chosen a better wording – like victims instead of sacrifices – but either way is true. It's not something you have to accept as an everyday part of this world, but it is an undeniable injustice we must work to change. Sydney knows that better than any of us, and I'm sure she didn't mean any of what she said out of anger."

Kent stepped in, "There's no sugar coating to it, no innocent white lies. Siven has entered survival mode. If you want to live, you have to fight. If you turn the other cheek, you die. You either stand beside me or get out of my path. Now which will it be?"

I eyed the sorcerer, and a mask of seriousness stared back. "I have people to protect," I said, turning on my heels for the door.

Kent grabbed my forearm with a relentless grip and held tight. His fingers dug into my skin and refused to let go even after I attempted to shake free. It wasn't until my head snapped back to glare at him that he said, "How would you like to protect all of Siven?"

I warily eyed him, "What are you talking about?"

Kent released his grip, allowing my hand to fall to my side. "Let's just say my chess pieces are preparing for checkmate. The only two still rogue are my king and queen, partially due to a great miscalculation on my part. I'd deeply appreciate them returning to my side before too many pawns or another knight is sacrificed." His eyes flicked to Fallon. "I don't want another fatherless child asking where daddy is or when her mother and sisters are coming home. That must be prevented at all costs, but to do so,

I need my king and queen."

I glanced between the three of them – the child of tragic incident, the man of comforting protection, and the sorcerer of planned retaliation. The last two stared at me, one pleading and the other calm and collected. One knight murdered, pawns constantly slaughtered, and his king and queen fighting a battle of their own – yet his eyes held nothing but confidence, as if he was sure of the answer to come.

But he never waited to hear one. "I don't need an answer now. Think about it. Talk it over with William. When you free him from the spell, come back with your decision."

"Why us?"

Kent reached into the front pocket of his pants and dug out a small envelope folded into a square. "You know the answer. The two of you were obvious choices to reunite Siven, but there is something more." He slipped the envelope into my palm. "William and Sydney hold more power than they are aware of. The contents of the envelope will reveal what is hidden, but do not open it without William. He has to see it, not just hear it. Understand?"

I clenched the envelope and nodded before slipping the paper into my back pocket.

"Good, then get out to the livery and apologize to Sydney."

Bewildered, I asked, "What?"

Kent sighed in irritation and pushed me toward the door. "She tailed you these past few weeks, so apologize and get back to your mission. The sooner you accomplish that, the sooner I get my king and queen. Now go." He pried the door open and shoved me into the dim hallway.

I reached the door to the stairs before Kent pushed the other one shut, leaving me in the dark hall. One hand flat against the wall, I maneuvered the stairs a single, hesitant step at a time. The light outlining the bottom of the door guided my slow steps as my other hand blindly sought the door. Fumbling for the knob, my hand bumped into it, and I pushed the door open to return to the main floor of the tavern.

Once I exited the bar, the livery was only a hop, skip, and a jump away. A short walk across the dusty road had me standing beneath its thick white sign. I stepped through the open door and searched for the familiar face.

Her head poked up beside Cobalt as she stroked the equine's neck. Her lips formed words far too quiet for me to hear, but Cobalt's ears flicked at the whispers. He nudged Sydney's shoulder with his nose, and she quietly laughed before rubbing the pegasus' long face.

I stepped down the aisle, my boots crunching on straw strewed through the livery. Cobalt's ears pricked in my direction, and he whinnied to me. I stopped in my tracks when Sydney whipped around and spotted me. Staring at the ground, I scratched the nape of my neck as I said, "I'm sorry.

104

I let my emotions get the best of me, and I took it out on you. Sydney, I am so, so sorry."

Shaking arms enveloped me in a tight embrace, hands clutching the fabric of my shirt. Her head fell to my shoulder with her cheek resting against my collarbone. "No, I'm sorry. It's my fault. I shouldn't have said what I did. I didn't mean any of it – not a single word. I'm sorry. I'm sorry. I'm–"

"Sydney, stop," I breathed softly. "We both got too heated. I'm sorry. You're sorry. Let's move forward and leave that in the past. Okay?"

Sydney nodded and released me from her embrace. She smiled while wiping at the corners of her eyes with the heels of her hands. "Where to?" she asked.

FILTHY MOUTH

My teeth chattered as the icy wind bit at my cheeks. The frigid air attacked and invaded every crevice in my many layers of clothing, spreading like a wild fire from my head to my toes. Even within the heavy wool gloves, my fingers tingled with the first onset of numbness as wet flakes of snow soaked into the fibers.

The cover of the forest did little to insulate against the swirling flurries of snow. Needle-covered branches shook with the howling wind to scatter the snow blanketed atop them. The flakes flew on the gust of air, weaving around tree trunks and snaking past clawing branches. They collided into my face and stung my already freezing skin.

"How much farther?" Sydney asked, her breath visible in the winter air.

I shielded my eyes from the onslaught of the mini blizzard as I glanced at her bundled form. "A half hour or so."

Sydney groaned as she pulled her scarlet scarf up to cover her nose. "Why does it have to be so cold?" she whined as she let the reins slacken in her grasp in order to fervently rub her gloved hands together.

"Winter tends to be cold."

She glared at me, her brows furrowed beneath the bottom of a knit hat and the hood of her cloak. "Has anyone ever told you you're funny?"

I pondered that for a moment, going so far as to rub my chin in thought. "A few."

"They lied."

"Oh, Sydney," I laughed, "you just have to lighten up."

She hummed, not necessarily in agreement as much as to appease me. "If anything should lighten up, it's this weather. I'd rather be burning under the summer sun than freezing my butt off out here."

"I'll remember that when you complain of the heat next summer."

Sydney clicked her tongue. "I wouldn't expect anything less."

Two sets of hooves crunched on the layer of settled snow as we rode closer to the eastern outskirts of the city of Stratwood. Clouds barricaded the sun, allowing little light to escape their grip, but the howling wind gradually died down to an uncomfortable breeze to become more bearable and less miserably stinging. The bitter snow floated to the earth from

106

above, no longer racing through the trees or slamming against my cheeks.

With the mini blizzard calm, the large stacks of cut logs were visible through the entangled branches. Sydney and I dismounted the pegasi and left them tied to the tree branches before I trudged a path toward the lumber yard, Sydney following in my exact tracks. Once out of the tree cover, I took quick, leaping strides across the powdery snow until I almost fell into the backside of a log stack. I braced myself against the wood to peek my head around the corner.

My cheek slammed into the snow-crusted wood as Sydney plowed into me. She knocked me into the powdery snow, her elbow digging into my side. Flustered, she scurried to the side and managed to sprinkle me with a dusting of flakes. She hastily brushed me free from the snow and pulled me back to my feet. "I'm so sorry," she apologized.

I smirked and patted Sydney's back. "Miss a step?"

"Kind of," she said, absentmindedly clutching her own forearm. "Sorry."

"It's fine." I patted my own jacket to dislodge the remaining snow. "No harm done." My throbbing cheek didn't agree with that last statement, but Sydney didn't need to know that.

She seemed satisfied with my answer and leaned around the lumber stack. "Is the coast clear?"

"Doesn't matter," I shrugged, stepping past Sydney and the piled wood. "We've already made too much noise."

"Sorry."

I glanced over my shoulder to see Sydney stock still where I left her. She stared at her feet as I peered around the lumber yard. "It's okay. There's not a soul in sight."

Sydney perked up almost immediately and jogged to my side. She gazed at the numerous stacks of planks and logs, spinning in a complete circle. Stopping with her back to me, her hands rose to level with the tops of snow-covered planks. They moved up and down – a few millimeters at most – until they locked position. "What do you think? The one on the left?"

I squinted at the piles of wood, gauging their heights without the layer of snow blanketed on top. "I think so, but worst comes to worst, we search both of them."

Sydney nodded in agreement, and the two of us trudged through the fresh snow to stand next to the tallest pile of wood. The stack towered multiple feet above our heads, and the occasional dusting of flakes fell upon us.

"Can I get a boost?" I asked.

Sydney complied, stooping low with her right hand cupped beneath her left. I placed my foot in her hands, and we counted to three together. As the third number tumbled from our lips in unison, I jumped straight up with Sydney propelling me higher. My hands reached for the sky and grabbed hold to the top layer of snow and the planks beneath. Digging my elbows into the snow, I wiggled my way atop the pile, my feet sliding for traction. My body plopped into the powdery fluff, and I lay still for a moment to catch my breath.

"Are you okay up there?" Sydney called from below.

I swiveled in the snow to peer down at her. She was covered from head to toe in the snow my climb shook free. "Just fine," I said, beaming down at her. "And yourself?"

Sydney shook her head, a flurry of flakes tumbling from her hat. She brushed the dusting of snow from her shoulders and looked up at me with a childish pout. "I'm cold. Can you find it fast?"

I smiled fondly. "Will do," I said before crawling through the snow with my gloves sifting through the layer of flakes. I nudged the snow into manageable mounds, sweeping it away to reveal the slumbering wood beneath. After constant brushing and swiping away of the numbing snow, a tiny metal tip peeked its head above the sea of white.

I snatched it from its freezing prison and unzipped my coat to tuck it into my breast pocket. Shuffling to the pile's edge, my feet dangled over the side. I pushed off the wood, and gravity pulled me to the earth with a muffled thud of boots pounding into the ground. "Fast enough?" I asked.

Sydney jumped at my unexpected arrival. "You found it?" she asked in surprise.

"She always does," Will announced himself. "It's the last one, right? I get to come home." His voice was light, airy with innocent cheerfulness, and it rang like tinkling bells.

"Soon," I said. "Real soon, but there's still one more piece. This one completes the blade, but a sapphire accent is missing. Give us another couple days, and you'll be back where you belong."

"And where's that?" Will asked with a hint of both mischief and curiosity.

"Anywhere you want it to be."

"So a warm bed?"

"William," Sydney chided. "Please remember your sister can hear you."

He whined, "That's not what I meant. I just want to sleep again. I don't even remember what it feels like to have a fluffy pillow beneath my head."

"You and me both," Sydney commented.

I said, "It's not that bad. We've managed to bunk down in abandoned barns or camp in the woods."

"And which of those are we doing tonight?" Sydney asked.

"Neither. There are a few caves a little to the east of here we can bed down in."

"Let's get going then. It's cold out here," Sydney said.

Our boots crunched through the snow as we retraced our steps. We hopped in our old tracks, stretching our legs to reach the next footprint within the snow. Sydney stumbled and missed one of the prints, almost falling face first to the ground.

"You know what?" she said, stopping in the tracks. "All I want is a warm fireplace to curl up next to. Is that too much to ask?"

I was about to retort, but an echoing voice beat me to it. "Then you shouldn't have deserted!"

I spun around, eyes wide with frantic dread; and every muscle in my body froze. My racing heart jumped in my chest, pounding against my ribcage in every last effort to breathe. My breath came as deep huffs through my nose, trying to calm the erratic heartbeats and sooth the angry adrenaline coursing through my veins. My palms twitched until they curled into fists, clenched so tightly at my sides that they shook and trembled with the strain.

Standing tall and proud to the point of domineering, the copper eyes of a knight blazed with the intent to kill. A feral grin sat upon his lips, his teeth bared in a snarl with wisps of smoke drifting into the air with each breath he took. Spikes of coarse, black hair contrasted boldly against both the snowy landscape and the metallic gray of royal armor. Two golden stars were etched into his chest place, one at each side of his collarbone.

The man's gloved hand rose, and with not a word spoken, three subordinates – each male – stepped out from behind stacks of lumber. They stood silently behind their leader, one fanned out to each side and the other directly behind. Each knight's face – the leader's included – twisted into a sadistic leer.

"Oh, how the tables have turned, Lockwood," the captain said, eerily calm with a demented sickness to it.

Mustering up as much toxicity and animosity as I could, I spat back, "What are you doing here, Drake?"

"That's Commander Chief Bolton to you," he sneered. He drew his sword from its place at his hip and lined it up to my chest. He went on as if talking to the shimmering blade, "King Caldwell and Queen Ember have ordered your life to end. You see, you have become quite the nuisance and tarnish upon the good name of the crown. Lockwood, you have started something you shouldn't have. You are to blame for the defiance in this kingdom. All their deaths are on your hands.

"That fellow...what was his name? Oh yes, McCadden, your good for nothing lap dog. He was nothing special. I don't know what you saw in that sentimental bastard. He was too soft, couldn't even kill a few beggars littering the streets. He's not even worth the effort I had to put in to slice through his neck. His family, too. They were a pain with all their pleas of mercy. I did the world a justice disposing of those fleas.

"And then we have Ms. Bates cowering in her boots behind you. As lovely as always, although I do believe crimson is her color. She's not as beautiful without the blood staining her cheeks. Ah, I can remember it. What a fond memory it is!"

"Shut your filthy mouth!"

Drake startled, faltering back a step as his head swiveled like an owl, eyeing every last pile of wood. "I wasn't informed William was back," he said. He glanced over his shoulder and ordered to his nearest subordinate, "Find him. He dies too." The knight scurried off to do as told.

A shaky, trembling hand grasped the back of my coat, tugging lightly like a scared child would hold tight to a mother. "We need to leave." Sydney's voice hitched and cracked with every word, a whisper transforming into a desperate plea. Her eyes watered and shined in the light, but the tears never overflowed. Her bottom lip quivered between the bite of her teeth. "Please."

"Sydney," I said, calm and composed, "lend me your sword."

The trembling grip on my coat loosened but did not falter. Her eyes stared at me but at the same time saw nothing. Her limbs froze, and only sharp gasps and pants fell from her lips.

In one fluid motion, I drew the sword from her hip and pushed her back. "Go! Run!" I yelled. She blinked at me, but with a final push to motion, she scurried into the trees.

I lunged at Drake, pushing my weight into the sword as it collided with his. Not fazed in the slightest, Drake didn't budge an inch. He eyed my blade as if it was nothing but a pestering fly. With a swift lick of his lips and a flash of glinting malice crossing copper orbs, he shoved forward with overpowering strength to free our clashing blades. There was no time to recover before Drake thrust his blade at my chest with a cry of, "You've got this coming!"

I dashed to the side, the tip of his blade just barely nicking mine. An enraged fury burned within his demented eyes, and every ounce of sanity drained from his being. He swung wildly, almost blindly, and charged like a seething bull on a rampage. Half his violent swings cut through the air with an audible whistle and missed me entirely. The others struck my blade in a ferocious flurry of metal clashes.

I ducked and jumped a few feet to my right, narrowly missing a slash to the neck. When I thought I was out of harm's reach long enough to suck in a deep pant of air, a seething pain shot through the right side of my torso. My opposite hand left the sword's hilt to clutch at the source of the searing fire, a small amount of crimson dampening my fingers.

"Stay out of this, you son of a bitch!" the infuriated bellow rang off the surrounding trees in a shrill echo. The demon of a commander lunged at his own subordinate, his blade slicing across the young man's cheek to produce nothing more than a shallow scratch. "My revenge means nothing if you interfere! That goes for you too!" he roared, taking a preliminary swing at the second knight. "Make yourselves useful and capture Ms. Bates! I want her alive so I can drain the life from her eyes myself!"

The two startled knights raced past their leader to follow Sydney's tracks. "No!" I pleaded and ran a few strides to cut them off.

Drake leapt in my path, forcing me to stumble backward. His feral grin returned with a vengeance, and it sent an involuntary chill down my spine. "Your opponent is me!" he snarled, baring his teeth like a rabid wolf. Once more, he charged with unwavering power and madly sliced through the air.

I scrambled back, both hands clutching tightly to my sword's hilt. The powdery snow kicked up a flurry as my feet shuffled rapidly through it. They knocked into each other, tripping on my own feet, and my back slammed into the layer of flakes. I scuttled back, my elbows and feet digging into the snow in a hasty attempt to flee.

Drake caught up to me and stood over my legs. He thrust his sword down, impaling the snow beside my head. Towering over my body, he maliciously leered at me and snickered callously. "Look at you! What a pitiful excuse of a human being! You don't deserve to walk on this earth! Why don't you roll over and die already?"

"As nice as the offer is, I'm afraid I'll have to decline," I spitefully panted. I kicked my leg up and nailed Drake in his unprotected groin. The man grunted and stumbled back a step. His grip on the impaled sword wavered before he doubled over in the snow.

I scrambled to my feet and dashed for the forest, following the trail of Sydney's footsteps. Before I reached the cover of the trees, a blur of black and white flapped its feathery wings. The equine barreled through branches with a second at its tail. Its hooves collided with snow, but its galloping pace did not falter. With blind and most likely stupid hope, I ran as he caught up. I reached for the saddle horn and leapt into the saddle.

I landed hard in the saddle's seat. My knees gripped the sides of the saddle as my feet hung down, not even attempting to find the stirrups. Gathering the reins in one hand, I steered Cobalt across the lumber yard to enter the forest once more. The equine's wings extended with a mighty flap before compacting as close to his body as they could to avoid tangling in the maze of tree trunks.

A final scream rang from the lumber yard, angry and vengeful. "I'll find you, Lockwood, and when I do, I'll kill you!" The enraged threat echoed off the trees before being swept away with the chilling winter breeze.

Cobalt flew with the same frenzied desperation I felt. Midnight hooves nicked branches and shook needles free. The equine nose-dived into the brush and zigzagged around the trees and their ensnaring arms. They passed in no more than a quick blur; and a few too many times for comfort, the tree trunks popped up in our path. I braced myself for the collisions that never came and thanked every entity of every practiced worship that Cobalt had sharper senses than me. I trusted my mount to maneuver through the labyrinth of nature and held on for dear life.

When the dark mouth of the cave appeared at the end of the tunnel, I took control from Cobalt and steered us around the couple trees in our path. I pulled the reins back with a gentle yet forceful yank, but Cobalt didn't slow. He stampeded headlong toward the cavern. His wings flailed at his sides as his hooves dug into the snow. The equine slid into the darkened cave until his hooves found greater traction on the cave's rock floor. His forelegs locked, and he abruptly stopped.

I was dislodged from the saddle and thrown over Cobalt's neck. The sword clanked against the rocky ground as I somersaulted into the face of a protruding boulder. My back crashed against stone, knocking the breath right from my lungs. Curled in on myself, I stared dizzily at the cavern's jagged ceiling and clenched at my side. The searing fire had returned and was joined by the pounding of my head and the aching stab of my lower back.

The crunching of hooves outside the cave neared, turning to steady clops once they stepped upon the stone. A pair of boots thudded against the floor and scampered to my side. "Dawn," Sydney called, dropping to her knees beside me. Her eyes scanned my face before traveling lower. Once they spotted the slice and discoloration of my coat, they widened in shock. "What happened?" she asked with poorly masked panic. Her hands nudged mine aside and pressed against the wound.

I sucked in a hiss of air through clenched teeth. My eyes squeezed shut as I bit my bottom lip.

William's concerned voice spoke up in question, "What's going on? Are you two okay?"

"Dawn's hurt," Sydney said as she slipped out of her cloak and didn't hesitate to tear it in long, wide strips.

"I'm fine," I insisted.

"What happened? Where are you hurt? How bad is it?"

"William," I interrupted his rather panicky string of questions. "I'm fine. It's doesn't even – Ah! Take it easy."

Sydney's fingers trembled as she fumbled with the zipper of my coat. "I'm sorry," she mumbled weakly as she pushed the jacket aside. "Can you sit up?" I obliged, slowly and surely with as few hisses of pain as possible, and Sydney held a shaky hand on my shoulder. She shimmied the hem of my shirt up far enough to pass the slice in my flesh and handed me the bundle of fabric to hold. Collecting the ripped strips of her cape, she carefully wrapped them one by one around my abdomen, tying each to the next. "I'm sorry," she said again, her eyes focusing on the trembling of her fingers.

"It's okay. The cut is shallow. I'll live," I said.

"I'm sorry,"

I reached out to touch her forearm, and she flinched under the contact but didn't pull away. "Why are you apologizing? You've done nothing wrong."

Sydney's fingers froze halfway through looping two ends of fabric together. Downturned eyes stared at the stilled fingers and gradually raised in short, hesitant jerks. They paused at the bandages, continued up, and stopped at the folds of my shirt. When the earthy orbs reached my neck, they raised no further. They stared past me into the dark recesses of the cave, empty and hidden behind a fog, as if her eyes had always been so void and detached from her inner psyche. "It's nothing." Her monotonous voice was as destitute as he eyes.

"Sydney," William's serene concern echoed off the cavern's walls.

Her eyes blinked, sudden realization flooding the orbs. Her fingers sprang into action and hastily tied off the last strip of fabric. "That should do it," she said with a final tug of the makeshift bandages.

She rose to her feet and turned her back to me. Her boots thudded against the rocky ground as she stepped toward the mouth of the cave. She stopped and stood just shy of the snow. Her body visibly quaked with a single shiver before she wrapped her arms around her own midsection. "What do we do?" she asked, her voice barely a whisper on the wind.

I smoothed my shirt back in place and carefully shrugged on my coat. Pushing myself to my feet, I retrieved the fallen sword and walked to stand beside Sydney. "They can't be far behind," I said, peering into the vast, snow covered forest. "We have to be stealthy and silent to avoid them at all costs."

"What if we can't avoid them?"

I held the sword out for Sydney to take. "We fight."

NOT ALONE

"Are you sure about this?" William asked in a hesitant whisper.

"Yes," I answered just as quietly. "We'll be fine, but you need to be silent no matter what happens. Okay?"

There was a pause where the only sound was the soft whistle of the wind before William finally answered. His voice was even quieter, not loud enough to be a whisper but not as hushed as a murmur. It was almost dejected, as if his very presence was useless. "I understand."

"Thank you," I said, hoping to ease his worries even if only a little.

My worries, on the other hand, had only just begun. Each beat of a hoof was unnaturally loud, and my head shot from side to side. The entangled branches and deep thickets blocked my vision and concealed any potential threat. The wind whistled through the trees, mocking my heightened senses. Every miniscule movement – the subtle shifting of twigs and the smallest flake of snow landing on my exposed skin – had my breath hitching in my chest. The anticipation of the inevitable suffocated and drowned me in my own debilitating fear.

Goosebumps speckled my arms, but they had nothing to do with the freezing temperature. My throat was dry and scratchy as if I traveled through deserts of sand and not blankets of snow. My gut twisted with a sickness that wasn't physical, my own mind forcing my stomach into knots, and the winter wind couldn't cool the uncomfortable warmth burning the back of my neck. Begging for more oxygen, I struggled to keep my breath even, to steady the short, ragged gasps of air.

They were here – watching us – waiting for an opportune moment to strike, like a cat stalking a mouse. They caught us, played with us, and released us only to come back for more. They were the hunter, and we unwillingly filled the role of their prey. It was maddening. Their eyes scorched my skin, but I failed to spot them. I couldn't pinpoint their direction. It felt like they already cornered us within the secrets of the forest, and we were helpless to escape their clutches.

I hated the vulnerability, the pathetic feeling of being powerless – like I had no choice but to sit back and wait for our demise.

I eyed Sydney in hope of finding some form of comfort – something,

114

anything to calm my paranoia. Not a single limb twitched. Her head stared forward, never peering over her shoulder at me or glancing to the side to investigate a rustle of branches. Shoulders rose and fell with her rhythmic breathing, and to an outsider, Sydney would be the very picture of calm and collected. That wasn't the case though. Her statue-like posture meant only one thing.

Sydney was terrified, even more than me.

Whether it was the excess adrenaline coursing through my veins or the unnerving paranoia gnawing at my mind, I couldn't cool my head. They were here somewhere. Their eyes bored into me, piercing my very core. That was a fact. Deep down, I knew it to be true. Call it a sixth sense or even natural instinct – either way, they waited for us just out of sight.

Or so they thought.

The shining glint of metal I grew to despise appeared in my peripheral vision. Between two thick tree trunks, a shoulder guard gleamed beneath the rays of the evening sun. On further inspection, the swishing of a snow-colored tail stirred up a flurry of flakes near the base of the tree. With him to the right, I assumed the others boxed us in on all sides.

"Sydney," I called her as if we weren't in potentially fatal danger. She peered over her shoulder, and void eyes immediately widened with apprehension. We stared at each other, a silent understanding passing between us. I nodded to the sky and mouthed the count to three.

At the signaling number, I dug my heels into Cobalt's sides and steered him straight up. I burst through the treetops with a spray of pine needles and snapped twigs falling beneath me. My head whipped to the left and then right in search of Sydney. She broke through the treetops with two arrows whizzing on either side of her. The one of her left grazed her shoulder, slicing the cotton of her coat, but the pointed tip missed her flesh.

Branches snapped as deathly white royal pegasi charged to the sky, one on each side to box us in. The two knights on the left and right steadied their bows, each reaching for another arrow while Drake and the man in front of us blocked an easy escape. But the sky was a vast, endless possibility of escapes. Forward and backward weren't the only options it had to offer.

Cobalt dipped down, allowing gravity to pull us back to the earth. His wings folded into his body, and we nose-dived toward the treetops. When his hooves skimmed the uppermost branches, his wings extended with a powerful flap. We surged forward with each quick flap of feathers and bolted through the sky with all the speed my mount could muster.

My head snapped back as my eyes sought Sydney. A rushed breath of relief blew from my lips upon seeing her a few feet behind me. The relief was short lived, though, because the knights were right on our tails. From the looks of sheer determination and unadulterated malice, the knights had no intention of bringing us back alive.

Arrows shot through the air in a wild, reckless array. Strings taut and arrows drawn back, the knights released them in rapid succession, forgetting the importance of aiming altogether. The projectiles veered in every direction but straight as if they had no intention of doing anything more harmful than winging us. The killing intent of their swords was not found in the arrows, but it was there in the smug grin of the captain hanging back to enjoy the show.

It got tiring – this game. Was all this really necessary? Had my offenses been so extreme as to drag others into my atonement? Had I even done anything wrong to deserve such atonement? There was no law on the books that prohibited protecting one's family. I was guilty of one thing and one thing only – desertion. Even so, in all my years of service to the crown, desertion never led to a man hunt. They were willingly let go, released of the chains binding them to the crown, and written off as those undeserving of their title. Why was I any different? Why did they fight so hard to silence me and to kill anyone involved? What were they afraid of?

As the bombardment of arrows continued, the knights' precision increased. With each one getting closer and closer to their targets, I couldn't risk another injury. I drew the sword – only one minute shard missing from its blade – and swung at a too close for comfort arrow to send it spiraling to the forest floor. The arrows came faster as the knights closed the gap between us. At this rate, the sky was far too open.

With a firm hold on the reins, I steered Cobalt sharply to the right and urged him to descend into the thicket of branches. Cobalt charged brashly into the grasp of the trees, heedless to their entrapping hold. Branches cried as they snapped beneath the equine's weight and retaliated by scratching his winter coat of fur. Twigs and needles tangled in his mane and imbedded themselves into my clothes, but we pushed on, racing around the tree trunks in a frantic dash.

Cobalt burst through the thick brush into a small clearing. As he bolted across the clearing – snow flurrying in our wake – I twisted in the saddle, desperately seeking any sign of Sydney. I peered into the web of branches and held my breath as I waited for the vibrant red of her scarf or the deep blue of her hat. The flurry of snowflakes settled back to the ground, and there was still no sign of Sydney. I reeled Cobalt back, slowing our pace until the equine slid to a stop atop the snow. Turning him back the way we came, Cobalt pawed at the ground as I held him in check.

The wind whistled, seeping into every crevice and fold of fabric covering my body. A shiver ran down my spine as Cobalt snorted puffs of white smoke from his flared nostrils. The crunch of snow beneath the pegasus' hoof echoed with the wind, its constant noise flooding my ears. The wind didn't carry any other sound – no flaps of wings, clashing of swords, or screams of help.

Something was wrong.

I spurred Cobalt to the sky, and he quickly rose above the trees. The vast sky was empty. No matter which direction I looked, Sydney couldn't be found. The glint of metal didn't shine beneath the sun's rays, and the wind didn't blow through snowy feathers.

Cobalt raced back to the clearing and dove into the thicket without hesitation. We followed the broken branches and the occasional divot in the snow to retrace our path. My eyes darted from side to side, erratically scanning for the smallest amount of color against the endless white and dull gray of the snow frosted trees; but the forest blurred into a hypnotic mess. Pulling back on the reins, I slowed Cobalt. I blinked until the whites and grays no longer merged together and the straight trunks of the trees no longer curled in on themselves.

"Wrong answer."

Drake's voice had my head snapping to the left, and I spotted the man towering over Sydney where she had fallen from her pegasus. Blood dripped from Sydney's arm, drops plummeting to stain the snow crimson. Her body shook and quivered as she inched her way backward. She backed herself into a tree, and Drake stalked after with his sword poised to strike.

With a firm kick, Cobalt surged forward, but it was too late. The gleaming blade stabbed into Sydney's abdomen, puncturing both layers of fabric and flesh all the same. A crying gasp spilled from her lips as Drake pushed his weight against the weapon, not stopping until the blade's tip hit bark. He withdrew the blade with a spray of blood splattering the snow and a sadistic grin plastered to his face. His finger ran along the sword's blade, smearing the blood over his glove. He leered down at the gasping, writhing Sydney and reached out to her with his blood stained hand.

Cobalt stormed the scene, charging straight at Drake. The knight leapt back as I jumped from the saddle and landed beside Sydney. With Cobalt as a protective wall, I rushed to Sydney and knelt at her side. My hands flung to cover the gaping wound. An almost inaudible whimper rang in my ears as I applied pressure. "Sydney," I called her name.

Earthy orbs, once as wild and free as a raging tornado, became dazed behind heavy eyelids. Her cheeks paled, draining of the slightest color. Forced pants of air scratched their way to her lungs as her eyes began to close.

"Sydney, stay with me. Come on, Sydney. Look at me. Keep your eyes open. Please, I'm here for you. I'll get you out of here, and you'll be okay. Just please, don't close your eyes."

Her head lolled back against the tree, and her hand slowly, shakily rose to cover both of mine. Eyelids veiled her eyes almost completely, leaving only a sliver of brown visible. "Leave me," she coughed weakly. "Save yourself."

"No. I won't abandon you. Family means we don't forsake each other, and you're family. You always have been and always will be."

Sydney shook her head back and forth, painfully slow. "We both know... that I... won't make it."

I blinked against the tears pooling at the corners of my eyes, and I could hear the sniffling sobs from the pendant, muffled on his side but still audible. "You'll live, Sydney. You'll be there when William finally comes home. You'll help fix this country and rebuild it from the ground up. You'll be beside us in it all. You have to be."

A sharp click of a tongue alerted me to our audience. I could only see Drake's legs behind Cobalt, but I knew that scoff belonged to him. "How touching," he mocked, "but it's a sin to lie. Her time on this earth has expired. We all can see that."

"Shut up! You're wrong, you coward! I was your target! Why did you go after Sydney?"

"Don't flatter yourself, Lockwood. You're nothing compared to her. She was a weeping angel beneath me while you were a parasite on my back." His boots scuffled in the snow, stepping away from Cobalt. "Only she can satisfy my thirst. Killing you would only taint her blood with yours." There was more shuffling and the squeak of leather as multiple knights mounted their pegasi. "Carter, once Ms. Bates dies, kill Lockwood. Understood?"

"Yes, sir," the subordinate replied as armor clanked together to salute.

Drake was wrong. He had to be. Sydney wouldn't die. I wouldn't lose another family member. I couldn't. I held tight to her remaining life, refusing to let it slip through my grasp. Not this time. Not ever again. She was my friend – my sister – and I would protect her.

"You're too late," Drake said before departing with two knights in tow.

Sydney's fingers lightly squeezed mine. Her pointer finger rubbed my knuckles in short, jerky strokes. She sucked in a rough gasp of air, and her eyelids fell shut. Her name tumbled from my lips in a desperate cry before her eyes fluttered open. Her lips parted, words on the tip of her tongue.

"Stop worrying. It'll be fine."

William breathed out a stuttering breath as he tugged at the collar of his white button up. He rubbed at the nape of his neck before his finger grasped the hem of his shirt, fumbling with the fabric. "What if she blames me? What if I walk in the house and can't handle the guilt? What would happen if I left her again?" He was like a scared child, his hands shaking and his eyes watering with fear.

I collected the carriage horse's reins in one hand and placed the other on William's thigh. "William," I said with a gentle squeeze of my hand, "Sydney reached out to you. She wrote you all those letters and you wrote back. Your episodes have been getting better, and you've been having far fewer of them. Think of this as a step forward. It's a good thing. Remember that I'm here for you, and if it becomes too much, you can always back out."

William inhaled deeply and blew the breath out his lips. "You're right," he said, squeezing my hand in his. "She said she doesn't blame me, but I keep overthinking it. My mind won't stop. It keeps going back to that."

"Why don't you ask her in person?" I suggested as I steered the carriage onto the private path. The dirt trail wove its way through the forest. Trees neatly lined its perimeter, and their branches overhung, crisp leaves dotting their shadows on the road. The occasional bloom of white daisies clustered near the base of the trees, and vines snaked their way up the trunks. Being early afternoon, the sun fought to shine upon the road, struggling to break through the abundance of foliage overhead. It otherwise would have been an uncomfortably hot day, but the almost constant shade – only broken by the light sprinkling of the sun's rays – shielded us from much of the heat. The soft caress of a refreshing breeze helped too.

After about a fifteen minute drive at a leisurely walk, the forest parted to enclose a beautifully quaint yet intricately detailed dwelling. Tucked back on the left stood a barn brimming with character. Bold, bright red paint covered the structure with a contrasting white outlining every door and window. A line of three outer stalls had their top halves unlatched to rest against the barn, and the long face of an equine poked out of each one. A corral of whitewashed wood was empty on the opposite side of the barn, and behind that, a few head of dairy cows and calves grazed between the trees of the forest.

Angled toward the barn on its right was a single story, ranch-style house. Stones of every shade of gray, tan, and even red lined the outer walls of a protruding entry while the rest of the home was a deep walnut. Wrapping the entry, a platform porch ran along the entire front of the home with a crafted porch swing and set of accompanying chairs atop it. Gently rocking back and forth in the swing sat the very woman we came to see.

With hands clasped together in her lap, she twiddled her thumbs as she stared at them. She fidgeted, the rhythmic rocking of the swing faltering with each shift of her weight. Loose bangs shielded her downcast eyes as her hand abandoned the twirling of thumbs in favor of skimming her fingers against the single braid of hair hanging over her right shoulder. Her eyes closed as her head lolled back, her chest rising with a deep intake of breath. When the breath blew out her nose, deep sable orbs opened and landed on our approaching carriage. Her body stilled, feet planting firmly on the porch.

Beside me, I felt William's leg shaking against mine, but it wasn't just his leg. As his eyes met equally apprehensive ones, his entire body trembled with the fear of all the insurmountable and unwarranted guilt threatening to overflow. His hand sought mine, and I willingly offered it to him. Our fingers laced together as my other hand pulled back on the reins. We stopped with a slight jostle, and I pushed the brake lever to lock the wheels, haphazardly wrapping the reins around it.

I twisted my upper body to look at William and gave his hand a gentle squeeze. "Are you ready?"

His reply was quiet, weak. "No."

I gave his hand another comforting squeeze. "But will you do it?"

He swallowed hard. Eyes shining with dampness, he turned to me. While biting his bottom lip, he nodded.

"Alright. Shall we then?"

William's fingers slowly uncurled from around mine. He withdrew into himself, no doubt collecting his rampant thoughts as he hopped down from the seat of the carriage. Turning back to me, he extended his hand to help me to the ground, but then his attention solely focused on the still frozen figure on the porch swing.

William took a single step in her direction and stopped, his eyes never leaving her face. He stepped again, only one stride. As he took his third step, the woman slowly but steadily rose. When he walked two more paces, the woman descended the two stairs from the porch. Each hesitant step mirrored the other's as if they were perfect reflections, each pause and continuation precise. There was a thickness to the air around them that seemed to hold them back by invisible strings — as if they were human puppets. But in an instant easily missed by blinking, they severed the other's strings and freed themselves from the growing tension.

They ran to each other, closing the short yet immensely large gap in a few hurried heartbeats. Arms flung around the other and gripped to fabric like their lives depended on it, like the other was the only thing giving them breath under water. The woman's head fell to William's shoulder with tears overflowing from her eyes. Her breaths came in short gasps of air that verged on sobs, and William's own choked cries mingled with hers.

"I'm so sorry," the words spilled from Will's lips. "It's my fault. All of it is my fault. None of this would've happened if it wasn't for me."

The woman's head rose to stare at William as she vehemently shook it back and forth. "No, it's not. It never was. I never blamed you."

"But I—"

"William," she said, her small voice silencing the other. "I didn't ask you here to blame you or to put more guilt upon your shoulders. I just want my little brother back. Please, William, stop shutting me out. Stop shutting out everyone from your past."

William's shoulders tensed, and his body went rigid. Hands fell to his side, and he shifted back a step. "I... I can't," he struggled for words. His head tipped forward and he rubbed at the nape of his neck. "I don't know how."

"You're not in this alone. You wrote me that yourself. Turn around," she said, her hands assisting in spinning William to face me. "Dawn is your support, and if you'd let me, I'd like to be as well."

A single breath of air rushed from his chest in a quiet laugh as his lips upturned into a smile, the edges of his eyes crinkling. "You're right, Sydney," he nodded.

Sydney smirked and nudged his side lightly with her elbow. "I always am." She grasped her brother's forearm and pulled him toward me. When she stood beside me, she pushed William at the carriage. "Put it in the barn. You two are staying for dinner," she said, leaving no room for argument.

William hopped up into the carriage, grabbed the reins, and released the brake. His smile turned mischievous, lopsided. "I hope you're not cooking."

"Hey, I'm not that bad of a cook!" Sydney protested, swatting at her brother's shoulder.

William slid out of Sydney's reach and clicked his tongue to the horse. When he was a safe distance away, he called over his shoulder with a hearty laugh, "Says the one that almost burned the house down!"

"That was one time!" Sydney defended herself to which William cackled louder.

A hand fell upon my shoulder, and my eyes met earthy orbs glimmering with gratitude. "I haven't heard that laugh in over a millennium," she said, her eyes flicking to William's back with a warm smile. They locked on me a second later. "Thank you for being there for him when he thought no one was. It means the world to me to see him happy again. I only hope I can be part of that happiness."

"You already are," I said.

She eyed me skeptically. "But it's only been a few minutes."

I shook my head. "It's been much longer than that. He probably won't admit it, but he jumped around like a child on a sugar rush every time one of your letters arrived. Trust me, you are already a big part of his happiness."

Sydney smiled, genuine and face splitting. The innocent lift of lips morphed into a devious grin when William exited the barn, sliding the door shut behind him. "Could you somehow bring up the sugar rush thing over dinner conversation?"

"Well, of course," I said, innocently waving to William.

Sydney's hand covered her mouth to muffle the musical laugh threatening to bubble over, but the few escaping giggles did not miss William's attention. He quirked an eyebrow and paused midstep. "Should I be afraid?" he asked warily.

"Not at all," Sydney called back as she swung an arm around my shoulders and pulled me close. "I'm getting to know my new sister."

"So I should be terrified," Will said. "Nothing good ever comes from that look in your eyes."

"What look?" Sydney feigned innocence.

William shook his head and smirked. "All I'm going to say is two can play whatever game you're gearing up for. You better be prepared."

"Oh, we are," Sydney taunted as she squeezed me close. When William walked into her reach, Sydney slung her free arm around him and hugged him close to her side as well. Her hand slid up the back of his neck to ruffle his messy mop of hair. "It's good to have you back."

William swatted at her hand but smiled nonetheless. "It's good to be back."

Her mouth opened and shut, failing to make any noise other than short gasps. Fingers dug into my hand as she clung to my warmth. Orbs of dark walnut fluttered and squeezed shut before managing to stare at my face. Her lips parted, and at first, only a sharp breath sounded from her mouth. She gulped and coughed before trying again, and her voice – although weak and quiet – finally formed the words she had been searching for. "I'm happy... I wasn't...alone."

BLIND

Choking sobs rang painfully in my ears, sharp and stabbing from the far off void, no longer muffled on his side. The fingers clenched tightly to my hands slackened, slowly at first, and then all the pressure – the clinging to life – disappeared. The rough, ragged gasps of breath stilled in her unmoving lungs, and the hazy sheen to her eyes vanished, leaving unblinking orbs cracked open to stare at nothing at all. Untidy bangs fell upon her pale forehead, the hairs' ends fluttering with the cold breeze. Blood stopped pumping to the gaping wound to her midsection, and the already shed crimson liquid quickly dried and crusted in the cold wind. The red that once signified life stained my hands with death.

It happened again. I couldn't protect her. How many people would have to die before I finally saved one? My father, the little girl, and Sydney were all innocent. Who would be next – Raven, Charlie, or maybe even Rose? Could I even save William? Sydney was right beside me. I felt her life drain from her body, and I was powerless to fight against it, to force her soul to stay in this life – her life.

I wanted to cry and shout until my throat was raw and my voice wavered. My humanity wished to join William in his muffled sobs and low whimpers, but the tears never came. The quivering sorrow and trembling grief hung low in the background, willingly offering the main stage to ravenous anger. My limbs shook with fury, not unspeakable anguish. The unbound wrath bottling in my body sought a release, and it would be given it.

The squeak of shifting armor had my rage bristling. Snow crunched beneath boots with each impatient transfer of weight. The knight dared to clear his throat as if Sydney's death was an inconvenience to him, as if he hadn't had a role in murdering her. To him, this was a simple waste of time better spent kissing Drake's ass. If he wanted to be on his way, I'd send him straight to hell where he could spend the rest of his days having his liver clawed from his body by a ravenous eagle.

My hand trailed to Sydney's face to brush over her eyes, blood smearing pale skin as eyelids closed. I rose to my feet. The heartwrenching cries still rang in my ears as I stared at the broken shell of a life. There was a foreign peace upon the colorless face that didn't belong. It was the peace of those that lived long after their lives should have expired, those that passed without pain, those without an ounce of regret. It didn't belong. The dull aura of peace couldn't compare to the pink flush of carefree elation or the sparkling gleam of overflowing ecstasy. Where was the sassy spark of mischief or the flare of growing irritation? Those belonged on her face, not empty peace.

Fingers curled around the hilt of the fallen sword, and I dragged it through the snow, the jagged tip trailing behind. The cold steel trembled in my grip, and the grief of his soul surged through his embodiment. Every quaking tear engraved itself into the golden labyrinth upon the blade and dripped down its edge. His anguish not only echoed in my ears but raced up the blade and climbed over the guard to huddle under the warmth of my hand.

I stepped around Cobalt and stalked toward the knight. His lips turned up in a sneer and parted as he spoke. Whatever taunt he uttered went unheard, the words missing my ears altogether. His voice failed to register, but each minute movement did. Muddy eyes flicked to Sydney before locking on my blood stained hands. They narrowed at the sword dragging through the snow.

When he spoke again, his domineering voice broke through the static ringing in my head. "Drop the sword," he ordered as he drew his own from his hip. He took a single step in my direction.

The floodgates holding back my wrath burst. Both hands gripped the hilt as I lunged, swinging at his side with the force of an experienced captain. The knight's eyes darkened as he raised his own blade to deflect the blow. It didn't deter me. I thrust at his armored chest, and he readied his sword in defense. Metal clashed and locked in a fight of power. He pushed his weight into the blade, but his boots lost traction on the powdery snow. When he stumbled, I shoved him back, releasing our blades.

I spun and swung the blunt edge of my blade at the back of his knee. The limb buckled under the force, and the knight fell to one knee. The tip of his blade dug into the layers of snow for support, and he leaned heavily on it. My leg shot out to kick the flat of the blade and knocked it from the knight's grip. The sword fell in a puff of snow. He reached for it, but I brought my boot down upon it to pin it to the frozen ground. The man leaned on the heels of his palms and skittered back.

I stalked after him like a cougar hunting a doe. The sword dragged a thin line behind me as the knight backed himself into a tree. He scurried to the left on his hands and knees, but he didn't get far. I smashed my boot into the plate of the knight's back. With a strangled gasp of air, he collapsed to the ground. His arms struggled to push himself up but shook under my weight.

"Please!" he resorted to begging. "I'll abandon the mission! Just let me go! Please!" He squirmed in the snow, his fingers clawing for leverage.

My foot slid down his side, rooted itself under him, and flipped him onto his back. The momentary look of relief morphed into wide-eyed panic when my boot slammed into his chest plate. I stared down at him, eyebrows furrowed in anger. "You think I'm doing this for my life," I dryly laughed. "That's a foolish thought. If that were the case, I wouldn't be standing here now." I dug my heel against the metal, a sickening screech sounding from the armor.

Orbs flickered to the still form of my companion before narrowing at my face. "Killing me won't bring your friend back," he spat between grit teeth. "What's done is done. My life won't change that."

I leaned on my knee, bending over to glower mere inches from his face. "Do you hear that – the shattering of a man already broken? Can you hear the binding holding him together snap, the glue deteriorating as each piece falls? Are you deaf to the wails of a man being devoured by grief? Do you know what it's like to lose your parents and blame yourself, to estrange yourself from your only sibling, and then lose her only centuries after a reunion knowing you can't even say goodbye? Do you?"

The knight's eyes widened as I panted from my outburst. His head tilted, and he squinted in concentration. He squeezed his eyes shut and shook his head. "I don't hear anything," he said quietly.

"Of course, you don't!" I snapped. "He means nothing to you! She meant nothing to you, but they mean everything to me! Do you even know what it's like to love another human being? Does the black hole in your chest have the capacity to?"

The man squirmed and grabbed at the heel of my boot. Fingers curled into the worn leather. Just as quickly, the appendages released to cover his quaking face as I plunged the sword's point into the snow beside his ear. "You may be deaf to him, but I know you heard my question. Answer it."

He shrunk in on himself, both arms crossing his face to cover his eyes. His limbs trembled, and the metal armor clanked together. "What question?" he asked, voice shaky.

"Do you have the capacity to form any sort of bond with another human being?"

"Yes, yes," he cried. "I have a family and friends."

I tapped the guard on his arm with my pointer finger, and the knight flinched. When he made no other move, I pried his arms from his face and stared into terrified orbs. "So did she. The only difference is she can't go back."

The man's grim expression fell, a tiny ember of hope sparking. His eyebrows drew together as a shaky breath exhaled through his lips. Muddy eyes peered at my face with reserved optimism as he asked, "You're... you're letting me go?"

I straightened my back and withdrew the sword from the snow. "An eye for an eye will leave the whole world blind," I droned, gazing at the jagged indent at the sword's tip. Lifting my foot, I stepped back, and the knight slowly sat up. He leaned on his elbows before pushing to his hands. His lips parted to offer his gratitude, but I interrupted him. "And I've lost my sight." The sword stabbed between his legs, burying itself in the layers of snow.

He yelped out a deafening shriek and scurried back. In a flurry of snowflakes and clanking armor, the knight stumbled to his feet and tripped over himself in his haste. He scuttled through the snow and dashed to the last remaining royal pegasus. The equine crow-hopped as the man struggled to swing into the saddle. He wasn't even seated when he cried his command to motion. The pegasus took off in a hasty retreat, and the man didn't look back once.

When he disappeared from sight, a heaviness fell upon my body. My shoulders slumped, and my grip on the sword's hilt loosened. Mind fuzzy, a constant ringing in my ears drowned out the whistle of the wind and the quiet whimpers from the void. My eyes burned as they blinked against the accumulating liquid. I trudged to Sydney's still form, dropping to my knees before her.

"I'm so sorry," I apologized as my vision blurred. "I'm sorry."

My hand shakily fished in my pocket. It retrieved the tiny shard of metal with the jagged piece pinched between my fingers. "Thank you," I whispered hoarsely. "Without you, I'd be rotting away in the dungeon. You made this possible, and I'm so sorry I couldn't repay you. You deserve so much more."

It both surprised and pained me not to hear Sydney's voice in return. I half expected her earthy orbs to snap open and flicker to my face. The edges of her mouth would turn up, and her lips would part. Her hand would settle upon my shoulder and ease its trembling. A musical laugh would echo in the trees as she waved off my gratitude and insisted it was a team effort. But no matter how long I sat waiting, Sydney never replied.

Seconds turned to minutes and minutes to hours. The afternoon sun set long ago to be replaced by a grieving crescent moon, and even the moon was consumed the following morning.

I didn't – no couldn't – register exactly where I was. Each tree looked the same as the rest as Cobalt maneuvered through the dense forest. Reins slack, my steed moved completely of his free will. The wind whistled through his pricked ears, his head high and far more alert than mine. Where he went, I didn't question. The cloudy haze that muffled my mind couldn't touch Cobalt. I trusted him. I had to. He was the only one left.

My hand settled on the cold back of a lifeless body draped over the equine's withers, or maybe it had always been there. Either way, fingers attempted to curl into the stiff cloth, but the fabric didn't waver under the touch, not even a slight crumple, frozen from the biting cold. I felt nothing as I blankly stared at the unmoving back. There was no sadness, no grief, no pity, and even the burning anger had long since fizzled away with the flurry of snowflakes. I was void of emotion, unwilling to feel as I swallowed them down, stuffing them in the deepest part of my core. It was easier to not face them and bury them beneath a strong facade.

The cold breeze that gently blew against my cheeks grew more ferocious and whipped my hair against my neck. I jerked forward, narrowly keeping my butt in the saddle, when Cobalt came to a standstill. I shook my head and struggled to regain my bearings. Through a blurred vision, the silhouette of a two-story farmhouse towered over me, its oaken sides dusted with snow. Two fuzzy, unclear figures emerged from the silhouette while a third smaller one hung back. I swore I heard my name being called, but I couldn't be sure over the ringing of my ears.

The quickness of the bleary figures as the closer two rushed toward me had my already reeling head spinning even faster. Words failed to register in my mind and gradually faded altogether, drowned out by the resonating ring in my head. A cloud-covered, dreary sky engulfed my vision as it enveloped both the house and the approaching figures. The sky darkened, and the dim glow of the sun disappeared quicker than naturally possible. I welcomed the darkness, knowing full well I was surrounded by the safety of familiar faces.

"Stop fidgeting and take a seat already," a quiet voice – or what I assumed to be quiet – ordered with slight irritation.

"But–"

A heavy, fatigued sigh interrupted the person's rebuttal. "She's fine. Her wounds weren't nearly as bad as they looked. All the blood was superficial, and from the looks of Sydney, most of it probably wasn't hers. She's exhausted and will wake up when her body is good and ready to."

The explanation didn't satisfy the woman. "How am I supposed to sit around and do nothing? My only child barely made it home, Sydney is dead, William won't talk anymore, and Rose is waiting for both of her parents. I have every right to worry about my family's wellbeing."

Blood. Sydney. Dead. William. Reality slowly sunk into my empty mind, the events replaying behind closed eyelids as vivid as if I had jumped into the past.

"And what's worse," my mother continued, her voice taking on a sorrowful edge, "is that I believed she was dead."

Charlie consoled softly, "We were both foolish enough to. We should have known better than to believe the likes of him, although part of what he said was true. Sydney truly is dead, and Dawn was a walking corpse. Let's be thankful the knight didn't finish his job."

Me? Dead? Why would they..? Drake. It had to be him. What a pompous ass! The coward dared to bring unnecessary heartache to my family. If killing Sydney wasn't enough, he had to gloat. Her life wasn't a trophy kill. She was more than some stupid prize to be won, and Drake would rue the day he crossed my family.

Feet shuffled on the floorboards, and the scuffling grew distant away from me. "Let's leave them in peace," my uncle suggested. There was a moment of unwilling silence before Charlie added, "We can make lunch, and hopefully she'll be awake by the time we're done."

The floor squeaked as Raven shifted her weight before finally shuffling across the room. A quiet groan of protest sounded from the door as it clicked shut. The soft padding of footsteps grew lighter and lighter until their sound disappeared to leave a silent hallway.

Wait, them? Who was with me?

As much as I wanted to lie in a state of mindless bliss, I forced my eyes open. I blinked against the light pouring through the window until my hand came up to shield my eyes. The former ache of my limbs was nowhere to be felt as I pushed myself into a sitting position. My head fell into my hands, and I sat like that for some time. Eventually though, my eyes peeled open and met a bundle of small human and pale blue blanket.

Strawberry blonde braids poked out from beneath the thin blanket. Her head curled into the bundle, and toes stuck out from the bottom. Fingers held loosely to the violet blanket now pooled in my lap, a hairsbreadth from grasping my hand. Steady breaths had the blanket cocoon rising and falling as I tenderly stroked her hair.

Rose stirred, her head leaning into my touch. Arms disentangled from the blanket as her legs stretched out. Her fingers released the purple fabric, and she rolled to rest on her back, close enough to the bed's edge to fall off. When my arm wrapped around delicate shoulders, ochre orbs snapped open. Turning her head, her eyes brightened, not a single trace of drowsiness in them. With the energy of the excited child she was, Rose leapt into my lap and wrapped her arms around my torso. "Mom!" she cried as she buried her head in the crook on my neck.

I hugged my daughter tightly, one hand cupping the back of her head. Her warmth pressed to me and the breath exhaling against my neck eased every ounce of weariness left in my body. With Rose in my arms, it felt as if none of the tragedies had happened, as if time ceased to exist. Her pure innocence washed away the remaining darkness and cleansed the world's sins from my mind, because these passing ticks of time lasted an eternity with Rose nuzzled against my chest.

Orbs sparkling with dampness peered at me. Her arms loosened around me as she sidled into my side, fitting perfectly with her head resting on my shoulder. "Is... is Will back?" she asked, her voice barely a whisper.

I shook my head, and Rose buried hers in my neck. Glancing over her, my eyes fell upon the dresser, a metal shard and almost whole sword sitting atop the stained wood with the worn parchment lying beside them.

"William, can you hear me?" I asked.

Rose perked up, staring at me but staying silent. Both of us held our breaths as we waited, but he didn't answer. Peering up with an expectant gaze, she asked permission without words. I nodded, and she found her voice, albeit a little shaky. "When are you coming home, Dad?"

He broke. Strangled and choked sobs filled the small room, and Rose clung to me tighter. "William, please listen to me. There is one piece left, but to get that piece, I have to sever this connection. I know you're hurting right now, and I'm so sorry I can't take away your pain. I would if I could, but I can't. All I can do is get you home where you belong. Do you trust me to do that?"

The exasperated cry of *yes* was immediate.

I slid from the bed, leaving Rose to dangle her legs over the side. Padding to the dresser, I picked up both shard and sword. "This isn't goodbye, William," I said. "I'll see you soon." Touching the shard to the blade's tip, the two pieces melted into one. I didn't hesitate to unroll the parchment and read the words that would finally lead me to William.

I shine beneath the branches which protect the engraved proof of love.

My lips upturned, parting in an ear to ear smile. "Rose," I said, turning with the sword held tightly in my grasp. "Let's go free William."

Toothy grin plastering her face, Rose nodded with more enthusiasm than her small frame could contain. She hopped to the floor with an almost inaudible thud and skipped to my side. Her fingers slipped into my free hand, and she tugged me toward the door. Jiggling the knob, she pulled the door in. As we rushed into the hall, the knob collided with the room's wall. Judging by the crack of wood, it probably broke through the wall, but I couldn't care less.

William would be home by lunch, and that was all that mattered.

BRAIDED TOGETHER

Rose and I thumped down the stairs like a pair of stampeding horses. We rounded the landing – both of us sliding in our socks and nearly colliding with the floor – but we managed to stay upright all the way to the kitchen, Rose giggling the entire time. Our hands only parted to slip into coats and boots as we messily geared up for the winter expedition. I tossed a hat to Rose, and she pulled it on until the flaps covered her ears, strands of intertwined yarn hanging down with her braids.

"Dawn," my mother said, eyes wide as she stood in front of the stove, wooden spoon in hand. The utensil clattered to the floor. Before I knew it, her arms wrapped around me tightly. "Are you okay? What happened? Where are you going?" she asked, words fast and jumbled.

I rubbed her back and squeezed her shoulder lightly. "I'm fine, really, Mom," I said, pulling back from her embrace. "I'll explain later. Rose and I will be back within the hour. Make enough food for five."

Raven's head tilted as she contemplated my apparent miscalculation in the number of lunch participants. Her eyes flicked to the grinning Charlie at her side, then a giddy Rose itching to sprint out the door, and finally landed on me, a tender smile pulling at the corners of my lips. She gasped, her hand going to cover her mouth, as olive orbs brightened with moisture. Her lips parted to ask the question I knew was coming, but it never left her throat. Even so, I nodded to answer it.

With light pressure, her hand pushed me toward the door. "Go," she said. "Bring him back."

"Will do," I turned from my mother and ducked into the closet under the stairwell. I rummaged for a pair of gloves, and upon finding them, tossed them to Rose as I grabbed a heavy blanket off the shelf. I wrapped the sword in it, tucked the bundle under my arm, and hurried out of the house behind Rose.

We ventured into the late morning and ran across the yard, but not without a few almost-falls on the ice. Rose flung the barn door open, and I ran in after her. She made a beeline for the second stall on the right as I retrieved Cobalt. By the time I haltered my pegasus and led him out of the stable, Rose was already seated on the bare back of a dapple gray – Cam's personal mare. "Hurry, Mom," she said, beaming at me.

My heart swelled as my fingers curled in Cobalt's mane. I jumped onto his back and wiggled into place. "Follow me," I said. With a single cluck of encouragement, Cobalt broke into a canter, his wings unfolding and extending at his sides. We took flight with a few powerful flaps, leaving a flurry of snowflakes in our wake. Looking over my shoulder, I spotted Rose close behind – as natural atop the mare as my father ever was.

We flew over the northern part of my family's property, low enough to touch the treetops. The endless acres of pastures and fields wove with the trees, and we followed the swaying of the bare branches. It was a short ride, so short the chill of winter didn't get its chance to set it.

I tugged lightly on Cobalt's mane to request him to land. As his hooves gracefully touched down, my eyes locked in on a single tree among many. It stood solemnly beside a wooden fence post, its trunk the only one on the inside of the pasture. Sprinkled with tiny white flakes, the bare branches possessed a mesmeric beauty as they overlooked the clearing. In the dead of winter, a light dusting of snow concealed the proof of love.

After hopping off Cobalt's back, I unwrapped the sword and draped the blanket over Cobalt. My boots crunched through the snow with each frenzied step. Four steps at most and my hand reached out to the tree. My fingers brushed at the trunk, the thin layer of crusted snow crumbling beneath my touch. I wiped at the tree until the cut of letters could be seen. My finger traced each letter, and for being etched in bark by a dull pocket knife, the letters flowed smoothly into the next.

William

+

Dawn

Fingers tugged at my coat so I tore my eyes from the engraving and looked down at Rose. She pointed at the tangle of branches and asked, "What's that?" Ochre brown orbs flicked to the tree, and I followed their line of sight.

Not even a foot above the carving, the crust of snow dipped into a divot in the bark. Resting against the crisp white, a bulb of brilliant blue lounged in the crest of wood, its feet kicked up as it slumbered. "Good eye," I said as I smiled at Rose. I plucked the jewel from its hiding place and held it in my open palm.

"Would you like to do the honors?" I asked, offering the sapphire bulb to Rose.

Eyes lit up with all the delighted bliss of a lifelong dream come true. Her arm extended but paused halfway, hand open and poised to grab. Fingers flexed before moving closer to hover over the gem. Her touch was hesitant, ginger as if the jewel would crumble to dust or vanish right before her eyes. When her fingers finally curled around the droplet, her hand retreated to cradle the sapphire against her chest like a fragile baby.

I lifted the sword, carefully setting the flat of the blade against my palm. Holding tight to the hilt, I extended the sword to Rose. "Do you see the indent near the guard?"

Rose nodded.

"Press the sapphire into it."

Rose held the droplet between her thumb and pointer finger as she twisted it to line up in its rightful home. She set it in its indent and pressed down on the bulb until the gem slid into place with a pop.

The sapphire shined, more so than normal. Its rounded bulb glistened as it flattened against the steel, oozing out from the indentation. Liquid blue trickled down the blade like thick molasses and followed the golden labyrinth of cracks. The molten jewel split at each cross road to travel down every available track. Like a turtle race, each trail of sapphire inched its way down the length of the blade agonizingly slow. They continuously crossed and merged with each other, and the closer the paths came to the blade's tip, the more they merged to a single line. Every last trail converged into one before the liquid sapphire pooled and balanced at the metal point. When every ounce of blue joined the bulb – leaving the golden labyrinth unscathed – a single drop of the molten gem fell from the blade.

Before the droplet had the chance to splatter on the snow, a blinding yellow light burst from the sword. I dropped the sword and swept Rose into my arms. She pressed her face into my jacket as I turned my back to the unnatural brightness. My arms wrapped tightly around her as my eyes squeezed shut.

When the light stopped reflecting on the snow and bouncing against my eyelids, I peeked over my shoulder. Miniscule, glistening shavings of metal filled the air and gently floated to the ground like leaves falling from a tree. They rested atop the snow, and fell upon the shoulders of a man. He stared blankly at the ground, eyes wide with confusion.

"Dad!"

"William!"

Rose and I threw ourselves at Will, encasing him in a tangle of arms. Rose sniffled into his chest as she wiped at her teary eyes. My fingers clung to the cotton of his shirt and held on as if my life depended on it.

A shaky, tender touch pressed into my back as an arm snaked around my torso. "Where are we?" he breathed, barely a whisper as if any louder would send him back to the void. "Please tell me this isn't a dream I'm going to wake up from. If it is, I don't want to wake up."

Lifting my head from his shoulder, I released my grip on his shirt and cupped his face in my hands. "Does this feel like a dream?" I questioned before pressing my lips to his. Our noses pressed into each other's cheek, and the coldness of his lips sent a shiver down my spine. Breaths mingled to chase away the frozen chill before I pulled back to lose myself in a pair of swirling, dark walnut orbs.

William chuckled lightly, a smoky wisp of breath in the frigid air. "That proves nothing. I've had far more detailed dreams," he joked with a crooked smirk pulling up the corner of his lips, his cheeks reddening even more.

"Then how about her?" I asked, peering at Rose.

Rose glanced up at William, her tear-stained cheek pressed against his chest. Her hands fisted in his shirt, and her bottom lip quivered. When Will's other arm wrapped around her shoulders and pulled her even closer, Rose broke out in fresh tears. "Dad, I missed you so much!" she cried.

"I missed you too, my little flower," William said, on the verge of tears himself. He placed a soft kiss upon Rose's head before ruffling her hair with a quiet chuckle. "Have you been behaving for Grandma?"

Rose released William to wipe at her eyes and nose in an attempt to rub away the evidence of tears. She nodded her head and beamed brightly. "I'm on my best behavior."

"That's my girl," William said, ruffling strawberry blonde locks again only to have his hand swatted away.

"You're messing up my braids," Rose complained. She tried her best to keep a straight face, but a giggle slipped out.

William persisted in tousling her hair. "Don't worry. I'll redo them."

"Really?"

"Of course."

Rose sprung to her feet, tugging William and me up by our hands. "Let's go home then!" she bounced with excitement. "Dad can ride with me. I want to show him my new skills."

"As you request," William told her, allowing Rose to drag him to the dapple gray. Rose jumped upon the equine's back with the agility of an acrobat and scooted closer to the pegasus' withers before patting the available space behind her. William had a little more difficulty as he hefted himself in place, wiggling up on his belly. "You make it look easy," he said, a little out of breath.

Rose grinned and patted Will's knee. "I had a lot of practice."

I interrupted the two by tossing the blanket draped over Cobalt at William. It hit him in the face as he nearly fell over backward. When he disentangled and righted himself, he gaped down at the offending blanket. "Figured you might be cold," I said.

He blinked down at it before smiling at me in thanks. "Very," he said as he wrapped the blanket around his shoulders.

I hopped atop Cobalt, and the three of us journeyed back to the house. The flight wasn't the same frenzied rush I was used to, the hectic race to beat the clock. The clock stopped. Constant ticks and tocks no longer sounded in the recesses of my mind. There was no more time limit. William wouldn't vanish, his existence disappearing forever. He was safe and home where he belonged. For once, a life hadn't slipped through my fingers while I stood by powerless to grasp it and bind it to this world.

We flew into the yard. Flakes of tiny ice crystals swirled in the chilly breeze as two sets of hooves dug into the layered snow. Cobalt's wings fluttered lightly before folding into his sides. Stepping high through the snow, the pegasus pranced to the hitching post by the house and stood beside the gray mare.

As I slipped from Cobalt's back, the house's front door creaked open. I ducked under my pegasus' neck and met Raven and Charlie at the door. My lips stretched in a giddy grin as I beamed jubilantly. "We're home."

William and Rose popped up at my side, and Will said, "Hi, Raven."

My mother looked as if she would cry, her eyes glistening, but she blinked the tears away. "Come in before you freeze to death," she strained to keep her voice steady. She took hold of his shivering arm and ushered him into the warmth of the house. Pulling him through the kitchen, she towed him into the family room and didn't hesitate to push him down into the plush chair closest to the stoked fire. "A little better?" she asked in the gentlest, most motherly tone I'd ever heard.

William's face flushed at the attention, the tips of his ears burning brighter than they did in the cold. "Greatly. Thank you," he said as Rose plopped down in his lap.

Raven smiled tenderly, her eyes crinkling as she bent to place a quick peck to William's forehead. "It's good to have you back," she said. She straightened and turned to the kitchen. "I'll call when lunch is ready." With that, she returned to tend the stove.

Rose squirmed in Will's lap as I walked up behind them to lean on the back of the chair. "Will you fix my braids?" Rose asked, giving William her best puppy dog eyes.

Will nodded. "Go get a brush." Rose squealed in glee before scampering off his lap and dashing up the stairs.

William sighed contently as he sunk back in the chair. He toed off his boots, and stretched his feet closer to the fire. Eyes squeezed shut, and his head lolled back, groaning in satisfaction. "It feels so good," he breathed, burrowing deeper into the chair.

I wrapped my arms around his shoulders. "What does?" I asked, whispering in his ear.

"Everything," he blissfully sighed, walnut orbs still veiled. "My frozen toes and fingers thawing, the softness in which Rose calls me *dad*, the straining pull of my muscles trying to balance on the bare back of a pegasus, the pressure of your lips on mine – all of it feels so surreal, so new. It's as if

I'm experiencing life all over again." His eyes blinked open, and he peered at me, a bittersweet sheen to dark orbs. "It helps."

"Do you want to talk about it?"

He shook his head. "Not right now."

"Alright," I said as I kissed his cheek.

An eager cry of *Dad!* rang through the room as Rose noisily thudded down the stairs. She rounded the bottom step and dashed to plop down on the floor between William's legs, her back resting against the chair. Not looking behind her, she held the brush up and waved it until William took it from her grasp.

He wiggled in the chair until he was leaning forward, his elbows pressing into his knees. Fingers gently rolled the band off one braid and tossed it at me to hold, doing the same with the second braid. William ran his hands through the soft locks as the hair unwove in supple waves. As he began to brush in long strokes, he asked, "What adventures have you been up to these last few centuries?"

I sat on the armrest while Rose jumped into storytelling mode, a brilliant grin consuming her face. She retold a tale of fishing with Raven and Cam, frequently flailing her arms for emphasis, and insisted she caught the biggest fish. She admitted to asking Cam to bait her hook but reassured us she did it on her own every fishing trip after that. Jumping topics, Rose gushed about being Cam's riding buddy and Raven's cooking assistant. Her chest puffed out when she recalled helping Charlie stack wood for this winter.

She went on, "He split the logs while I stacked them in piles, but some were really heavy so Uncle Charlie had to lift them. He even made snow angels with me when we were done. And then Grandma came out and helped us make a snowman. He even had a carrot nose, but one of the yearlings got out and ate it. I'll show you later."

William finished with the last braid and patted Rose's head. "Maybe we can replace its nose," he suggested as Rose hopped to her feet.

"Could we make another one too?" she asked, ochre orbs hopeful.

The answer came from the kitchen as Raven peeked her head around the corner. "We all can after lunch."

Rose squealed in glee and ran into the kitchen before William and I were even on our feet. Will draped an arm around my shoulders and lazily bumped into me with each step toward the kitchen. He tilted his head and smirked. "Are you up for a snowball fight later?"

I chuckled. "You're on."

RESPONSIBILITY

Two days after William's homecoming, there was a knock at the door in the early morning. When I went to answer it, no one waited for me on the other side. Instead of greeting a guest, I found a small package sitting on the doorstep. I eyed the stable yard for the sender, but not even a single footprint dusted the layer of fresh snow from the night before.

I picked up the small box and turned it in my hand. No name or address labeled the cardboard on any of its six faces, but its contents jumbled around within it. It didn't sound like anything dangerous, so I shrugged my shoulders and brought it inside.

As I pried one of the flaps open, I sat down at the kitchen table. I dumped its contents onto the tabletop.

A folded piece of parchment and a chess piece tumbled out of the box. I pinched the chess piece between my fingers to get a better look at it. Like a castle wall, the silver rook had tarnished and worn brinks engraved upon its body. A single crack ran from its base all the way up the tower, breaking into two before merging at the top.

I eyed the piece of paper and set down the rook. My hand reached for the parchment and unfolded it.

Dear Dawn, William, & Family;

Our humblest apologies go out to your loss. Sydney was irreplaceable to you, me, and the entire country of Siven. I am sorry.

Signed,
Kent, Darrel,
Kalli, Kaylynn,
Michael, & Fallon

Will and I departed for Brestone barely an hour later. We explained our intentions to Raven, Charlie, and Rose; and they willingly saw us off with the promise we'd be back soon. They waved goodbye as Will and I flew off in the early morning, the sun barely peeking its head above the treetops.

But before seeing Kent, we had a small detour to make. Only a short ride from the house, the Lockwood cemetery lay eerily silent. Snowcapped headstones stared blankly ahead, their sentiments lost to the material world. The only life this cemetery possessed suffocated under the weight of millions of compounded snowflakes, but there was a break in the endless white – a gray of ash and freshly turned sod signifying the newest victim who lost a fight against death. It was an eternal resting place, one so new there was yet a headstone to commemorate its occupant, but William and I knew who was laid to rest beneath the earth.

William tugged lightly on the reins and pulled his mount to a stop a few paces from the boundary between sod and snow. He swung from the saddle and stood stock still with his back to the grave. Reins slipped through his gloved fingers as the pegasus tossed its head. Slowly, he turned and stiffly stepped a short trail through the snow until he stood atop the mixture of ash and dirt. His shoulders rose and fell as he took deep, steady breaths, but the rhythm wavered. His body jerked, and his knees buckled. He fell to the cold, hard ground and ripped his glove off to dig his fingers into the dirt.

I quietly dismounted Cobalt and followed Will's footprints. Walking to stand at William's side, my hand fell to his shaking shoulder.

This was my fault. The reunion between brother and sister wasn't supposed to be grim and mournful. The tears shed should have been out of sheer joy, not stifling grief. Quivering lips should have been beaming grins, and eyes should have glistened with uncontainable glee. But none of that happened, and it was because of me. Sydney would still be alive and breathing if I would've had her back. All I had to do was glance over my shoulder – one quick look to see Sydney fall from the sky. If I would've reached her earlier, gotten between Drake's blade and her, then she'd be alive. Sydney would be smiling and laughing, and William would have his last remaining blood relative by his side.

William balanced on the edge of breaking, crumbling and shattering all over again. His fingers clung to the earth as if he'd float away without the anchor. Head bowed, chocolate bangs fell to veil equally dark orbs, and his shoulders continued to tremble. Shaky breaths were visible in the winter air, but the quiet gasps didn't escalate to cries. Soft, gentle murmurs passed between his lips, and in that breath-hitching moment, I realized I was wrong.

"There's so much I still haven't told you, so many stories I wished for you to hear. Fifteen hundred years is a long time after all, and I wanted to share what we had missed. I thought I had all the time in the world, but that's not the case. I find myself wondering which stories you'd want to hear, which would have you bursting into a fit of giggles like when we were kids, and which would earn me a smack upside my head.

"You know, when you wrote that first letter, I was afraid. I honestly thought you resented me, so it took weeks before I even opened it. You were the same big sister you always were, but I was still scared. You hadn't changed, but I was fearful that maybe I had. I wanted to be the little brother you grew up with, but I believed the me at that time would be a disappointment to you. And so I didn't write back at first. It was selfish on my part, but I wanted your unconditional love and kindness that I was spoiled with as a child.

"Perhaps my true fear was I hadn't matured enough to keep up with you." William shook his head, dismissing the idea with a faint shadow of a quivering smile. "Of course, you would have said my worries were unwarranted."

William paused, inhaling and exhaling a steady breath. His fingers flexed and dug even further into the dirt. "I know you wouldn't want us wasting precious time when there is work yet to be done, but there is one thing you must hear. Out of all the things I wish to tell you, I believe this is the most important." Long, slender fingers relaxed, releasing their grip on the earth. They splayed out and pushed into the ground as if there was a mirrored hand pushing back.

"Thank you," he whispered weakly as he choked back a sob. "Thank you for protecting me even when I pushed you away. Thank you for being strong enough to look after our parents' legacy and maintaining all the memories it holds. Thank you for reaching your hand out to me and bringing me home. But most of all," he began as he shakily rose to his feet. His arm wrapped tightly around my midsection and pulled me flush against his side. Cheek falling to rest atop my head, he nuzzled his nose in my hair.

"Thank you for rescuing the love of my life when I was ignorant to the danger she was in. You put your own wellbeing on the line and made the greatest and most tragic sacrifice any human ever could. For that, I am grateful and sorry that I couldn't prevent this end. I hope you'll be able to forgive my incompetence again, but even if you can't, you'll forever be in my heart. I promise to live a life you'd be proud of. I won't let your sacrifice go to waste."

William raised his head, and with one final glance at her grave, edged his way back to the snow with me in tow. When the heels of his boots crunched atop the snow, he turned away from the unmarked resting place and walked the few required steps to reach the pegasi. His hand reached up to wipe at the corner of my eye. "What are you crying for?" he asked, feebly smiling.

His words and smile weren't enough to mask the puffy redness of his own eyes. Tears pooled in their corners, giving the walnut orbs a shimmering shine. "You're one to talk," I said, meeting his gaze.

William ran his fingers through his exposed hair, careful not to disturb the earmuffs, as he diverted his eyes. "We should go," he said quietly.

I nodded, and we both silently mounted our steeds. We rode side by side and flew close to the treetops. Zigging and zagging, the two of us bypassed the slightest hint of civilian population, careful of even the smallest dwelling. We dipped into the forest and scouted out every road and path before crossing them without leaving a single track. It wasn't until we safely passed over the Kitoc River that I pulled a folded envelope from my coat pocket and handed it to William.

He stared at it quizzically before quirking an eyebrow at me. "What's this?" he asked even as he began unfolding it.

I shrugged. "I don't know. Kent said you and Sydney hold more power than any of us realize. I'm guessing it's that power."

William carefully lifted the envelope's flap and gingerly extracted a single piece of paper. "Power? What power could we possibly possess? We're not sorcerers like he is." He unfolded the paper and tilted his head. Holding it up for me to see, he asked, "What does a crest have to do with me? My family isn't noble."

Printed on the paper was a copy of a white shield. At its center stood a moline cross with an arrow shooting diagonally through it. At each of the cross' remaining corners, the sharp claws of a bird readied to attack when given the order. No name or fancy scroll work bordered the shield's edges. In fact, compared to most noble crests, this one was quite simple.

"Do you recognize it?" I asked.

William shook his head. "I'm familiar with most of Siven's crests but not this one. In my opinion, I don't think it's a family from Siven. It's far too modest. Siven's crests are showy and pretentious, but this one isn't. How is it related to me?" He stared at the paper, glaring at it as he tried to unravel the mystery.

"We'll just have to ask him. After all, we're almost there."

William accepted that, glaring at the paper a moment more. Not bothering to slip it into the envelope, he tucked it into his pocket and continued to stew over it.

By the time early evening set upon the earth, we landed a few minutes outside of the limits of Brestone. We rode down the beaten path as trees dwindled to open up to the small village. The closer we got, the more people stopped to stare in both wide-eyed shock and soft smiled relief, and there were a lot of people – more than the town could probably house. Men, women, and children of all ages mingled together and from the looks of it, were either refugees or their descendants. It was a welcomed change to the bigoted Centrielle under the watchful eye of the crown.

Many of the faces stared and gawked as William and I rode to the tavern at the village's center. As we swung from our saddles, the building's door creaked open with a deafening cry loud enough to silence any sound had the town not gone silent at our arrival.

"Ah, I thought it might be the two of you," Kent mused as he stepped across the threshold, Darrel and another man following.

To Kent's right, Darrel warmly smiled – his dark eyes bright – but his face had changed from the first time I met him. Running from the top of his left cheek bone to below the corner of his lip, a jagged slice marred his russet brown skin. On his forearms, too. With the sleeves of a gray sweater pushed up to his elbows, cuts of a blade scattered his skin. Despite that, Darrel was as friendly as ever and offered his calloused hand in greeting to William and me.

The same couldn't be said for the man standing on Kent's other side. He matched Darrel in height and stood with his shoulders squared. Dusty, dirty blond hair was slicked back, only a single strand hanging down to touch the bridge of his nose. Knavish, serpent-like orbs the color of amber bore mercilessly at William and me, eyeing us up and down like one would do to prey. If that wasn't enough, his lips turned up in a wry smirk.

The man's aura instilled an irrevocable distrust, but for the life of me, I couldn't explain why. Maybe it was his deceitful eyes, sly grin, or overconfident stance. Each was far too fallacious for my taste. I had no ground for this immediate distrust, but I'd proceed with caution like I would when handling a snake or tracking a fox.

"Payton," Kent addressed with utmost authority, "would you be so kind as to bed our guests' pegasi in the livery for the night?"

With a gruff nod, the human fox relieved William and me of our reins and led the equines away.

"Well then, shall we retire to my office where we can discuss the details of my prior offer?" Without waiting for an answer, Kent spun on his heels and led the way through the crowded tavern, leaving the three of us with no other option but to follow. He forged a path to the door by the bar and ushered for us to follow him up the stairs. When we entered the cramped hallway, Kent immediately showed us into the last room.

The room was simple, having the bare minimum to be called an office. A rectangular dining table took up most of the offered space and had six chairs seated around it. Documents and maps scattered the tabletop; and with the lack of a filing cabinet, stacks of paper lined the far wall.

"I hope you'll excuse the mess," Kent said as he waited for us to step in. Once the four of us were in the confines of the room, Kent pushed the door shut. His hand hovered over the lock but deciding against it, dropped to his side. He gestured to the table. "Please have a seat."

William and I complied as Kent and Darrel maneuvered around the table to sit opposite us. Both worked fast to gather the scattered documents into more manageable piles before relaxing into their seats. Kent crossed his arms over his chest, and his eyes stared first at me and then flicked to William. "We'll skip the unnecessary pleasantries and get right to the point. Will you or will you not accept my offer to succeed

Caldwell and Ember as king and queen?"

William dug in his jacket pocket and withdrew the single slip of paper. He slid it across the table before resting his elbows on the wood. "Explain what this is, and then we'll talk."

Kent glanced at Darrel and then the paper. His posture straightened as he heaved a sigh. "How much do you really know about your family, or more specifically, the family name your parents were forced to abandon?"

William's gaze fell to the table. His answer was barely a whisper. "Next to nothing."

"I see," Kent said. "Then we have a problem, because I cannot relay this information to you without jeopardizing the security of future plans. I need an answer to my offer before I show you my hand. I hope you understand that."

William didn't look up, didn't even acknowledge he had heard the man. My hand clasped his thigh, and walnut orbs peered at me. I tilted my head in question, and he nodded. I told Kent, "Our answer was always going to be yes, but we want to know your reasoning behind choosing us. What does William's family have to do with this, and what is the power you spoke of?"

Both Darrel and Kent breathed out relieved sighs as if they had been holding their breaths. Their lips stretched into celebratory smiles for a mere moment before vanishing beneath an unshakable seriousness. "Darrel, would you please grab the files — all of the files?" Kent asked before facing William and me. "What is shared in this room from this point on stays between the four of us and no one else. Understand?"

William and I nodded as Darrel stood and snatched numerous folders from the stacks of paper lined against the wall. One by one, he laid the manila folders on the table in a long row. Each file had a surname printed on its face. Diallo... Malik... Ortiz... Acker... Ngo... Nikitas... Belger... Karnik. Darrel held two more folders in his hand. He watched us carefully as he placed the last two directly in front of us. McCadden. Okabe.

"What is—"

Kent raised his hand to silence me. "I'd like both of you to refrain from asking any questions until I'm done with my explanation. Okay?"

When we nodded, Kent continued, "Upon first glance, these names only have one thing in common — they're foreign surnames. Most have been unwillingly abandoned and replaced with names of conformity.

"I'll use your family as an example. Rei and Nagisa Okabe fled from Arkaynai after the attempted assassination of the king and his family. Following the assassination attempt, a civil war broke out between the noble families. Each clan fought for power, and while many chose to die for honor, your parents chose to live. The two of them entered Siven as refugees and applied for citizenship soon after. They were approved but only after complying with a few stipulations. Among them was changing their names. On paper, they became Matthew and Natalie Bates. Skip forward a millennium or two, and they started a family together. In order to assure the future safety of their daughter and son, they gave them common names that could be found in any city of Siven.

"Now let me switch to the McCadden family. Spencer's paternal grandparents immigrated to Siven from Ezmarin during the famish. Back then, Siven was under the rule of King Baron and Queen Brook. Their reign was much more accepting than the current one, and they embraced the refugees. Because of that, it was easier to gain citizenship, and there were no stipulations involved. That's why we still see the McCadden name in Siven.

"I'm sure the other names are unfamiliar to you as I had to do substantial digging to find them. Each name is foreign, but they all hold immense power in their country of origin. Among these names are grand dukes, earls, renowned merchants, influential bankers, and even a princess next in line for the crown. They are people of class and wealth while relatives now residing in Siven are forced into hiding. You can imagine the tension building between Siven and our neighbors, but I plan to use that in our favor. Which is where you two, along with numerous citizens under my protection, come it."

Kent reached across the table and pinched the corner of the Okabe folder. Lifting its face and laying it flat, his pointer finger tapped the newly revealed piece of paper. On the top was the same picture of the crest Kent had given me. "This is the power your family holds, not in Siven, but in Arkaynai. Your father's brother survived the war between clans and continued the family name while holding onto his nobility. You have a cousin named Kenji Okabe, and he married the eldest daughter of Arkaynai's king. The two of them are next in line for the throne and have agreed to support the overthrow of Caldwell and Ember."

"Why?" William asked, barely a whisper. "He doesn't even know me."

Kent huffed irritably, but it was Darrel who answered. "We have spoken to Kenji personally, and to him, family is held close to his heart. He wants nothing but the safety and happiness of his family, and that includes you. Like all of us, he is disgusted by Caldwell's actions and believes the crowns' duty is to their people. You believe the same, do you not?"

William's chest heaved as he took a single deep breath to compose himself and nodded. "Let me see if I understand your thinking," he said once he found confidence in his voice. "You chose me because I have connections to Arkaynai, and with me, Dawn is a package deal. In my opinion, she's more valuable to you because her family is held in high regard and greatly trusted throughout Siven. You need her to gain the support of Siven's citizens and me for the support of our neighboring countries. If that thinking is true, then you plan to form a royal court that is equally mingled with citizens originating from all six countries, thus hearing the voices and having the support of as many people as possible. Am I right?"

Kent smirked, lips stretching with pride. "Bravo!" he clapped. "I expected nothing less from Siven's future king."

A knock at the door had all heads turning to it. Kent's hands paused mere millimeters apart in mid-clap. He calmly gathered all the files in a single pile and slid the short stack of folders to the side, flipping the top one to conceal the name printed on its face. "It's open," he called as he sifted through the other piles of documents. As the door's knob twisted, Kent found what he was after and unfolded a detailed map of Siven to lay it flat on the table.

The door pushed open, and the man from earlier – the snake-eyed fox – stepped in. He divested himself of a pair of black gloves, shoving them in his coat pocket, as his eyes fell upon William and me. "It's about time you two showed your faces," he scoffed. "Acting like damn royalty and making us wait. Pathetic."

Darrel cleared his throat, effectively gaining the new arrival's attention. "I suggest you hold your tongue and refrain from insulting the future rulers of Siven," he warned lowly, dark eyes narrowed.

Amber orbs bulged almost comically as the man gaped. Like a fish out of water, his mouth opened and closed, eyes flicking between every face in the room before finally landing on Kent. He glared accusingly at the straight-faced, calm sorcerer. "Wait a minute!" he protested. "You never told me they were going to be the king and queen! I thought there were specialized warriors you sent for to fight with us!" What started as flabbergasted shock easily morphed to rage at an alarming rate.

Kent shrugged off Payton's outburst. "It was on a need-to-know basis, and you didn't need to know." Ignoring the potentially violent altercation, Kent tapped his fingers on the map. "Shall we talk strategies?" he suggested as he keenly watched the fox from the corner of his eyes.

"You barely know them, and yet you trust these two with our attack strategies! Are you insane?" Payton continued his outburst, hands clenching into fists at his sides.

His voice a threateningly calm monotone, Kent stated, "It's not a matter of sanity. If it was, I wouldn't have trusted them to you."

Payton's mouth opened, ready to fire back a heated response, but one look at Kent had his jaw snapping shut. His lip curled in fury as he bit his tongue and slunk back. As he crossed beneath the threshold, he slammed the door behind him.

Kent sighed as his hand ran through the hair of his ponytail. He rubbed at his temple and with apologetic eyes, said, "You'll have to excuse that one.

He's on a short leash as it is."

"You have nothing to apologize for. I'm more interested in hearing your plan to achieve a new Siven," I said.

"Ah, yes," Kent smiled smugly. "It's quite simple. If all the pieces move accordingly, it will go off without a hitch, taking only a single day's work."

"Is that even possible?" I questioned, quirking an eyebrow. William stirred at my side, perking up at the possibility.

Kent nodded. "It is if we burn the castle to the ground."

Burn the castle? No, we couldn't do that. The one and only time it had been set ablaze during the Great World War was a massacre of the innocent. According to the history books, only a handful of people escaped. Servants, knights, and prisoners burned to ash – scorched beyond recognition. The queens at that time perished, and their youngest son was the only member of the royal family to survive. Siven nearly collapsed with the castle until the viceroy took charge. It was a tragic disaster.

"Your plan is to sacrifice the innocent living in the castle?" I asked incredulously. "I can't accept that."

Darrel shook his head. He answered gently, "That's not it at all. We have comrades undercover in the castle who will quietly and efficiently evacuate the castle when given the signal. The only casualties will be King Caldwell and Queen Ember. We will not allow innocent lives to be sacrificed. If we did, it would be a shaky foundation on which to rebuild Siven. We would be no better than Caldwell and Ember."

Kent leaned across the table, his palms pressed flat against its top. "That information is confidential and does not leave this room. I intend for it to stay that way, so do not utter a single word of it. Understood?" William and I nodded, and then Kent relaxed into his seat. "Good. Do you have any questions?"

William leaned forward, his long pointer finger falling upon a black dot on the map. "We are here," he said before trailing his finger up and to the right a couple inches. "How do you plan to get here?"

Tracing each path on the map with his finger, Kent explained, "Payton will lead a small force in the west and attack the western wall as a diversion. Darrel and I will lead the rest of our forces northeast. Once we cross the main road heading into Centrielle, Darrel will split off with the both of you. I will continue to the castle guardhouse as a second diversion while Darrel assists you to sneak into the inner courts. You must lock the king and queen in their chambers and set the castle aflame. Once done, we will rendezvous on the road to Centrielle."

"What if this plan fails?" William asked quietly.

"I won't allow that," Kent stated.

William persisted, "But if it does?"

Kent eyed the two of us, icy orbs flicking to Darrel momentarily. "Then the four of us take responsibility and will be executed as traitors." He said it so casually that it seemed the thought of failure had never crossed his mind, but his hand inched across the table to intertwine his and Darrel's fingers.

I glanced at William, but his eyes were downcast. "It seems failure is not an option," I said, and all attention turned to me. "When do we move out?"

The tension did not fully dissipate, and the change of topic couldn't wipe away the bitter taste of despair that hung in the room. "When the snow no longer sticks to the ground, I will send for you. Until then, go home and enjoy what might be the last of your days."

CRISIS OF THE SNAKE

Winter dragged on, and I began to think the world was stuck in the perpetual cold in order to give me a few more weeks of false peace. Even though the days gradually grew longer, they passed in a blur. One minute, the sun's rays peeked above the stables; and in the next, they descended behind the bare trees. The nights, though, ticked by relentlessly in a constant state of anxiety, the lack of sleep doing nothing to pull me under. After the euphoria of my family's reunion wore off, paranoia set in. The slightest sound in the dead of night had my body flinching involuntarily and my heartbeat racing. In my mind, it was only a matter of time before Drake murdered us in our sleep.

William fared no better. He'd wake at any hour, chest heaving and covered in sweat. The first night it happened – four days after returning from Brestone – I woke to find him hugging his knees, breaths coming in shallow gasps. His entire body trembled. It happened every night during the following week, not to the same extent as the first but far from improving. Then it went to every other night, but that was as good as it got. He refused to talk about it and played the part of a healthy and happy man in the light of day; but due to my own insomnia, I heard the pained murmurs he tried to hide.

That was why, three months later, we were grateful to hear the awaited knock at the door. Darrel waited patiently as William and I tacked our mounts and said what could be our last goodbyes to our family. He led us back to Brestone, and we were briefed on the next day's events before calling it an early night.

For the first time in nearly three months, William and I slept through it, not startling awake once.

Bustling to and fro in the crisp spring air, the entire village scurried about in preparation for a hopefully successful day. Hooves stirred up clouds of dust as every available equine was tacked and led to their riders. A continuous string of commands lingered all around, shouts of orders firing from every direction. The voices mixed into an almost overwhelming melody, but it was a tune of excitement, built up for this very day after millennia of oppression.

It was our turn to fight back.

In the midst of the barely controlled chaos, a small band of riders mounted their steeds in unison. Their commander – the human fox – stood at attention beside a chestnut horse and curtly saluted Kent. "We are ready to move out," he informed, his eyes never breaking contact with Kent.

The sorcerer scanned the small diversion group – only five men including Payton – before he nodded his approval. "Be careful of the castle sentries," he ordered.

"Yes, Sir," Payton said.

Kent, Darrel, William, and I watched in silence as the man mounted his horse. With a simple motion of his arm, the band of men followed their leader in nearly perfect unison. The synchronous movements were somewhat unsettling for a group of untrained men. It seemed too militaristic, too practiced, too in tune for a ragtag group of rebels.

As soon as the band of men was out of sight, Kent called across the yard, "Kalli! Kaylynn!"

Two women, only a century or two younger than me, bounded to our sides. Mirrored images of each other in everything but hairstyle, the two were adorned from head to toe in camouflaged clothing. The one on the right, with short blonde hair spiked on the top and cropped short on the back and sides, held her twin still as she bounced about in excitement. The other shrugged off the unwanted hands and slid up to Kent's side, snaking an arm around her older brother's neck.

"Is it time to go yet?" she asked, her chiming tone near whining.

Kent nodded, not at all bothered by the arm clinging to him. He playfully tugged the golden ponytail on the left side of her head. "You need to take this seriously, Kalli," he admonished but held no heat behind his words.

"I am!" Kalli retorted.

"No, you're not," her twin mumbled.

"Am too!"

"Come on, you two. Focus," Kent said. He shrugged off Kalli's arm, and for the slightest of seconds, fear swam within the depths of his icy blue orbs. "You need to take this seriously, or you might get caught."

"I know. I'm sorry," Kalli said, bowing her head. "We won't let you down. Right, Kaylynn?"

Kaylynn clicked her tongue. "Of course," she stated as if there could be no other answer.

"I never doubted you," Kent said. He wrapped an arm around Kalli and extended the other to Kaylynn. The latter stepped forward reluctantly and allowed Kent to pull both sisters into a tight embrace. "Demon and Angel are tied out back, tacked and waiting. Be careful."

The twins pulled away. Kalli waved a goodbye to all of us and gave Darrel a quick hug before running to catch up with the stoic Kaylynn. They squeezed through the bustling crowds of people and ducked between the tavern and the adjacent apartments, Kent's eyes following the entire time.

Icy orbs stared after them for a long moment before they flicked to William and me, all former fear wiped clean. "Follow me," he said as he stepped past us and entered the tavern. He wasted no time in climbing the achy stairs and leading the three of us into his office.

"I've prearranged all the necessary supplies you may need," Kent informed as he gestured to the two bulky shoulder bags sitting atop the table. He tossed one to William and briefly explained its contents. His hands then reached for the second bag, gingerly pulling it across the tabletop. Deft fingers slowly unzipped it, and his hand dipped inside to withdraw a single vial of an opaque white liquid. "This is an extremely unstable and highly flammable substance designed by yours truly," Kent boosted, flashing a pearly white grin in pride.

I eyed the small vial in cautious awe, "How does it work?"

"It's quite simple. Break the glass, and the liquid will combust," Kent answered. He must've seen the confused wonder on not only my face but William's as well because he quickly elaborated, "The substance is designed to combust when exposed to the slightest amount of oxygen. One of these vials will be enough to singe the king and queen's chamber. In other words, don't break them without some sort of safety precaution first. You will burn to a crisp if you don't proceed with caution."

"How many are in there?" William asked, peering into the depths of the opened bag.

"Fifty," Kent said. He gently set the vial back within the confines of the bag. Zipping it shut, he gave his final instructions, "Use every last one. Don't bring a single vial back with you."

After another hour of final preparations, everything was in place, minus the commander himself. Darrel, William, and I mounted our equines and took our places at the front of the mass of rebels. Behind us, a mixture of mounted and on-foot volunteers – about two hundred altogether – waited patiently and a little antsy for their leader, an excited hype in the air. The many layers of rambunctious murmurs died to absolute silence when the tavern's door squeaked open.

Kent stepped into the street, taking a moment to admire his militia, before strolling in front of Darrel and me. He stopped beside William's mount. "My future king," he addressed, "I've got one more thing you might need." The sorcerer grasped two straps slung over his shoulder and offered the twin blades, both sheathed in a simple harness, to William.

147

William graciously accepted it, wasting no time in slipping his arms through the straps. The swords settled against the middle of his back, a bit higher than he was used to. His hands reached up to his shoulders, and fingers curled around the worn leather of the grips. He drew both blades, adjusted to their weight and feel, and sheathed them on his back once more. "Thank you," he said.

"No thanks necessary. I can't have my future king and queen unarmed when entering the enemy's nest. It's only fair that you have a way to protect Dawn. We can't have her clashing swords while carrying the vials," Kent said.

At the reminder of that decision, the bag in my lap weighed against my legs even more, and the strap across my chest dug deeper into me. I didn't regret it though. I'd rather feel the crushing weight than put the burden upon Will's shoulders. I'd gladly combust one thousand times over if it meant protecting William from the possibility of a burn, and I trusted Will's swordsmanship skills to return the favor.

Kent twisted on the balls of his feet and retraced his steps to the awaiting pegasus beside Darrel. He swung into the saddle, and Darrel passed him the reins. With a soft click of his tongue, his mount strode forward a few paces before Kent turned to face the militia. His lips stretched into a face-splitting grin, and he made no attempt to hide his pride.

"Ladies, gentlemen, and everyone in between, we make history today! Let us stand together and create a country we will be proud to pass on to the next generation – one where we don't have to fear for our safety while walking down the street!" Above the roaring shouts and applause, Kent ordered, "Move out!"

With a final rally cry, the militia surged forward to take its first steps. Waves of goodbye and kisses blown through the air were exchanged between the volunteer members and the family and friends that would wait in the village for their return. Those on foot stole a few quick embraces with the promise of a better tomorrow. As we crossed the village limits, the remaining occupants cried out their support, the echoes ringing in our wake and pushing us forward with an excess of optimistic confidence.

The echoing cries slowly died out in favor of quiet murmurs when the group left the beaten path and spread out through the forest to weave around the trees and duck under their budding foliage. Midmorning light shined through the treetops and brightened the forest floor in a soft glow to welcome our intrusion. Periodically, riders at point rose above the trees or spanned farther on each side, disappearing among the brush, before returning with news of dwellings to be avoided. We adjusted easily as a unit and dodged the occasional farm, choosing to stay concealed in the trees instead of cutting across fields or pastures.

Kent dropped back in line with Darrel, William, and me. His icy orbs continuously scanned the forest, flicking to the sky and glancing over both shoulders, even as he conversed. "Have any of you put some thought into a more in-depth infiltration plan?"

Darrel spoke first, "It'd be easiest to scale one of the towers."

"We'll have to be careful of the sentries, though," William said. "They have an open view of the grounds. It will be difficult to find a blind spot."

"There won't be any sentries. They're on our side," Kent informed.

I studied the sorcerer quizzically. That wasn't what he told Payton. "But you said–"

Kent eyed me, the blue of his irises shining confidently. With his head tilted, I caught a gleam of a slanted smirk. "I know what I said," he interrupted, "but I'm telling you now. Don't worry about the sentries. They'll be long gone by the time you arrive." He flashed a warm grin, white teeth peeking through. "They're personal friends I entrusted to evacuate the castle. They won't give you any problems."

"In that case, it'll be easy getting in," Will said. "Each tower is equipped with multiple trap doors and hidden tunnels. They're meant for the king and queen to use as escape routes, but most knights know them like the back of their hands."

"Are you familiar with them?" Darrel asked, leaning forward in the saddle to peer around Kent.

Will chuckled lightly, a little forced, as his hand rubbed at the nape of his neck. A light tint colored his cheeks. "You could say they make a good escape for new recruits trying to skip training."

Kent and Darrel exchanged amused glances, and I couldn't help but laugh. "I never pegged you for a delinquent," Kent teased.

"And I thought you were good at digging up information. I guess we both were wrong," William countered, a lazy grin upon his face.

"Fair enough," Kent smirked. "Shall we forget about our king's delinquency problems –" William groaned "– and return to the matter at hand? How do you plan to find Caldwell and Ember?"

I said, "With the pace we are going, we should arrive around afternoon tea time so they should be close to their chamber if not in there."

Kent nodded and hummed approvingly. "Have you thought of an escape route?"

"The tunnels will be the safest," Will said.

"Good. It's reassuring to hear you both have put some thought into this," Kent said. He then fell silent, having no more questions to ask, and returned to observing every inch of the forest.

Darrel, William, and I followed suit. Once more, we adjusted west to avoid a hunting cabin. It wasn't long after that the gurgling of the Kitoc broke through the foliage. The closer we got, the louder the river roared.

When the front four of us stepped past the trees to the grassy strip before the sloping bank, we eyed each other, mutually understanding the dilemma.

With the extended winter and the heavy snowfall, the Kitoc filled to its brim with the melted runoff. The water lapped against the bank, forced onto the grass in constant splashes. In its center, its flow neared barbaric with the water clashing and fighting for position. The battle continued in the liquid for as far as the eye could see, never slowing its frantic race.

"Can you do something about this?" Darrel asked Kent as he stared warily at the water.

Kent shook his head. "I'm afraid not. If I cease its flow, even for only five minutes, the entire area will flood. I can attempt to slow its pace, but that's it."

"It's better than nothing," Darrel said.

Kent gazed at the Kitoc, his eyebrows drawing together in concentration. Eyelids closed as his head bowed in thought. Barely a moment later, his eyes snapped open; and he twisted in the saddle to face his militia. "Listen up!" he shouted. "No one crosses on foot. If you're on horseback, you will cross through the river carefully but quickly. Those with pegasi will double up in saddle and assist flying those on foot to the opposite bank. Understood?"

After a loud cry of comprehension, Kent swung from the saddle – leaving the reins to Darrel – and approached the river's bank. He knelt in the soggy grass, and both of his arms extended toward the water. The pads of fingers skimmed the water's surface, dipping into the chill river. The muscles in his back and shoulders tensed, and his eyes squeezed shut.

A span of about one hundred feet of river visibly slowed, the water no longer violently crashing together or overflowing onto the grass. But with the patch of water more docile, the river upstream protested the backup, its level spilling over the banks.

"Hurry!" Darrel ordered.

As the riders on horseback urged their mounts to the river's edge, William and I swung from our saddles and passed the reins to those on foot. Darrel did the same, and the three of us worked together to guide the volunteers across. When those on pegasi crossed safely and dismounted, I whistled for the equines. They flapped back riderless and were quickly given a new set of riders.

I sent another group of pegasi across when William called from the riverside, "Dawn, we have a problem!"

My head snapped in his direction. Beside Will, a frightened horse planted its hooves in the earth and refused to step into the water. When an equally scared and disgruntled young man urged his mount forward, the horse half reared and backed even farther away from the riverbank.

I hurried to the pair, careful not to spook the horse even more. My fingers curled around its bridle and rubbed the equine's cheek. "Shh. It's okay. Calm down," I cooed softly. When the bay overo relaxed, I led him away from the water's side and instructed the next rider to cross. "I'll take care of this, Will," I said, and he nodded.

I looked up at the still frightened young man. "What's your name?" I asked.

"Ariano," he answered quietly.

"Okay, Ariano, this is what we're going to do. I want you to take a few deep breaths to calm yourself. If you're calm, your horse will be too." I paused for him to do just that. "Good. Now we're going to try to cross together. I will lead you and your horse through the water with my pegasus. Having a confident partner should help your horse be more willing to enter the water. Okay?"

Ariano nodded.

"Wait here," I told him as I stepped away to find Cobalt. I spotted him on the opposite bank and called his name. His head shot up with his ears pricked. He flew to my side, and I wasted no time in swinging into the saddle.

I rode back to Ariano and took the reins from him. After leading the pair to the riverbank, I urged Cobalt into the water. He didn't hesitate to step forward. As the pegasus took a second step, I tugged lightly on the overo's reins. The horse hesitated for a moment before taking a small step and then another. The pair followed close behind as the cold water rose to touch my knees. We slowly crossed the middle and then began climbing the opposite bank.

When both sets of hooves stepped upon dry land, I handed the reins back to Ariano. "Thanks," he said sheepishly, ducking his head to the side as color dusted his tawny brown cheeks.

"You're welcome."

I turned to fly back to the other side, but I saw it wasn't needed. William and Darrel sat atop their pegasi as Kent stood and wiped his hands on his trousers. The sorcerer hopped on his equine, and the three soared over the river.

"Crisis averted. Let's move out," Kent said. He flew above the militia to regain his lead with Darrel, William, and me right behind. The sorcerer began heading out when he came to an abrupt halt.

"Kent!" a shrill cry echoed from the forest. "Kent, you were right!" The thunder of hooves shook the trees as the black beast burst through the branches, his nostrils flared. The unicorn's rider waved maniacally as she pulled the beast beneath her to a sliding stop. "He's a traitor, Kent! A low down, dirty two-timer!"

"Kalli, calm down. Tell me what happened," Kent said.

Kalli took a single breath, but it did little to calm her. Her words fast and jumbled, she spoke, "We followed Payton like you said to. He and his men diverged from the plan and rode straight to Centrielle. He met up with Drake and told him your plans, and now they're planning to lay in wait on the eastern side of the castle." She huffed from her quick explanation, her lips still parted.

"It's okay," Kent said calmly.

Okay? Our plan was jeopardized, all our cards laid bare. "How is that okay?" I demanded.

Kent eyed me, confident grin plastered to his face. "I have already accounted for the snake's bite."

"Then what do you suggest we do?" I questioned.

"You and William will go alone to the west side of the castle. I will take half the forces to the east, and Darrel will lead the rest to the guardhouse. We will box Drake's men in and take care of them. All you two have to worry about is Caldwell and Ember."

"So you expected this?" I asked.

"Well, of course," Kent boasted. "I do my research after all."

MONSTER AND DARKNESS

Hidden within the foliage and tangling branches at the forest's edge, William and I halted to gaze upon the desolate castle, its outer walls staring back. Eerily silent, the gray stone rose into the sky, looming far overhead. Two towers faced us but stood empty, the glint of armor not shining through a single arrow loop. Atop each tower, a white flag proudly displaying an attacking lion flapped in the gentle breeze. The golden-maned cat bared its claws and hissed, ready to pounce, but it was harmless in every essence of the word. It did not protect Siven but instead played guard dog for Caldwell and Ember. The beast lacked its instinctual courage and had no pride to fall back on.

"The coast is clear," William said, drawing my attention. He peered at me, eyes bright with both shaky anticipation and hardened determination. "Are you ready?"

"As I'll ever be."

Our pegasi stepped into the small stretch of meadow. Hooves crunched over the crisp grass until the tower's shadow engulfed us. Will and I exchanged a final glance, nodding, before urging the pegasi skyward. The equines unfolded their wings and flapped, each flutter of feathers propelling us up. We passed each arrow loop and found them to be indeed empty with not a soul in sight. Once we ascended above the tower's highest stone guards, we flew over them and landed beside the lion's flag pole.

William swung from his mount first, grabbing the shoulder bag hanging around the saddle horn and tossing it to the ground. He walked to my side and placed both hands firmly but gently around the bag in my lap. I shrugged off its strap to allow Will to gingerly set it beside the other, and then I freely hopped off Cobalt's back.

To our right was the tower's entrance – a simple wooden slab with a wrought iron handle. After taking the few strides to reach it, I stooped down and wrapped my fingers around the sturdy ring. With my feet firmly planted on the stone, I heaved with all my might. The wood croaked with deafening moans sounding at each pull. The door suddenly flew open with a final tug that sent me stumbling back.

"Careful!" William warned with a pair of firm hands pressing against my

MORGAN BRIESE

shoulder blades to prevent my fall.

I glanced behind me and saw both supply bags sitting a couple feet back. "That could have been bad."

A rush of air blew past Will's lips in amusement. "Let's try not to go up in flames," he said.

"Deal."

William's hands slipped from my back, and he attempted to sling the safer of the two bags over his shoulder. "Hand it over," I said. He blinked, pausing with the strap in his hand. I continued, "You're the one with swords that can fight if things turn south. Carrying extra weight will slow you down, so hand it over. I'll take both of them."

He hesitated only a moment before realizing I was right. With bag still in hand, he took a single step to my side and placed the strap over my shoulders, resting the bulk against my back. Nimble fingers unzipped it, pulled some of the contents free, and pulled the zipper back in place. He handed me the torch and a pack of matches before lifting the second bag from the ground. Being as careful as one would with a priceless and fragile family heirloom, Will brushed the ends of my hair to the side and situated the strap around the back of my neck, the many vials flush against my belly.

"Promise me you'll watch your every step," he whispered, walnut orbs gazing into my emerald ones.

"I promise," I said.

His eyes closed for a mere moment, just long enough to collect himself, before snapping open. His hand slid the pack of matches from my grip and pulled out a single stick. Swiping it against the backside of his boot, fire fizzled to life, and he lit the torch in my hand. He dropped the match after blowing out the flame and relieved me of the torch. "Shall we?" he asked, stepping toward the unwelcoming darkness within the tower.

William led the way into the stone pillar, descending the twisting stairs with me a step behind. The hand not carrying the torch sought the cold, rough stone of the wall surrounding us. His knuckles rapped against the dreary gray and paused between each tap. With each step down, he repeated the knocking, but the only answer received was a dull, monotonous thud. We made two complete circles descending the spiraling staircase before the rapping knuckles sounded hollow, as if the noise drifted off behind the stone. Tapping a few more times, William confirmed the slight variation between knocks.

"The highest tunnel leads to the hall outside their chamber. It's behind this stone," William said. Descending two more stairs, he continued tapping the stone until he was satisfied. "Please step back a bit," he requested, and I quickly complied.

His hand pushed against the stone as he leaned into the wall. The rock gradually receded under the weight but stubbornly ground to a halt after a mere inch of movement. Rocking back on his heels, he withdrew his hand and tucked it against his abdomen. Will slammed his shoulder against the stones, and the whole wall shook, a large indentation jutting in where flesh met rock. He didn't hesitate to ram into the wall again. With his second attempt, a few of the center stones dislodged, creating a domino effect where the wall crumbled and sent up a cloud of dust. After a few moments of choking for air, the sediment settled upon the rubble, and a long passageway stood before us.

"That's one way to do it," I said as I followed William into the tunnel, carefully stepping over the pile of stones.

Massaging his shoulder, he turned to me with a teasing grin. "It's faster than stacking them in a neat little pile."

I laughed at the image that statement conjured but immediately clapped a hand over my mouth when my amused giggles echoed. "Sorry."

"It's fine. Let's go. If we hurry, we'll be able to cut off any and all escape routes." His hand clasped mine and tugged gently until I followed him.

We walked as fast as we could without jostling the vials I held to my stomach, the light of the torch barely illuminating our path. Only being able to see a few feet ahead of ourselves, we ran into numerous cobwebs and struggled to wipe away the intricately spun threads. We ducked and dodged to the best of our abilities but managed to walk through just about all of them. A few even homed fat spiders – the large bodied kind found in ancient barns. One ended up on William's cheek, and in a near panic, he slapped his face so hard he left a bright red handprint. After that, both of us itched and scratched at any exposed skin, completely convinced a nest of spiders crawled all over us.

That's why when we found the passage's end, the two of us sighed in relief. William hurled his weight at the wall and crashed through on the first try. He tumbled with the falling stones, the torch flying from his grasp to be buried beneath the rubble, and he landed roughly on his side.

I rushed to him, my hand offered for him to take. "Are you okay?"

A low groan fell from his parted lips as he graciously took my hand. "I'll live," he grunted as I pulled him to his feet. He rubbed a sore spot on his torso and winced. "Hopefully," he added with a small, upward twitch of his lips. He rolled his shoulders and after one last rub to his side, Will's eyes met mine, so many emotions and sentiments swirling in them.

We were really going to do this. There was no turning back, no denying the importance of our role. Lives depended on us. The citizens of Siven, the deteriorating relationship with the surrounding countries, our family, the rebels, Kent and Darrel – they all needed this mission to be a success. It was life or death, oppression or freedom, discrimination or equality. The importance of what we were about to do would either rebuild Siven or destroy any hope of a new tomorrow. We had two possible endings – survive to be heroes or die as traitors.

"Let's go," William said. His fingers entwined with mine squeezed lightly, and walnut orbs shined with resolve.

If I didn't know any better, I'd say that was the look of a hero.

We walked down the hall side by side, the light of day seeping through the arrow loops. Banners and portraits covered the stone walls at even intervals with golden torch mounts between them. Each painting of Caldwell and Ember lacked bright colors, the shades as dull as the gray stone. The banners, too, were lackluster strips of fabric, each embellished with different flowers – white petunias, yellow carnations, orange marigolds, and pink snapdragons. They lined both walls, a portrait always opposite a banner.

An obnoxious, echoing creak rang through the hall. William and I froze midstep as the aching noise rounded the sharp turn not far ahead of us and bounced off the walls to linger in the corridor. William released my hand and drew both blades from his back, stepping in front of me and inching toward the corner. As he pressed himself flush against the wall, I followed behind him.

"That incompetent fool!" Ember shrieked. "How dare he allow that lowlife scum so close to the castle! Does he consider this to be handling it?"

Caldwell snapped, "Enough! Let him perish with the rest! I don't care who lives or dies as long as I escape!"

William's grip tightened on the hilts as he chuckled dryly. "As long as you escape?" William menacingly questioned as he stepped around the corner. I followed him as he took two slow, deliberate steps to close the gap between him and the targets. "You would sacrifice your people to save your lousy hides, and yet you call yourselves king and queen. If you want an escape so badly, I'll give you a permanent one."

Orbs of copper and honey widened dramatically before both sets of eyes narrowed. Caldwell scrutinized William from head to toe before glaring at the sharp points of the swords. His lip twitched angrily as he snarled between grit teeth, "Stand down!"

Taking another step forward, William raised the blade in his hand and pointed the tip directly at the man's chest.

"That's an order!" Caldwell warned as he hesitantly stepped back toward his chamber.

"You're not the one giving orders anymore," Will said, uncannily calm. "I'm going to tell you once and only once. Go back to your chamber."

Ember grimaced in distaste but quickly backed away. She pushed the chamber door open with another resounding creak and slipped inside the room. William and I forced a sneering Caldwell to stumble into the overly extravagant chamber, and the man boiling with anger stood defiantly beside his wife.

"I expect an explanation right this moment," the aging man demanded. "Where has your loyalty gone?"

William sheathed one of his blades and scratched at his chin in mock contemplation. "That's a rather interesting thought. You seem to believe I'm still your loyal captain, but then why did you abandon me and discard my partner?" Will's burning orbs flicked to me before hardening at Caldwell. "You, who has abandoned all loyalty to his people, do not have the right to question my loyalty."

"Excuse me," Ember cut in, her voice nasally. "We have not abandoned *our* people. Those deemed useful to our society have been protected. All others are nothing more than hindrances."

Hindrances? How could she even consider a living being to be a hindrance? Life was precious no matter how one chose or didn't choose to live it. Didn't we, as human beings, all walk our own paths through life that would lead to individual happiness? Who was she to say another person didn't have enough value to society in order to chase after their own personal fulfillment? Simply by being alive and breathing, each human being possessed immeasurable value to the world.

"You can't deem someone worthy of living. A person's value can't be determined by anyone but them, least of all by you," I spat.

Ember scowled, honey orbs narrowing and head tilting. The anger quickly dissipated, though, as her lips stretched into a smug grin. She stepped toward me, stopping only after Will blocked her path. She raised her hands up in defense until William lowered his blade. "But I already have. How's your father been?" she asked with far too much feigned innocence.

My eyes bulged, and my breath caught in my throat. She didn't. Darting between Ember and Caldwell, I spotted matching smirks on the two wrinkled faces. They did.

Ember continued, "You must miss him, what with his untimely passing, but I can't say the same. The stubborn mule threatened to terminate his contract if you weren't released from custody, and he did too. I never thought he'd go through with it, but apparently his little *buckaroo* was worth more than his life. In all honesty, you killed your own father."

I froze, my limbs locked in place. That's not what my mother told me. Caldwell terminated the contract. Didn't he? It wasn't Cam. He wouldn't– no he would. He did... because of me. My father died... because of–

"She didn't!" William shouted.

Ember blinked, turning her attention to the man she had seemingly forgotten. "You would believe that, wouldn't you – the man whose parents had a horrible carriage accident while trying to find him?" William tensed.

"At least they were near the barracks and were found rather quickly." Will's body began to tremble. "Oh, that's right. You were among the trainees who heard the crash and rushed to the scene. I recall hearing how much of a bloody and mangled—"

"Stop!" Chest heaving, I slipped the dangerous vials from around my neck and placed them on the floor. My feet moved without being told to, stalking toward Ember. The woman backed away, but I pursued her retreat until cornering her against the wall.

Standing before her, I breathed deeply as my hands relaxed, fingers uncurling from the fists they had been at my sides. I spoke, my voice level and calm, "I believe people are inherently good. No one is born evil. It's humans that turn other humans into monsters. Their societal injustices and unrealistic standards corrupt an innocent mind to believe they are the problem. They get pushed too far, believe they are a mutation – an abnormality – only to snap and lash out against everyone – both friend and foe. Knowing this, I'd hate to image what you have gone through to become the monster I see now."

I turned on my heels, leaving Ember slack-jawed, and slowly approached William. His outstretched hand shook, the length of the blade quivering too. His other clenched into a tight fist with his fingernails digging into his palm. Brushing my hand against his, he finally looked at me, lips twisted in agony and walnut orbs pleading for refuge. "Let's end this," I whispered, loud enough for only him to hear.

William swallowed the lump in his throat and nodded. After taking a deep breath, his shoulders squared, and the trepidation of his limbs – while still there – lessened significantly. "It's time to repay your debt to humanity," he said.

"What debt?" Caldwell demanded. "We've done nothing wrong!"

He didn't receive an answer.

William watched over the two of them, sword at the ready, while I scanned the room. Deciding they would suffice, I grabbed the backs of two wooden chairs on my right and dragged the miniature thrones across the marble floor. Their legs scraped and scratched the stone until I positioned them back to back in the center of the room.

As I turned to William, he ushered Caldwell and Ember over. The latter crossed the room with her head held high, sitting in the nearest chair with her hands crossed daintily in her lap. Caldwell, on the other hand, planted his feet on the ground and refused to move; but upon feeling the sharp point of a sword against his protruding stomach, he shuffled to the vacant chair. The back of his legs bumped into the wooden seat. He crossed his arms over his chest and maliciously glared at William.

Will planted a firm hand against Caldwell's sternum. With minimal effort, he pushed the man, and Caldwell dropped to the chair with a dull thud.

"How dare you treat your king and queen with such disrespect!" Caldwell protested.

As I slipped the second bag from my shoulders, William surprised me, scoffing with a single dry laugh at Caldwell's words. He lashed out with the sword and thrust the blade above the man's head. The tip knocked not only one but both bejeweled crowns from their heads, and the hunks of gold clattered to the floor. "You're nothing more than dictators."

Unzipping the bag, I emptied its contents onto the floor and grabbed the bundle of rope. I hastily secured Ember and Caldwell to their seats, the latter protesting the entire time. With his wrists and ankles tied tightly to the chair, Caldwell struggled against the binds. He rocked back and forth, snarling and grunting, until the chair fell on its side. He seethed with animosity on the floor, and Ember glanced at his unsightly predicament, the same condescending gleam to her eyes she had often directed at me.

"This is blasphemy! Let me go right this instant!" Caldwell wailed.

The man was ignored as William sheathed his sword. He joined me as I knelt beside the other bag and carefully pulled on its zipper. Once open, my fingers gingerly clasped a vial to withdraw it from the confines of the bag. William grabbed one as well, and the two of us stood. With a silent understanding, we encircled Caldwell and Ember in a ring of vials, far enough away so Caldwell's thrashings wouldn't break them. We covered the room – the bed, the dressers, and the upholstered sitting chairs.

With about twenty of the combustible vials scattered throughout the room, William and I began backing out the door. William placed a vial beneath the threshold, and we turned to leave.

"Stop! You can't abandon us!" Caldwell yelled.

I paused my departure and turned to stand just outside the room. Caldwell sneered at me, his head lifted off the floor as far as it could be. "It was you who abandoned your people first."

"I did not! I protected them from those heathens trying to overrun my country!" Caldwell yelled.

I glanced at Will, but he adverted his gaze to the ground. As much as I wanted to leave, to end this, I couldn't let this go. For William and Sydney and Rose, for Spencer and his family, for Darrel and Michael, for the rebels, for the baker and his wife, for the children on the streets, for everyone ever told that the person they were born as was wrong – I would give this man a lesson in human decency.

"Those people you call heathens have the same right to this country as you do. It was not close-minded conformists like you that built Siven. Our country was carved onto the map by people seeking freedom – a home where they could live the life they wanted to without judgment. That is Siven's foundation. It doesn't matter how much time passes or how much society changes as people discover themselves. That foundation is the same. Each and every person deserves to have the same chance at happiness as anyone else. The only heathen I see is you."

I turned my back to Caldwell, deaf to whatever protests he cried, and clasped William's hand, tugging him into motion. We rounded the corner, pausing to place a vial on the floor, before continuing down the portrait-clad hall. Every twenty feet or so, we stopped to set another vial on the ground. After placing two more vials, William dug up the fallen torch, lit it, and led the way through the tunnel. We continued our trail of dominoes all the way up the tower until the light of day shined upon our faces.

"How many are left?" William asked as I laid another vial on the tower's top step.

I peered into the bag I held. "Six," I said.

"Alright, then you keep two to start the chain, and I'll drop the other four in the outer courts. Sound like a plan?"

I nodded and handed him the vials he requested. Will lifted the hem of his shirt to create a little pouch and nestled the dangerous substance against his stomach. He used one hand to swing into the saddle as I did the same.

"Signal when you're ready," William said. He then urged his pegasus to take flight and soared above the empty stables and servant quarters until hovering above the outer court. He looked at me expectantly.

I nudged Cobalt with my heels, and the equine extended his wings. He flapped his feathers, propelling us straight up with each beat of a wing. We rose high above the tower, nearly level with William's altitude.

Digging the two vials from the bag's depths, my fingers closed around them. I extended my hand over Cobalt's withers, holding the clenched fist in the gap between his feathers and neck. My opposite hand rose above my head and froze. Locking gazes with Will, I saw he was ready. I swung my arm through the air, waited a heartbeat, and dropped the vials.

As soon as the glass fell from my fingers, my legs squeezed Cobalt's sides. My steed bolted forward, frantically fleeing for the treetops. With each flap of feathers, we made it that much closer to freedom; but what seemed like hours was only seconds before the initial blast went off with a deafening bang. It was the onslaught of heat against my back that had my feet digging even further into Cobalt's sides. The speed of the pegasus' flaps increased tenfold as each stride elongated, his legs running through air.

The series of explosions continued in fast succession. Even after every vial went off, the ringing bangs sounded in my ears. The heat grew uncomfortable against my back, and the wind whipping past me did little to soothe it. The fire sent burning shadows to reflect on the grass and the fast approaching treetops, and the smell of rancid smoke burned my lungs.

When Cobalt's hooves passed over the budding branches of the forest, my head swiveled in search of William. I scanned the sky until finally spotting a lone rider soaring above the only road leading from the burning castle. Reining Cobalt in, I steered him to the left. He flew diagonally over the forest, racing to Will's side.

"William!" I shouted above the crackling of flames, or so I thought. With the constant buzz of ringing in my ears, what I knew to be a shout sounded like a mere whisper.

No matter how loud my call truly was, William heard it. His head whipped to the side, wisps of flames dancing in the depths of his walnut orbs. The warm breeze tousled chocolate locks of hair, his bangs sweeping to the opposite side than they normally did. With the brightest smile of relief I had ever seen, he extended his hand to me, and I wove my fingers with his the moment they came into my reach. Together, we gazed upon the fiery inferno that marked the end of an oppressive era.

Flowing flames engulfed the dark stone. Bursting through every arrow loop and paned window, fire scaled the castle walls as liquefied glass oozed intricately down cracks and grooves in the stone. Blazing orange leapt from stone to wood, not leaving a single crate unscathed. Flames cackled as they consumed the garden and stables to meet in the middle of the outer court. Burning fingers of fire climbed each tower, scorched the lions to ash, and clawed at the sky to leave scratches of billowing smoke. The thick clouds suffocated the innocent blue of the sky and rose to ghost over the sun.

Darkness veiled the light, and for once, fear couldn't be found.

William's fingers squeezed mine, and I turned my full attention to him. His lips parted, breathing two simple words that were probably much louder than the muffled whispers I heard. "It's over."

SWIMMING WITH DOLPHINS

Two pendants lay atop the dresser, their golden chains mingling together around the cracked chess piece. Sitting in front of a mirror, their images reflect along with my face.

"Your hair has gotten longer. It's almost as long as it was before." The words were quiet, not as muffled as they used to be, but still softer than they truly were. If I turned my head, angling my right ear to the speaker, the words would be as clear as a midmorning sky. But with the words coming from my left, each syllable struggled to be heard.

The stroke of the brush paused as I glanced over my shoulder at William. When my eyes fell upon him leaning against the door frame, the task of running bristles through hair was forgotten. Warmth bubbled in my chest and spread to every extremity, the familiar flush dusting my cheeks.

Under my appreciating gaze, Will straightened and scratched at his nape. His lips twitched in a small smile as pink lit up his face. "What do you think?" he asked quietly, walnut orbs flicking to meet mine.

His hands smoothed over the lapels of a black waistcoat, stumbling over a line of silver buttons, before falling to his sides. The pads of his fingers skimmed over black slacks that hugged his thighs quite nicely. The crisp white of a button up, complete with shining rose cufflinks, contrasted his dark attire. Tucked beneath the waistcoat, an emerald-colored tie, striped with crossing paths of white and black, failed to fall in a smooth line.

"Your tie is crooked," I said with a light chuckle.

Eyes darted down as his head tilted forward. He scrutinized the fabric in question, the corners of his eyes crinkling. Deciding that the tie was truly crooked, he reached for its knot and attempted to correct its alignment. He lightly tugged and pulled but only managed to free the tie's tail from beneath his waistcoat. After another minute of struggling to straighten the fabric, Will's hand fell dejectedly to his side, and his bottom lip jutted out in a child-like pout.

"You really should learn how to tie a tie properly," I said but stood and crossed the room to help nonetheless.

As I untied the failed attempt at a knot, William defended himself, "This is only my second time wearing one so give me some credit."

I hummed in agreement as I eyeballed the length of each side of fabric around his neck. "At least you tried this time. That's an improvement." His answering chuckle rumbled beneath my fingertips as I finished the new and improved knot. I tucked the tie beneath his waistcoat, smoothed over the fabric, and fixed his collar. Taking a single step back, I smiled warmly. "You look absolutely dashing."

Through his own light flush of cheeks, William wasted not a heartbeat to say, "But not nearly as breathtaking as you."

I had to agree, because I felt like the queen I had become, especially in the dress I wore for the day's long-awaited unveiling. White flowers of fabric wrapped around my neckline, tying together at my nape. As the flowers accentuated my breasts, the color of mint glittered the occasional petal, some dusted darker than others. The collage of flowers continued to my waist where it gave way to the flow of smooth silk. The fabric overlapped to create ridges that rippled diagonally down the dress. In a soft gradient, pure white transitioned to a deep shamrock as the tail brushed against the velvety carpeting.

"Thank you."

"No thanks necessary. I'm only stating the facts," Will said.

I shrugged, "I guess I'll go thank Darrel for picking out the dress then." I shifted my weight in a mock attempt to step around William.

"Okay, wait," Will sputtered. "I humbly accept your gratitude with the utmost appreciation."

"Again, thank you," I laughed.

William made a show of bowing, dramatically sweeping his arm through the air before tucking it against his torso. "You're very welcome," he said with an airy chuckle. As he straightened, he cocked his elbow and held it at his side. "Shall we go see if everyone else is ready?"

I answered him by slipping my arm through his and joining at our elbows. "To Rose's room we go."

"Ah, yes," Will said. "We will embark on the treacherous journey across the hall."

"But it may be," I laughed. "After all, the girls were prettying up the boys when we left. Poor Michael probably has his fingernails painted by now, and if it's the color Fallon chose, it won't go with his bow tie."

"I don't think we have to worry about mismatched colors. Fallon was heading for Kent so if anything, at least the pinks will match," William chuckled.

"And what about you?" I asked, eyeing his curled fingers. "Did Rose get to you?"

"I actually asked her to," he informed as he splayed his fingers, wiggling them for extra effect. The nails were painted perfectly, obvious care on Rose's part so as not to make a mess, and the colors grew darker, starting with white on the thumb and ending with a deep forest green on the pinky.

"They match my dress."

"Of course," Will said. He continued as we passed straight through our bedroom and into the hall, "The king and queen can't unveil the new symbol of Siven to our people without being sophisticatedly dressed. It would be a disgrace for our color to be green but my nails to be purple, pink, or even yellow."

"Remind me next time to wear a rainbow dress."

William chuckled as we stopped in front of the oaken door of Rose's bedroom. Twisting the knob, he began to push the door open. "Our people may think we have a touch of insanity." He stepped into the room only to pause after one stride. "I take that back. They will be certain of how much sanity we lack."

From one glance, Rose's room looked like a circus. Every occupant – which in this case was quite a few – froze in whatever motion they were doing to turn their heads to the door. Darrel lounged back in the bed against the left wall, his hands behind his head and a broad grin stretching his lips, while his younger brother assisted Fallon in pinning flowers and ribbons into Kent's ponytail. The sorcerer, while not completely happy but far from grumpy and unwillingly, sat perfectly still while Michael tied off a pale pink ribbon much to Fallon's excitement. Giggles erupted from behind Kent, the younger of his two sisters finding his predicament to be downright hilarious, while Kaylynn did her best to ignore Kalli's fit of laughter. On the opposite side of the room, Charlie and Raven shared a single chair – both close to falling off – and Rose sat on her knees in front of the two. Two sets of deft fingers braided strawberry blonde hair. Charlie finished his braid first, tying it with a light blue bow, and Raven quickly added a second to match.

The minute Rose was free of the hands in her hair, she leapt to her feet. She bounced to William and me to wrap an arm around each of our waists. "Is it time yet? Can I go play by the fountain until everyone else is ready?" Rose asked.

"Me too! Me too!" Fallon piped in, abandoning her task of prettying up Kent in favor of racing on her little legs to Rose's side.

"Just be careful not to get too dirty." Before my words were fully spoken, Rose clasped Fallon's hand, and the two dashed around William. They were well down the hall, merely two blurs of light blue and pale red, before I called after them, "And no swimming in the fountain!"

Protesting whines echoed back to me, but the pair continued to bound over the bright carpeting. Curls of fiery red and braids of strawberry gold bounced against their retreating backs as they reached the end of the hall and turned the corner. Their mischievous giggles lingered in the wide, brightly lit corridor even after their footfalls died away.

"I'll keep an eye on them."

"That would be greatly appreciated," I told Michael as he, too, abandoned the last few ribbons on the floor and left Kent's side. He ducked out of the pastel room and followed after the two girls.

Michael had been a secret, one only a select few knew existed. That tight circle had been kept to include only family and eventually William and me. Although Michael was at a fighting age a century ago, Darrel refused to let him join our attack against the old castle. It took the confirmation of Drake's death before Darrel even allowed Michael to leave his hideout in Brestone. It wasn't until after Siven accepted William and me as their king and queen that Darrel believed it to be safe to finally let his younger brother out into the world beyond the boundaries of the rebel village.

Michael never complained though. If anything, he seemed grateful to the protectiveness of his brother. No longer a boy but not quite a man, Michael was mature enough to know the danger he had been in by simply being alive. He had gone so far as to thank William and me for our part in giving him the freedom he longed for. They were words no human being should ever have to utter, like an apology for existing. He didn't have to thank anyone, let alone us, for the equality of a human being. But he did. And from that moment on, I vowed to never make another person utter those same words of gratitude for something they were given at birth.

"Is everyone ready?" William asked from beside me.

"Yes."

"No."

Kaylynn and Kalli eyed each other, the latter continuing to brush through her hair. She bundled her golden locks on the left side of her head and tied her hair with an orange band.

"How much longer are you going to take?" Kaylynn demanded of her twin.

"Long enough to pick out a pair of shoes."

"So another few hours?" Kent chimed in with a slanted smirk.

"Brother!" Kalli whined. "That's not true!"

The three rambled on in a low bicker until Darrel sighed and swung his legs off the bed. He stood and walked up behind the bantering siblings. After clearing his throat and gaining their undivided attention, he asked Kalli, "What are your options?"

"Options?" she mirrored.

"For shoes. What do you have to choose from?"

"Oh," she said as realization struck. Kalli spun to face the dresser she stood by and lifted the lids off of two separate boxes. Each of her hands reached into a different box and withdrew a pair of shoes. Both pairs were the same light beige and would have complemented the vibrant orange of her mini dress. "Heels or flats?" she asked, holding them up for Darrel to see.

"Heels," Darrel answered after only a moment of thought.

Kalli didn't question his decision and slipped her feet into the pair of heels. She adjusted the straps before straightening and announcing she was ready.

"Are you sure?" William asked hesitantly, peering at Kalli as he did so.

"Yep! Let's go!" Kalli beamed. She linked arms with Kaylynn, much to the sister's distaste, and all but dragged the older twin toward the door.

The two passed William and me as we stepped out of their way. Kent and Darrel followed, hands intertwined, and Darrel's finger brushed over the gold band on Kent's left ring finger. I pulled the door shut after Charlie and Raven exited the room. As a small group, with the twins squabbling back and forth at the lead, we walked down the corridor.

Raven turned to me, awestruck eyes bright with amazement. "It truly is beautiful," she said.

"It is," I agreed.

It took a full century to complete, but the palace stood as a magnificent symbol of Siven's rebirth – of the people's pride in their country. After the fire at the old castle burned itself out, all that remained was rubble and ash. Kent rounded up his rebel group to clean up the mess, but it was decided that the new palace would not rest atop the grave of the old. William was adamant about the potential threat of certain ghosts roaming the halls of a new palace, but his reasoning wasn't the only factor in moving the palace's location. The old castle had lain in the middle of nowhere, essentially cut off from the rest of Siven. As a consensus, the palace was built on the northern outskirts of Centrielle where it would be closer to the people it represented.

Once the location had been decided, construction began. Citizens of Siven worked through hell and high water to lay the palace's foundation. Masons erected pillars while bricklayers constructed fireplaces. Carpenters crafted furniture – everything from dining tables and chairs to dressers and bed frames. Artists painted murals on corridor walls, adding color wherever possible. Gardeners and landscapers planted and tended to trees and flowers. Anyone with any sort of trade who offered their skill was given a task, no matter how small or large it may have been.

Building the palace even turned the economy around and helped improve trade and relations with the surrounding countries. All the citizens who had a hand in its construction were compensated for their time and effort. It was an expensive venture, especially with Kent and William competing for the best design ideas, but it had quickly become clear that money would be no problem. Siven was not and had never been a poor country. We learned just how much Caldwell and Ember had hidden away in their treasury, and it was no wonder Siven's people had little money to spare with how much the former crown wearers had hoarded. Even after all the expenses of building the palace was tallied and paid for, barely a dent had been made in the treasury's stash.

The abundance of money meant Kent and William could go wild with extravagant designs, and they did. Chandeliers hung in almost every room, each handcrafted to be unique from the others. Some, like the ones in each of the many bedrooms, gleamed with the sheen of different colors, pinks and greens and blues tinting the glass bulbs. Each long length of corridor sported different colored walls, thus receiving their names for easier navigation around the large palace. Marble lined the floors, and deep red carpets sat atop them, falling down the stairs to lead all the way to the front entrance. The whole palace's crown molding was inlaid with gold, and the dark oak stair rails were painstakingly engraved by hand.

My hand slid over those very handrails – the wood smooth beneath my touch – as I stepped down each stair. Coming to the bottom of the grand staircase, we followed the scarlet carpet to the enormous front doors. The noon sun shone through the thick glass bordering the double doors. Once Kalli pulled the cast iron handles, the doors effortlessly opened to allow even more light to pour into the entryway. Leaving the doors wide open, we each walked out onto the speckled white marble of another staircase.

If the palace's interior was considered extravagant, its exterior was downright breathtaking. The marble stairs opened up to a pathway of lightly colored slate stones. Red, white, and pink petunias bordered the stone in a precise row, their colors mingling together. Trimmed grass spread out behind the splash of color, and footpaths of stone trailed across the lawn. Rose bushes lined the palace walls, and hedges cut in the shape of animals dotted the grass. A small orchard of apple trees grew on the left side of the palace, only a few trunks visible from the front.

But the most meaningful feature sat in the center of the stone, directly in front of the palace entrance. Shaped as a star, beige stone protruded from the ground and rose to about my mid-thigh. The ledge, wide enough for a person to comfortably sit on to listen to the soft babble of water, held the names of persecuted victims that had fallen prey to the former king and queen. A circular stand rose from the pool of water, covered in blue tinted tiles. Atop the stand, three stone dolphins leapt into the air – frozen mid jump.

Rose, Fallon, and Michael sat atop the fountain's ledge, and the former two dipped their hands into the pool. Our little group joined the three, and many small conversations erupted at once. Kaylynn yelled at Kalli after being flicked with the chill water. Kent and Darrel knelt at the fountain's ledge to listen to Fallon gush about how much fun she was having. Rose dragged Charlie and Raven down one of the stone paths to show them her favorite hedge trimmed in the shape of a pegasus.

But none of those conversations grabbed my attention as much as William's silent gaze at the dolphins did. His eyes locked on the first dolphin's right fin, fixed on the name engraved upon the stone. *Rei Okabe.* Orbs of walnut flicked to the second dolphin. *Nagisa Okabe.* The center dolphin – the one jumping highest among the cascading water – drew Will's gaze. Eyes bright and smile soft at the corners, William breathed in a light breath as he stared at the precious statue. *Sydney Okabe.*

His lips parted to speak mere whispers, "Did you know dolphins are popular in Arkaynai? Apparently they inhabit the coastal waters and are friendly enough to swim side by side with humans. I remember my parents telling Sydney and me stories of when they swam with them and how gentle and playful they were. Sydney dreamed of going to the beaches of Arkaynai one day to experience it for herself, but travel between countries was never permitted. Her dream of experiencing the ocean will never be realized."

"That's not true," I spoke as softly as he had. His head tilted toward me, but his eyes never left the statue. "You said it yourself. Sydney will always be in your heart. Anything you experience, she experiences."

William peered at me, shining orbs finally tearing away from the dolphin. "Will you come with?"

"We all will. Once summer arrives, we'll take a trip to Arkaynai and see the ocean."

"And swim with dolphins?"

"Yes," I laughed. "We will definitely swim with the dolphins."

"I should ask Kenji about it later. Maybe he'd be able to show us all the best spots," William beamed.

I nodded. "But for now, let's open the gates, and give the people their palace."

ABOUT THE AUTHOR

Morgan Briese always had a wild imagination and indulged in storytelling from a young age. She dabbles in a little bit of everything and has experience writing poetry, essays, short stories, and novels. Her specialty is in young adult fiction.
Morgan enjoys horseback riding, anime, and cooking. She currently lives in the rural countryside of Wisconsin.

For more information and bonus content, visit her website.
morganbriesewrites.com